Why readers love

HER PERFECT ESCAPE

'Immerses you in luxury and intrigue on a stunning Greek island... Perfect reading escapism.'
HEATHER CRITCHLOW

'I devoured this tense glittering, gilded knot of a Mykonos mystery... The rich behaving badly, and a taut, twisty thriller.'
ANGELA CLARKE

'What a ride! Twists and turns, secrets and lies... A brilliant beach read.'
SAM HOLLAND

'Relentless and breathtaking – another of the propulsive thrillers we've come to expect from this powerful, masterful writer.'
KATE SIMANTS

'A sultry, gripping read and perfect for fans of *The White Lotus*.'
CASS GREEN

'Thrilling... Soaked in sunshine. Dripping with glamour and privilege.'
S.E. LYNES

Also by Rachel Wolf

Sun Trap
Five Nights

As Rachael Blok

Under the Ice
The Scorched Earth
Into the Fire
The Fall

HER PERFECT ESCAPE

RACHEL WOLF

An Aries Book

First published in the UK in 2026 by Head of Zeus,
part of Bloomsbury Publishing Plc

Copyright © Rachel Wolf, 2026

The moral right of Rachel Wolf to be identified
as the author of this work has been asserted in accordance with
the Copyright, Designs and Patents Act of 1988.

All rights reserved. No part of this publication may be: i) reproduced or transmitted
in any form, electronic or mechanical, including photocopying, recording or by means
of any information storage or retrieval system without prior permission in writing from
the publishers; or ii) used or reproduced in any way for the training, development or
operation of artificial intelligence (AI) technologies, including generative AI
technologies. The rights holders expressly reserve this publication from the
text and data mining exception as per Article 4(3) of the Digital
Single Market Directive (EU) 2019/790.

This is a work of fiction. All characters, organizations, and events portrayed
in this novel are either products of the author's imagination or are used fictitiously.

9 7 5 3 1 2 4 6 8

A catalogue record for this book is available from the British Library.

ISBN (PB): 9781035916863
ISBN (E): 9781035916870

Cover design: Simon Michele | Head of Zeus

Printed and bound in Great Britain by Clays Ltd, Elcograf S.p.A.

Bloomsbury Publishing Plc
50 Bedford Square, London, WC1B 3DP, UK
Bloomsbury Publishing Ireland Limited,
29 Earlsfort Terrace, Dublin 2, D02 AY28, Ireland

HEAD OF ZEUS LTD
5–8 Hardwick Street
London, EC1R 4RG

To find out more about our authors and books
visit www.headofzeus.com
For product safety related questions contact productsafety@bloomsbury.com

For Aine

Prologue

Greece

Friday night/Saturday morning

There's a stillness to a summer's night. A stillness to a calm sea. A stillness to this death.

The sea laps gently as the body expels its last puff of air. The sky black; the bright stars blinking a vigil.

You are not alone. We are watching.

A figure on the beach. Silent.

Does judgement await?

Greece has its own names for its gods, but they can be cruel; maybe this is the safest place for this to happen. The oldest of all the deities. They've been overseeing for so long. They must hold the best secrets.

Taking a life corrodes something within you, and the figure – hands clenched; cheeks tear-stained; blood thudding loudly behind the ears; cloaked in the same darkness that shrouds the floating form – desperately wants to rewind the last half an hour. Could it have been avoided?

A pain inside so sharp it could cut.

One step backwards, from the gluey, sinking sand by the water's edge to the warmer grains further up the beach. The footsteps sink in on themselves. The beach covering up the clues.

I was never here.

The pain again, a sliver of ice on such a hot night, lodging itself in the heart.

Greece will know what to do. Greece is not a stranger to blood on the beaches.

The party is – should have been – tomorrow. Or is that today?

How did it come to this?

1

Tash

Present

Friday morning

Tash thinks she sees her.

The Acropolis is flooded with people at 8 a.m., and it's 32 degrees Celsius. It isn't the first time Tash's been here. It's a well-trodden vigil, and it's not just the heat that makes her legs heavy as she climbs.

People queue to ascend and descend the steps. Families gather for photos. Swarms hover and collect up the hill – guides holding folders aloft to gather their tours.

She stands looking out over the city in the early sun, her back to the history everyone clamours to see. The Acropolis – the highest point. If there's anywhere she can spot her from, it's here.

This is where she saw her sister last. A year ago. She'd barely touched her as she'd said goodbye. Blown a kiss, watched her laugh as she waved.

There. Up ahead.

Her eyes fix on the young woman – is she too young? She follows the fall of blond hair. Curls. Of course, she's older now. She'd be twenty-five. Maybe she's dyed her hair.

But the laugh. It's the same.

A blue dress against the bleached stone, marble, sand and path. The tourists with cameras, phones, hats, guides – all the languages around her twisting tongues in different vowels, reeling out facts that have been told for centuries to those paying to hear them for the first time.

She's sure. Can't breathe.

'Emma!' she shouts.

But she's gone.

Tash runs, chest tight. Pushing up and against the crowds, someone shouts, *Hey, watch it*. She trips on a stone – the ground uneven and some of the original marble slippery. There are gasps as she bangs her head, and when she opens her eyes, she can't move right away. One of her shoes has come off. The white, bright surrounds spin, and strangers come to check she's OK.

An ambulance is called. A path parts, and her head aches in the light. People often faint up here. The heat and the climbing aren't easy for anyone.

She'd come on her own. She'd taken the public boat, first thing, wearing dark glasses and a hat. She hadn't got Stani to bring her on the yacht or taken the helicopter on the trip from the island.

She hadn't told Megan, her other sister. Megan is the only guest who's already at the villa. Everyone else arrives later today or tomorrow. If she can just find Emma today – bring her back for Dom's party on Sunday. His actual birthday on Monday. Persuade her to come a year after she vanished.

Megan is convinced Emma died at sea last year – the same day she went missing. Tash hates the look on Meg's face when she talks about the hope that Emma is alive somewhere. Kind of blank. Partly scathing.

Tash had wanted to blend into the crowd, like it might shake loose secrets. She's convinced that Emma swam away and faked her death, though who knows why?

It's not the first time she's thought she's seen her. The numbers run into the thousands. Sometimes the footfall on a street. Not just in Greece, but at home, in London. On the island in the Caribbean. In the villa in Italy.

It's just another day. Another sighting. Can she be sure this time is any different?

The same weekend last year held all the clues. She just needs to unpick them. Almost everyone who was here last year will be here again this weekend. Dom's birthday weekend. Bookmarked.

She sees their faces last year at the villa, round the table: her son Dom, his friend Theo, Mark – her now (almost) ex-husband, Sam – their friend and colleague, and Megan.

Nancy, Theo's mother will be missed – she'd died around Christmas time. Tash can't bear Theo's father, Richard. He's too busy with the senate anyway. She hasn't seen him since Nancy's funeral. So almost all the same people. Plus a few new ones. Dom and Theo are bringing girlfriends, and now Mark is bringing his.

Tash had wanted so desperately to prove she didn't care that Mark has moved on, she'd been almost militant about inviting this new girlfriend of only three months. Her husband of fifteen years.

But Dom's birthday weekend is the anniversary of Emma's vanishing – her younger sister going missing. That's the only thing that really counts.

Something seismic must happen in the next few days.

So much has happened this year. The world has turned upside down.

If she's right, and Emma is still alive, then why is she hiding?
This weekend will shake out its secrets.

There's a banging on the gates to the walled secrecy of it all. Some hidden clue one of these visitors must know. A truth that will creep out when no one is looking and stir up justice.

If not, then Tash is ready to burn it all down.

2

Tash

'I think I saw Emma,' Tash says, standing atop the hospital, looking out across the gleaming white of Athens and the blue of the sea. The helicopter is in view, blades lashing, and she raises her voice. 'I'll be back soon.'

'You should have told me you were going! I woke, and you'd vanished! Are you OK?' Megan is shouting now to be heard. Tash can't tell if she's cross or concerned.

'Yes!' It's harder to hear. The helicopter is so loud. 'Look, I'll see you in half an hour!'

The ambulance had taken her to the hospital, and after she'd been scanned and checked, she'd signed herself out and summoned the helicopter back to the villa.

She looks down at the sea as they fly back to her home. She's so sure Emma isn't buried on the seabed. So sure.

Emma had been a late surprise to her parents. Seventeen years younger than Tash. With Megan she'd grown up with all the usual sibling rivalry. With Emma, she'd just felt protective, particularly after her parents died.

Megan waits near the helipad at the villa as Tash lands. Tash pulls off her seatbelt and jumps down.

The emptiness and peace of this space, one of her favourite homes, is a relief after the busyness of the capital. It will be even quieter in a few moments, once the helicopter has left. This spot looks down on the white villa, the pool, the private beach – her sanctuary.

Megan cradles a coffee, looking out over the sea of the Greek island, then back to Tash who ducks her head a little. She hates the beating of the air. It's aggression she could do without today.

Behind Megan, the sea lies flat and blue like an iced pancake. It's late morning now, and everyone will begin to arrive.

'Come on. I bet you haven't eaten.' Megan takes a sip of her coffee and then tucks her other arm through Tash's. 'You were quick. Next time, tell me if you're going. Of course I'd come.'

The housekeeping staff are discreet as they move quietly, preparing for the house guests and the birthday weekend.

Megan slides a plate to Tash, and they sit at the kitchen island, its smooth cold granite a relief after the sun. Megan looks at her, expressionless.

'Thanks,' Tash says, watching her sister, whose dark hair gleams and is perfectly tied up in a loose bun. She wears a white bikini, covered by a tasselled throw. She's already nut brown and small diamonds sit at her ears, catching the sun.

'This is delicious.' Tash chews smoked salmon and contemplates the fact that she has felt her own shine slip away this year, but Megan, if anything, has heightened hers. Instead of six years older, Tash feels twenty. At thirty-six, Megan exudes sophistication and is stunning. At forty-two, Tash has lost her taste for fine clothes, for expensive shopping. She's as fit and active as she ever was. But the idea of having her nails done, of sitting beneath the hands of a hairstylist for blow-drying feels exhausting.

She's stepped away from their company. It was up and launched in the States by last Christmas. They'd had Mark's old college roommate – Richard Fowler – to thank in part for smoothing their path, but it had been her husband, Mark (the now almost ex-husband, which today gives her pause), who had leaned in and tackled everything with gusto when she'd frozen after the summer. They'd got in Sam as the new CEO for the US firm once it was launched, quietly alleviating the pressure on Mark, the vacuum of Tash, empty in her grief for Emma, sucking him briefly dry. Once Emma had been lost, she'd had no time for Mark.

Autumn through to winter had been a crazy time for the firm, and Tash had walked the streets in Washington and Boston as the snow fell and lost herself in the white drenching. The zeal she'd had for the company faded. The zeal for her marriage – for Mark – had iced over. Emma had drowned, and Dom had gone to university. She'd hung on to who she'd been as long as she could.

It wasn't so much that she'd stepped away from Mark and work, more that she'd slid. Slipped and glided away. It had been beyond her control.

But there's a spark in her now. This weekend. Surely it will turn the key to this time last year. She knows she missed something. It's almost a year to the day that Emma vanished. Today is Friday. Dom's party is Sunday, then he turns twenty-one on Monday.

Megan had been the first guest to arrive, and Tash had been overjoyed to see her.

Her sister is more likely than anyone to pull her up short.

Megan tops up their water glasses, and says, 'Go on then. I know you want to tell me – you thought you'd seen her?'

Tash nods. She lowers her fork. 'I'm sure I did. There was something ... I'm sure it was her.' She tells Megan about seeing Emma to test out the truth of what she saw, and already, she is disappointed – from the look on Meg's face, it starts to feel unreal.

Megan has a mouth half-pursed and her shiny slick lips clamped shut, preventing anything from slipping out.

'Aren't you going to say anything?' Tash asks, frustrated. She'd been unable to talk in the ambulance, her tongue thick and useless, her head aching. She'd wanted to tell them to go and look for Emma.

Then, when the doctors checked her, sent her away with a list of instructions, she felt silly. Had she really seen her at all? When she'd landed back at the villa, she'd been both pleased to be home and devastated to have felt so close but so far.

'Was that before or after the fall?' Megan asks, blowing on another coffee.

Tash shakes her head. 'Before. Of course. I tripped – I'm sure it ...'

Megan nods. She waits a moment. 'It won't have been,' she says, softly.

Tash looks away, out across the sea, touching the two identical bracelets she wears. She squeezes her eyes against the tears that bead up, and she shakes her head quickly, decisively. Then she stands. She's so sick of being alone in this. She will not be wrong-footed. 'I'm going for a walk.'

'Natasha,' Megan says.

She rarely uses her full name. Tash pauses.

'I'm not trying to be cruel. You know that. Emma is gone. You've banged your head – the doctor said to take it easy for the next few days. It's Dom's birthday. I mean, I know how much Emma ... hurts. It hurts me too. She was my sister as well. But your only son is about to turn twenty-one. Don't make this weekend about Emma. I mean, you were twenty-one when you had him and you've aced it – this mothering business. Let him have his celebration and you have yours. It's going to be hard enough for you as it is with Mark bringing his new girlfriend. It's practically abuse, asking you to spend the weekend with her. You've got enough to deal with. Maybe ...'

But Tash doesn't hear anything else. Megan has told her enough times how stupid she's being, letting the new girlfriend of her ex-husband come here, to her home.

She doesn't hear her because the sound of the laugh at the Acropolis is loud in her ears, and it's all very well for Megan. Ever the killer lawyer, she can dole out advice like the best of them.

Once again, she marvels that Megan is able to put Emma behind her.

We've moved on. We have to! Megan had screamed at her about six months ago. Or maybe accused, or disrespected (*a Megan word*), or blamed.

And as for Mark bringing his new girlfriend, well, she said it would be fine. The divorce is almost done. Mark needs to be here for Dom. If he's got someone new, then they may as well push past the hard part quickly.

Tash carries Emma like an open wound. If she was cut and bleeding right now, she's pretty sure no one would tell her to just ignore it.

'Tash!' Megan's call falls behind her.

'I'll just check the beach towels.' She forces herself to sound cheery and pushes out into the sun, striding past the outdoor pool, with its bleached wood loungers and stone-coloured furnishings. She takes the steps down to the beach. Their private bay is inaccessible from any other point other than by boat. The cove is sheltered and quiet. The sea calm.

She pulls off her clothes, wading in to the cool water until it's up to her neck, washing off the antiseptic hospital smell. She ignores the doctor's advice about taking things easy, doesn't care she's the only one here. The beach is her sanctuary.

A ferry travels at speed in the distance, taking hordes of people from Athens to Mykonos, to Santorini. Greece has six thousand islands, perfect and tranquil. So many tourists choosing just a few of them. This island is quiet. It's why they'd bought the villa years ago. When the popular tourist islands had built up quickly, springing five-star hotels out of the sand and filling tiny roads with huge SUVs, this island had retained its serenity. A small village half an hour away by car, near the port. A few villas like theirs, but the centre of the island is rocky, and they don't get any footfall. The only visitors who wind their way down the main road to the villa are invited. Close to the bigger islands, the party islands. And their boat, named *Lulu* after Tash's mum, with Stani, its skipper, can take them anywhere. Plus the helicopter if they need it. The bonus of wealth. Their tech company, huge in Britain, stretching across Europe and now the US.

She lets herself float, the sun hot, and she closes her eyes.

Mark. For years, they'd been a team. The two of them together had grown a tech empire, making gaming consoles successful enough to rival the biggest of names. It's eased their lives in ways she hadn't thought possible. She'd designed products with him and watched them fly. They'd met in London, living out of a tiny flat, and now they'd spread worldwide. Even after the divorce, there'll be hundreds of millions in her bank.

She's asked Mark to buy her out of the firm. She couldn't care about it any more, after Emma. They had so much. There was no need to push for more.

It had been wealth rather than fame they were after. They still have their anonymity. Neither of them had ever wanted notoriety. It's why their houses are secluded. Business isn't like the media. She is rarely recognised – not for the money anyway.

Sometimes for Emma. The media had let in a crack of cameras and eyes, staring back at her.

She lets her head dip back under water, appreciating the cool.

'Tash!' A man's shout flies easily across the water.

Sam. He's been able to come after all. Thank God. Something loosens inside of her.

'Hey!' She waves and swims in to shore. She walks out to the beach, heading for her dress before she hugs him. His blond hair is bright in the sun, and he wears a white shirt and blue shorts. He must have hit the beach in the States before getting here – he's tanned already and looks relaxed.

He averts his gaze. But Sam is her best friend and she's not embarrassed. They've skinny dipped plenty of times before after late night wine on holiday. She trusts him completely. He'd saved her after Mark had left. He'd picked up the pieces more than anyone else. Her rock. Her best friend.

'Sam,' she says, pulling her dress over her head and wrapping her arms around his chest, broad and strong. 'You came.'

'Of course.' He drops a kiss in her hair. 'I mean, can you imagine me staying away?'

She breathes out her first full exhale since the morning.

He smiles and hooks a strand of wet hair, fallen on her cheek, back behind her ear. 'Of course I came.'

3

Jaz

Friday

'Why did we fly commercial again?' Theo says, bored in the passport queue. Blond hair almost platinum, tall, in pale chino shorts and a blue patterned shirt, Hawaiian in style but clearly designer, open at the collar and loose. He checks his watch again. Jaz doesn't know the brand, but it's heavy with some sports timer thing round the sides.

'You know everyone else just calls it flying,' Jaz says and Dom laughs.

'She's right, mate. Come on, relax.' Dom squints at Theo. 'What happened to you on the flight since Boston? You were in such a good mood about coming here. Then I turned around and you were drinking so much I'm surprised you're not horizontal right now. It's barely time for lunch here in Greece.'

'Maybe I've developed a fear of flying.' Theo looks like he's forcing a smile.

'That's new!' Dom says.

'I've even got minis in my pocket.' Theo taps his shorts' pocket. 'For the helicopter.'

'No thank you,' Becki says, her Canadian lilt sunny and upbeat. She fingers the necklace Theo gave her for her birthday. 'If I'm meeting the great Natasha Cadel, then I'm going to be on best behaviour. Did you know she designed the Zen 3000? Awesome.'

'She's my mum, yeah?' Dom says, laughing. 'Of course I know.' His brow wrinkles. 'I think she's leaving the company, but I can't keep track.'

Jaz touches his arm as they move forward. Someone in the queue points at Theo. They hold a newspaper, and she can see his dad on the front. He had been plastered all over the papers handed out on the plane from Boston: *Senator Richard Fowler the next Vice President?* Theo is his spitting image, and there'd been a photo of Theo standing next to his father at a function on the inside story, near an article about a body being pulled from the Charles River in Boston – probably a drunk student, Jaz had thought. There were a few of those.

Excited chatter follows the pointing finger, but Theo remains determinedly oblivious. His face devoid of expression.

'Dude, is it true your dad's bringing his girlfriend?' Theo turns his back on the line behind them and faces Dom directly.

Jaz takes Dom's hand and squeezes it as he grimaces and nods. 'Yup.'

'What the fuck?' Theo says, shaking his head. 'I mean, I'm not exactly the Tact King, but even I get that it's crazy.'

'I don't get any of it,' Dom says. 'I haven't met her. Camilla or something. He said I'll be *surprised*.'

They separate and show passports. Jaz manages a *Kalimera* to the officer who returns a smile.

Following signs to collect their luggage, they step through the cool airport, the Athens' sun bright through the glass.

Jaz pulls out the pink sunglasses she'd picked up at a thrift store. They complement her hair.

'Your dad is losing it. Why would he bring a girlfriend? I thought he wanted to get your mom back?'

'I think he does.' Dom shrugs. 'Pass me one of those minis. I've changed my mind.'

Theo flips one out of his pocket, and Jaz watches it arc in the air and land in Dom's palm.

Dom has his mother's dark hair. Slightly shorter than Theo, but he carries more muscle. They both row competitively; Dom spends time in the gym too.

Jaz catches Dom's eye. She's waiting to see what he'll say when he gets there – how much he'll tell his parents. He's told no one but her. They'd spent the summer backpacking in Europe, and it had been a chance to get away from it all. But there's a ticking clock counting down, and Dom doesn't have long left. She's not surprised he needs a drink the closer he gets to the villa.

They head down the escalator to collect their baggage as he knocks the drink back in one.

Jaz watches Theo do the same. Becki catches her eye, the same tight expression on her face that she'd worn earlier in the year. Recently Becki has seemed much more relaxed. This look makes Jaz nervous.

When Becki and Theo had first got together it was like the dream. Meeting through the rowing club, they'd all hung out, always laughing, competing. They'd never make the number one university team, but they were good, and it had all been … fun.

Theo and Dom hadn't been as close since Dom switched dorm rooms, but they've been getting on much better since Easter. They've started to hang out as a four again towards the end of last term.

For the middle part of the academic year, it had been like the fun had run out – like the sand in a sand timer, once it's gone ... and it did seem to be gone. Theo lost his mom at Christmas in a car accident in a snowstorm. He'd been thrown clear, but she'd fallen in an icy lake, looking for help. They'd all been devastated, and Jaz doesn't know if that was what had seemed to run Theo off the rails. Clear grief, maybe some survivor's guilt.

For a while, whenever Jaz saw Becki, the gleam about her had seemed dimmer – whatever she was helping Theo to cope with was eating her up. And they hadn't gelled as a group. Whenever Jaz saw them, Theo was drunk, and Becki was tense. For a while, they'd gone through the motions as friends. Theo had lost his mom only recently, but Dom and Theo weren't the same. And Jaz wasn't sure that it didn't predate his mom's death. It was like there was something else between them that hadn't been there before.

But then the sun had come out, and they'd switched back to how they'd been. Like the timer had been turned. Theo had started drinking less; they'd all got on again.

It's a bad sign seeing him back on the booze.

Is he going to stop? Jaz wonders, watching Theo drink another. This is the first time in the last few months he and Dom have hung out and Theo has been drinking like this.

When she first met Dom, he and Theo were best friends and roommates before something cracked. She always supposes they must have argued, but Dom won't talk about it.

'Jaz,' Becki hisses, pulling her back.

The boys walk on, and Jaz feels Becki's fingers dig in her arm.

'The new girlfriend,' Becki says quietly, following the path of the boys with her eyes.

'You mean Dom's dad's girlfriend?'

Becki nods. 'I saw them together. They were out in Boston one night, having dinner. He was holding her hand.' Her eyes close briefly.

'What – is it someone we know?'

'No ... but I think –'

'Becki!' Theo leaps up behind them, grabs Becki round the waist. His blond hair flops forward as he picks her up and spins her. 'We've got the bags; we're good to go! I need to stop and grab something from the shops, but it won't take long.' He kisses her on the cheek, and the tension on her face melts to nothing. She laughs as he spins her again.

A few travellers nearby smile. Theo can make anyone fall in love with him, Jaz thinks. Who can resist those baby blues and the confidence he carries?

This break is what they all need.

Piling into the waiting car, sleek and with a uniformed driver, Theo asks for a stop when they pass a busy street just outside of Athens.

'Get me a coke?' Becki calls as Theo jumps out of the car and disappears into a market.

'What does he need?' Dom asks, checking his watch. 'He can't need more booze! Mum's sent the helicopter. We should get a move on.'

Just as the sun starts burrowing its way into Jaz's arm, as she sits by the window, Theo bounces back into the car.

'Gifts for your mom,' he says.

He carries a few bags. Some are bulky.

'Ready!' Dom says to the driver and lays his head back against the seat, leaning on Jaz. 'Not long to go!'

4

Tash

'Mum?' Dom's shout is loud in the whitewashed entrance hall. It's almost 2 p.m. now and she's been keeping track of where they are. Tash runs down the winding stairs. She'd been watching the car approach from her balcony.

'Sweetheart!' Tash wraps her arms around him, squeezing him, breathing him in. God, she's missed him.

She'd only been twenty-one when she'd had him, and it had just been the two of them for the first few years, before Mark. Their bond is tight, like the cord has never been cut.

'You're taller still!' She stands back to look at him and ruffles his hair. She couldn't stop the smile cracking wide over her face if she wanted to. 'Look at you. How was the flight?'

'Good. Delayed out of Boston, but thank God we're away. The summer's been great. Not looking forward to going back to Harvard. The exams were hard. Mum, you remember Jaz?'

Tash watches the touch of pride on his face as he pulls this red-haired beauty of a girl forward. Her hair lies in curls down her back.

It hurts just a little. This letting him go.

'Ms Cadel, how lovely to see you again.' Jaz hands her a jar of something pretty, some kind of jam. A mid-western twang to her accent, her expression eager to please. 'Dom said you like the farm jams the best. I made it when I was last home.'

'Thank you. Call me Natasha.' She hugs Jaz. She's only met her a few times but if she's important to Dom, she needs to make an effort.

Tash has dressed carefully. Tidying herself up after the swim, she wears white with some jewellery. Megan always dresses like she's photo shoot ready, and Tash had not wanted to be outdone: she is the hostess after all. Her hair isn't as glossy or as well looked after as Megan's, but she's dried it straight and shiny.

She wants to look her best, particularly with Mark arriving tomorrow. Just in case he comes early. With this girlfriend, she didn't want to be caught out looking like a forty-two-year-old in some divorcee novel. With Megan's arrival, Tash has made more effort with her appearance. The basics are there – she runs most days, she swims all the time, she does yoga. She feels confident she can hold her own – if she can just force herself to care.

She's on edge this weekend. So much to prove. It's important Dom has a good birthday. Important his friends like her. Important Mark's new girlfriend doesn't pity her.

Important she tries to make peace with last year, one way or the other.

Thank God for Sam. He walks in from the kitchen now, holding a tray of drinks, his strawberry blond hair falling forward into his eyes. 'Mojitos?' He holds out the tray, adopting a croaky older tone. 'Do young people like mojitos or are they old fashioned?'

'Thank you, Sir,' Theo says dropping his bag and stepping forward.

'*Sir*, he won't like that!' Tash laughs. 'Call him Sam. You must remember him from last summer?' She puts a hand on his arm. 'I'm sorry about your mum. I hope you're doing OK.'

Theo smiles at her as he takes a drink but doesn't say anything.

Tash had been to the funeral – the last time she'd spoken to Theo. He'd been quiet there too. Something has vanished from his face – nothing she can put her finger on, but he's paler now, despite the sun. His eyes more veiled.

She needs to keep an eye on him.

There's laughter as the drinks are taken, and Tash sips hers, her eyes flicking back to her son.

Dom is already back-slapping Sam. 'How did that date turn out?' he asks him, and Sam laughs, rolling his eyes.

'Let's just say we decided to leave it at one. I think she was too good-looking for me.' Sam laughs.

'Is that a thing?' Tash says. 'Anyone would be lucky to have you!'

'Sam's been buying me lunches recently since he's been working in Boston, but I think it's just to try to get access to some of my tutors. The fit ones.' Dom lifts a mojito and hands one to Jaz. 'They love his English accent.'

'I might leave,' Sam says, rolling his eyes comically.

'I hope you're not leading him astray. Godfathers have an example to set,' Tash says, grinning at them.

'Dom is the one trying to lead me astray!' Sam says. 'He's determined to parade me around like a prize cow.'

Sam had married Tash's best friend after university. They'd all been close. When Tash and Mark had tied the knot, they'd holidayed together, had New Years together. His wife made a shock exit and left him, and Tash had made even more space in her life for Sam.

Since Mark left, Sam has returned the favour. Four down to two.

'You be kind to Sam – he's not getting any younger,' she says, pulling her son in for one more hug. Wanting him to herself. 'Want to get changed and we'll head to the pool? Dinner's later, you've got a few hours before sunset drinks.'

'Ms Cadel, this is Becki.' Theo, in his Ivy League American accent, sounds ever charming as he introduces a blond-haired girl wearing a crop top and her hair pulled up into a high bun. She's slight, but her eyes are blue and burst out of her face as she smiles; she fills the room. 'It's so good of you to invite me, Ms Cadel. I'm a huge fan of your work.' The lilt of Canadian.

'Natasha, please. You're at school with them too?'

She nods. 'We met on the rowing team. I'm a cox.'

'Well, we'll have to get you out sailing while you're here.' Tash smiles, but now that Dom is heading out of the room, she feels tired. Her head aches a little, and she touches the edge of her brow where she made contact with the marble ground in Athens, all those hours ago. The bruise hides beneath an expensive concealer borrowed from Megan. The touch makes her think of Emma and Tash feels her smile stick to her face, to keep it from dropping.

'We'll see you by the pool.'

They disappear up the stairs and Sam looks at her. 'You OK?'

She nods. For Sam she doesn't need to make an effort.

'What is it?' His eyes narrow a little, looking at her. 'Is it Mark? I can't believe he's doing this to you. Surely coming would be hard enough, but bringing a girlfriend?'

Tash opens her mouth, grapples with the words stuck in her throat.

'Not him. I think I saw Emma this morning.'

5

Tash

'You think it was really Emma?' Sam asks, out in the sun and ready for her to say yes or no and believe her either way, and Tash is so grateful for this she could cry.

They sit by the pool on loungers, cocktail in hand.

'I don't know.' Her shoulders almost sag, but she holds them up. Resolve firm. 'I'm going to try to work out what happened last year. This weekend might help things come to light. It wasn't all smooth then – you remember – Richard was drunk and behaving badly, you were kind to Nancy. Emma, Theo and Dom spent most of the time on *Lulu*, diving, swimming and exploring. But something must have happened. I'm sure she didn't drown. I can feel it. I've missed something – there is more to Emma vanishing, I'm certain.' She fingers the bracelets. 'I know Meg and I don't agree, but I'm so sure she left this on purpose.'

When their parents had died years ago in a car accident, the sisters had bought themselves matching bracelets – thin gold chains with the birthstones of their parents set either side of the clasp. Tash never took hers off. She's sure Emma didn't either. When Emma had vanished, Tash had found Emma's on her dressing table. It had been hours later, when Tash was searching for some clue. Emma had removed it and taken it into Tash's room for her to find.

'No one wants to mention Emma this weekend,' Sam says quietly. 'Megan has asked them all to try to leave her in peace and just focus on Dom's birthday. She doesn't want you upset. I think there's been some tacit agreement to focus on Dom and try to honour Emma by letting her lie in peace.' He speaks softly, but the words are like tiny needles in a wound for Tash. He glances at the bracelet. 'You know Megan thinks that if the bracelet was left for any reason, it was a goodbye. She thinks maybe Emma swam out not intending to come back. She must have had some bad news about her boyfriend. Her behaviour was a little erratic last year.'

'I'm so sure Meg's wrong. Emma must have left it for me as reassurance.' Tash shakes her head quickly in frustration.

There's just no way Emma would leave her. Not like that. Tash feels it in her bones. The bracelet was a message of reassurance. Nothing else.

Tash has phoned the police so frequently with possible sightings of Emma she hears their sigh at the other end of the line. She'd been declared lost at sea a few months ago, and a memorial had been held for her. But Tash has never given up hope. She could have been rescued – even if she had swum out with the saddest of intentions. She could be somewhere – waiting for her big sister to come and get her.

'There's no point phoning the police. They think I'm mad.' Her eyes close briefly and she rubs at her head, where the throb from the bang earlier still aches. 'I asked them to follow a lead about six months ago. It came to nothing, but there was a sighting in Italy.'

'Who saw her?' Sam asks.

Tash stares down at the pool. 'Me,' she says, in a small voice. I was on the ferry to Brindisi. Sometimes I take a tourist route, go on the cheap seats and look for her. I really thought it was her – in the crowds as we were getting off. It didn't come to anything, but the CCTV looked like a possible – I was convinced. The police weren't. I just –' She looks at Sam. 'I just can't let her go.'

There is shouting and laughter bursting out of the villa. Dom leads, almost hurling himself down the steps, with Jaz shrieking behind him. Theo follows, picking up Becki and jumping straight into the pool with her. Water flies everywhere and Tash smiles, sitting back on the lounger and feeling herself really start to relax. Twenty-one years ago today, she'd been a terrified twenty-one-year-old swollen up to the size of a house. Now he's out in the world and thriving. It's strange how her heart can balance such love for Dom and grief for Emma. She's capable of being happy and enjoying life, and carrying an ache. Here particularly. The heart is more than a muscle: the scope of a universe, the lightness of breath.

Megan sits down, and Tash puts out her hand onto her sister's by way of an apology for striding away earlier.

Her sister's brutal honesty is part of why she loves her.

'Sam,' Megan says, smiling at him. 'Been working out?'

Sam blushes and laughs. 'Blame Dom. He told me it was about time I got serious about the gym. I've been paying for membership like the money itself is doing all the hard lifting.'

Tash glances at Sam. Megan is right. There are muscles, toned and prominent, she doesn't remember seeing before. 'Are you sure that date you went on hasn't got any future?' she says, lifting her eyebrows. 'You haven't been working out a bit more for a reason? There must be someone new for all this hard work.'

'Right!' Sam says, standing. 'I'm going to swim to get away from all this badgering!'

Tash sees Megan watch him dive into the pool. 'What about you? Any new love interests?'

'Oh Christ, New York is not the place to date. I thought it would be amazing. I've been there six months now but it's worse than London! Anyway, being partner now takes up so much time.'

Megan has never needed Tash's sympathy. Tash thinks of Mark arriving soon with his new girlfriend. Who would want the complexity a relationship can bring?

'Mum, let's head out on *Lulu* – Mykonos windmills for sunset? Then back for a late dinner here?' Dom shouts. 'Is Stani around?'

Tash nods. 'Yes, I asked him if he could keep this weekend free for us. I'll let him know.'

She calls the captain of their boat. They only use the villa a few months each year, so she'd had to make sure he was around. He works for a few families with villas here. He's known Dom since he was small, and Emma too. He's almost part of the family. When Mark and Tash got married, they came here for part of their honeymoon – the villa a wedding present from Mark – and Stani took them round hundreds of the islands.

When Mark had left, she'd come here to recover, and he'd taken her out on a similar trip treading the same path – it had been catharsis at sea.

There's no place like Greece for catharsis.

'A late lunch first,' she says, putting the phone down. 'I'll head in and tell Maria. You stay and swim,' she tells Megan.

Tash looks out at the blue sky, where the golden sun has dropped a touch lower.

Then there's a loud bellow of, 'Dom!' as Mark steps out onto the poolside and her stomach drops like a stone.

Mark and his girlfriend.

Too late, she realises this isn't such a good idea after all.

6

Tash

Tash feels Megan's hand tighten on hers, and despite being sure she was ready for this, her mouth is too dry to speak. She's grateful to Dom and Sam who approach Mark to say hello and give her a few minutes.

Mark enters like only Mark can. Sure of himself, six foot two, lean, dark hair and eyes almost black. Not handsome exactly – his face lacks symmetry, and that unsettles his crisp features. But usually happy, with an eager air and eyes that dart to the next thing. To the next challenge. The next race. And now, the next woman.

If she knows him well enough – and she does – there's the tiniest touch of hesitancy to what he does next. He's clearly thinking maybe this wasn't such a great idea.

'This is Kiki,' Mark says, and from behind him steps a young woman in a short green dress with thin shoulder straps and blond hair that reaches all the way down her back in waves.

Long tanned legs. An ankle bracelet. A diamond necklace that has *gift from Mark* written all over it. He always did make the obvious choices. *Classic*, he'd say.

There is a collective pause for just a second. Even a gasp from one or two. All eyes on this woman who is young enough to be his daughter, tanned and some kind of shimmer spray on her arms and chest, perfectly turned out, Insta ready.

Tash shoots a look at Dom – he stares at Kiki in disbelief, before masking his face in a smile of welcome as he hugs his dad.

'Fuck, what is she, twenty-five? Twenty-six?' Megan hisses, next to Tash. 'I wonder what she sees in the forty-five-year-old millionaire? He's such a classic twat.'

Shit, Tash thinks. She should have known.

'Come on,' Tash says, quietly to Megan, finding her voice. 'I need to get this over with.'

Rising, she swallows hard and finds her smile. This is her house. She has invited them here – and she needs to remember why she did it. Dom needs both parents around for his birthday. She's determined to be civilised about this. It's time to move on. All the reasons they'd split up still stand. Even if he's rubbing her nose in it right now, to clearly punish her. To win.

'Mark!' she says, and she leans in for a hug. There's an awkward moment where Mark goes to kiss her on the cheek, and they bump faces. Colour rises in his cheeks as he looks to Kiki and back to Tash.

'Tash, meet Kiki. You said it was OK if she came ...' There's a catch in his voice. He looks briefly like he wishes the ground would swallow him up. No matter what his thinking – and she's pretty sure it was about winning – he seems to be regretting it right now. She knows him so well. He would have planned it when he was angry, then in the moment his innate sense of decency would point out to him that it is the behaviour of a prick.

'Kiki, how lovely to meet you. I'm Natasha,' Tash says, thinking that if she calls her Tash, she'll punch her in the face. It's not this woman's fault, and yet she can still fuck off if she thinks Tash is making space for her.

'You're early!' She turns back to Mark.

'We caught an earlier flight.' He opens his mouth to say something else but whatever it is runs dry.

He came early to put her on the back foot. Off course he did. Overall, the divorce has been fairly straightforward. No huge rows, money and property divided cleanly. More than enough for them to share and not feel a pinch, or the need to fight.

But the feelings …

The feelings are raw. They'd both been floored. And Tash knows Mark. Gentle, kind, intelligent, but ambitious – and with the need to win. He would try and win anything and everything. The hint of competition – the merest whiff. Right now, he's proving in the divorce race he's acing who can recover the fastest. Move on the quickest.

Well, he can have this one.

Sam steps up and puts his arm around her shoulders and says, 'Mark, hi! Been ages.'

Thank God for Sam. She sees Mark's eyes flick from her to Sam and back. There's never been anything between them, but it won't hurt Mark to question it. Particularly with Sam looking so good, standing with his newly acquired tanned six pack, in swim shorts, with legs that have sprouted muscles like he's been airbrushed.

She sees Kiki give him a quick glance. Sam beams at her for a second then looks straight back to Mark.

Take all the time you need, she thinks. And she lets Sam's arm lie over her shoulder rather than move to offer drinks.

'Sam runs our US office,' Tash says to Kiki, and as she thought, Kiki's gaze homes in on Sam a little more. 'He's moved to Boston to sort out the office there. Says he prefers the coffee.'

Kiki's eyes hang on to Sam as Tash slips out of his arm and moves to the safety of the kitchen. All this positioning is exhausting. She's not with Sam, and she doesn't want to be with Mark. Why should she care if he has a new girlfriend almost half her age?

Yet she finds she does.

It's a most unwelcome surprise.

7

Jaz

'Jaz, can you talk?' Becki speaks quietly, glancing round the room for Dom.

'He's in the shower,' Jaz says. 'Come in. What's wrong?'

She leads Becki through the large, cool bedroom. They'd eaten by the pool and were changing for the trip to Mykonos. It was an hour by boat apparently. Jaz was looking forward to being out on the sea.

Two sleek modern armchairs sit either side of a coffee table by the window. The view looks out onto the Aegean Sea, flat and still. Perfect.

'Theo?' Jaz asks, pouring them water from the carafe.

Becki nods. She collapses in the chair and lets loose her hair before tying it up again. Her eyes are the colour of the sea behind her, but her brows are low as she frowns. 'His dad called him when we arrived. He didn't pick up to start with. But then he phoned three times in a row. I thought, when we got here, he'd started to relax, but he took the call in the bathroom and when he came out he was ... different.'

'What do you mean?'

'He was like it when his mom died. I waited for him to start talking to me, or to someone. But he didn't. He just kind of went quiet – kind of blank. And he drank. Then he went away for a few weeks at Easter, and he seemed to have come round. He's been great. I mean, not with his dad – every conversation I've ever heard him have with his dad ends in a fight. But he started drinking on the plane, and it's like he's back to where he was at the start of the year. He spoke to his dad before the flight, and then again now. He downed another drink immediately after it ended and left the room. He's just grunted at me. If he's going to go back to how he was, then I'll wish I hadn't come.' Her eyes close and she takes a quick breath.

Jaz doesn't know what to say. Theo has been upbeat in public – polite. 'I hadn't realised he was being a douche.'

Becki shakes her head, retying her hair. 'No – don't get me wrong. He's not horrible. He's just gone back to being – distant. It makes me uneasy. He bought something from the shops when we stopped after the airport, and I teased him earlier, pretending to look in the bag and he snatched it back off me.'

'A present for you?' Jaz suggests.

'Not that kind of snatch – kind of nervous. I'm going to look later. I'm not going to just sit around and worry about this. Not on top of everything else. He's going to be wasted tonight, on the boat. I just hope it's good, party-time wasted and not moody, unreachable. Can you help, if it gets tricky?'

Jaz wraps her arms around Becki, releasing the faint whiff of chlorine now rather than plane-scented staleness. 'Of course! Look, go and have a shower. Change. The sun is gorgeous outside, and the sunset will be stunning. Dom said Mykonos is beautiful – busy, but worth it. You're not on your own. We're here, and we can distract Theo.' Even as Jaz says this she feels like she's skimming over Becki's worries.

If she's honest, she knows it goes further back. Theo was weird before Christmas. Dom too. And Dom had pulled out of a few nights out when he knew Theo would be there. She thought that was all behind them. She forces herself to smile. 'You deserve a break. Let's just try to enjoy this weekend. His dad will be busy so shouldn't be bothering Theo – he's all over the press and is always doing interviews. He never stops campaigning.'

Becki nods. 'Thanks, Jaz.' She's still pale. She rises, hands fidgeting with her necklace – the one Theo had bought her for her birthday just after they got together. She never takes it off.

Jaz walks her to the door, and as she closes it, she turns and looks back out at the startling blue, the gold of the sun.

She hopes what she said to Becki is right – he might be drinking too much, but that's it. It's not like Theo is *dangerous*. He's just acting erratic right now. But his mom is dead only this year, making his dad, the grieving widower, the darling of the party, and the darling of America. That's a lot.

Greece will help them all.

8

Tash

The sea is a touch darker as they climb aboard *Lulu*, stepping off the edge of the jetty, which leads out from their beach.

The vessel is sleek with a high-tech kitchen and dining table at the stern, with cushioned seats arcing round the edge of the covered kitchen, above which Stani sits at the wheel. Below deck there are two bedrooms with en suites. Up on the bow, there are two other levels. A slightly raised area where they mainly lie in the sun or sit cross-legged and eat picnic-style if the sun isn't too hot. At the prow, there are loungers before the boat comes to a point. Rails run round the edges. It will fit about twenty at most, in various seated arrangements. It's perfect for the islands – it will sail into shallow waters and dock easily just offshore. They keep a dinghy tied up on the rails to the port side, which seats five at the most. It enables them to drop anchor at remote beaches and head right onto the beach. That way they can avoid the busy ports.

Tash watches Kiki climb up the steps from the lower deck and call to Mark, sitting up front where the sun drops its rays. Kiki is dazzling – she's changed into a tiny bikini and wears a crocheted cover-up. Tash sighs.

Megan also looks amazing – she's pulled on a black throw and has piled her hair up on her head.

'You look as though you're dressed for dinner,' Tash says, as Megan slips her arm through hers as they follow the others onto *Lulu*. The scent of citronella rises from the candles that line the walkway.

'Ah, you don't pay top dollar to look cheap!' Megan smiles. 'If I'm going to have a baby before it's too late, I suppose I better get on with meeting someone, yes? Can't hurt to look the part. What happens if we crash into some billionaire's yacht tonight?'

'Who wouldn't want you?' Tash says, always surprised at her sister's seemingly permanent single status.

'Stani is looking pretty good,' Megan whispers as the captain of *Lulu* walks towards them, arm held out to help them on board.

'Evening, Tash.' Stani speaks in a low, gravelly voice. His Greek accent lilting.

'Stani, you remember my sister, Meg?'

Tash buries a laugh, watching Stani extend his arm to Megan, who preens. Stani is ever the gent. Weathered and quiet, the strong silent type, he smiles as she cracks a joke and flashes her white, white teeth.

Dom runs up from behind them, taking the gap between the walkway and *Lulu* in a single leap and bear hugs Stani as the women step aboard.

'My God, those eyes!' Megan says, as they climb up to the deck.

'Single, I think,' Tash says. 'Mid fifties. Those eyes are a bit of the ocean, aren't they?'

'He's fucking gorgeous. Silver fox, but that body – not an ounce of flab. Have you ever thought ... you must have!'

'Might have crossed my mind,' Tash laughs.

'Champagne?' Mark says, standing at the bow of *Lulu*, and he opens a bottle, deft and sure, catching the first spray of fizz in a glass and filling them all. 'Dom, you lazy sod, come and make yourself useful.' Now that the initial introductions are over, he's relaxed into the familiar surroundings of the boat, the sea his second home. He looks like the real Mark again – the one she could write the book about. He reaches out to ruffle Dom's hair as he holds out the coupes.

That's it, Tash thinks. The reason she could never hate him. The bond between Mark and Dom. She'd struck gold when she'd married him. They'd been a unit so tight nothing could split them up – until Emma disappeared, and they'd fallen apart as cleanly as if they'd been severed by a blade.

'One for me?' she says, climbing up next to him and kissing him on the cheek. 'I'm pleased you came,' she says, taking the next glass.

'It's good to see you, T,' he says, softly. The sun lowers a touch behind his head, and his black eyes look darker. 'You look good. The sun suits you. And I just want to say it once, but I'll be thinking about Emma this weekend; focusing on Dom, obviously, but I know it will hurt, and I miss her too.'

'One for me too?' Kiki calls, and Mark's eyes hold Tash's for a second longer, before he steps away.

Tash can't speak for a moment. She swallows hard. Every now and again, there is the flash of the Mark she had forgotten about.

'One for all of you!' he says. 'Jaz, Becki. It's ladies first.'

'So old fashioned, Dad!' Dom groans. 'They're not weak women.'

'Chivalry, not old-fashioned,' Mark says, reaching for another bottle as he sees Theo is still empty.

Dom fiddles with his phone, and music stretches out across the sea. A chilled-out beat.

The boat glides out to skirt the southern tip of the island, before it heads further out to sea and towards Mykonos. The songs change, and the island slips by on their right, the salted air of the sea more pronounced in the light breeze.

Stani shouts out that there are snacks lower down if anyone wants as he steers *Lulu*. He looks across at Tash and smiles.

She and Mark have known Stani for fifteen years, sailing out with him every time they came over to Greece. She has no idea what he does when she's not here, and she doesn't care. He manages to slip in and out of their lives with ease, never showing more interest in anything than she's willing to share. Dom knows him like an uncle.

'Think I could have me some Greek captain as a holiday treat?' Megan says, sitting cross-legged up next to Tash at the front of the bow of *Lulu*. The deck has a half-circular array of chairs behind them with a low coffee table and then ample space at the front for sunbathing. Steps lead down to the water from the left.

'Give it a shot. There are two cabins below – you could make use of those later,' Tash says. She deadpans a serious face. 'But keep it down, why don't you? Don't be all *loud* – I don't want to *hear* it.'

Megan bats her lightly and closes her eyes, lifting her face to the falling sun. 'Shut up. I'm demure, as the kids would say. Not tonight anyway. Tonight, I want to chill with you and drink you dry of champagne.'

'All the way!' The others call to the left, and Tash sees Theo, Dom and Becki surrounding Jaz who is attempting a handstand on the moving boat.

'Waves incoming!' Stani calls, and Jaz topples right, falling on Dom who grabs her and kisses her. 'Almost. My turn. First person up straight wins, and you have to hold it for three seconds.'

'Out of the way, dude, let me,' Theo says, lowering his arms in preparation.

'Handstands? You're having a handstand competition?' Sam says. 'What about shots until you drop?'

'We're not stuck in the 80s,' Theo says. 'Shots later. We're doing upper body strength with the rowing team to stay supple. I'm fucking killing it.'

Arms locked he bends forward and rises. Dom glances up at Stani, nodding towards Theo.

Tash sees Stani send him a wink, and just as Theo swings his legs fully up, *Lulu* swerves to the left. 'Sorry, debris!' Stani shouts.

Theo topples over and jumps up to his feet. There's a flash of anger on his face, which quickly slips away. 'You did that on purpose, man,' he says to Dom.

'I ain't driving the boat, dude.' Dom shrugs. Then lets out a bay of laughter. 'Come on. Best dive? Stani!' he shouts up at the captain. 'Can you stop? Can we swim before we head out on the ocean to Mykonos, just for half an hour?'

Stani taps his hand to his forehead in a mock salute, and the boat slows.

Dom unhooks the chain that crosses above the rail of steps and pulls off his T-shirt. 'See you in there!' He stands facing inwards and springs up and back, arcing over in a perfect backwards dive, entering the water with barely a splash.

Theo runs and cannon-balls right next to him, water splashing up onto the boat deck.

'I'm soaked!' Kiki shouts.

'Come in then,' Theo calls.

She lifts the crotchet dress up and over her head, and in her tiny bikini, she walks to the edge of *Lulu* and turns to smile at Mark then dives in.

'Fuck, who do I have to kill for a twenty-year-old's body?' Megan says. Her legs stretch out in the falling sun, the heat still close. She's tied a scarf around her hair and with her huge sunglasses, *Jackie Onassis in her youth*, Tash thinks.

'I don't think I ever looked like that, but you've got boat-chic down good and proper,' Tash says, glancing out to the water where Kiki shrieks as Theo splashes her. Then she shrugs, forcing herself again to remember that she doesn't want Mark any more. 'Come on. Let's go in. I could do with cooling off.'

Diving in after the girls, Tash, Megan and Mark hit the water in quick succession.

The light is lower now – the sun has eased its heat a notch. It's not too far to the Windmills and Mykonos for the sunset. The music sings out across the water, and Tash lies back, floating – the only thing missing is Emma. Pain stabs quickly below her chest, and she closes her eyes. She won't make a fuss in front of the others and take the shine from Dom's weekend.

Dom's birthday party is in two days. Two days to find the answers.

9

Jaz

The windmills at Mykonos are busy. Crowds preen for photos, but it's not a crush, thankfully – people breathe in the sunset, the sky billowing orange like a spilled paint pot.

'Smile!' Natasha says, as they all cluster together.

'Again!' Dom shouts, and bends for Jaz to jump on his back.

Becki follows suit with Theo and the girls hold hands, arms aloft.

'Perfect!' Natasha calls.

Jumping down, Dom grabs her by the waist. 'Come on, let's get a drink before we sail home. There's a great bar up on the road.'

The four of them run up between white houses and shops, painted white and blue. Jewellery stands line up outside, along with T-shirts and caps.

Mykonos isn't tourist tat though – she notes the expensive labels on some of the shops, the fancy bags and jewellery on the tourists.

'I'll catch up,' Jaz says. She wants a few minutes browsing the stalls.

She tries on a bracelet with dark red beads. It will match her hair. She loves everything red. Becki is all about the blues, but Jaz likes the dark tones. She pays for it and moves to the next stall.

'That's pretty!' Kiki steps towards the rack of rings Jaz is looking at and picks one up. 'What do you think of this?'

'It's lovely,' Jaz says, feeling wrong-footed. Part of her wants to support Natasha out of loyalty to Dom, and being too friendly to Kiki feels wrong. But none of this is her fault. Mark and Natasha are big enough to run their own lives.

'I like the green one more,' Jaz says, picking a silver ring with a huge green stone. 'Try it. It matches your eyes.'

'Matches your eyes,' Kiki repeats in a mimic and bats her eyelashes. She laughs. 'Sorry, not taking the piss out of you.'

Jaz smiles. 'If my sis was here, she'd talk contouring too, if you need more accessory advice. She's a wannabee make-up artist. She posts videos on YouTube all the time. I'm lucky if I remember to wash my face when I go to bed.'

'I've invested in top of the range stuff for this trip. I knew I'd be *of interest*.' Kiki air quotes then picks out a beaded necklace and holds it up against her. 'What about this one?'

Jaz nods.

'I wasn't sure what it was going to be like – Mark said the four of you were at Harvard. I was worried it would be all pearls and roll necks.'

'It's not *exactly* like *Legally Blond*,' Jaz says. 'I mean, I don't wear a pink bikini to lectures and I don't own any pearls or Chanel. I could ace a bend and snap though, after a few shots.'

Kiki laughs and looks at her appraisingly. 'Jaz is a cool name.'

'Short for Jasmine. My sister is called Oregano.' She keeps her face deadpan.

'She's not!'

'Nah. Poppy. My mom likes flowers. And Kiki?'

'I'm really Camilla, but I've got a younger brother who couldn't say my name and Kiki kind of stuck.' She reaches for earrings and looks at herself in a mottled mirror, which hangs near the jewellery layout. 'You know, I feel like we've met before.'

Jaz shrugs a little. 'Really? Were you at Harvard at any point? It's a big campus. Oh, hang on, am I right you worked as a counsellor there?'

'Not any more. Got another line of income right now. Good job too, all that contouring powder costs as much as the flight over here. Gotta get going. I'm meeting Mark for a quick drink.' She holds Jaz's gaze for a moment. 'Thanks for the chat.'

'Here,' Jaz picks up the green ring. 'You should buy it. It suits you.'

Kiki nods.

Jaz watches her leave, her brain buzzing. Then her phone rings. 'Where are you?'

'Coming!' she says to Dom. 'Sorry!'

'Here!' Dom meets her with the others at the door, and they enter a bar, which has a balcony overlooking the sea. It's like magic – the view is gorgeous.

He's clearly known there, and the waitress seats them at a prominent table. Dom has a word with her then they all flop in their seats.

'I'd forgotten about this place,' Theo says, smiling across at Dom. 'We had a good time last year. With Emma too.'

'We did. I wish she was here this weekend.' Dom smiles.

'Me too.' Theo clinks Dom's glass, just once.

Jaz shoots Dom a look, checking in. But he seems to take this well. He's been talking about Emma a bit in the run up to the weekend, but he's wary about upsetting his mum and was trying not to mention her much.

'Good choice.' Theo takes Becki's hand and points out a few cruise ships sitting further out at sea and to the streets below that sit between them and the water. The harbour lies to the right, along a narrow road which wends up above the footpath that passes to the port through restaurants that are sea-scented and burn candles in this post-sunset amber half-light.

Jaz leans over the white balcony, looking down at the water. She can see Mark and Megan by a shop, browsing.

Kiki is on her own, near a designer shop, on the phone. Jaz wonders what her new job can be – when she'd seen Kiki she couldn't imagine her as a counsellor. But actually, after talking to her, Kiki is funny and seems pretty smart. First impressions can be a killer.

Natasha walks the opposite way along a narrow street, her arm looped through Sam's, and is laughing at Sam trying to eat an ice cream the size of his head.

'Sam's really nice,' she says.

Dom nods. 'He's the best. He works with Mum and Dad – he runs the US office since they've stepped back from the day to day running of the company. He was an investor early on, but he's never had anything to do with the design, that's all Mum and Dad.'

'It's good he's here – for your Mom. Now that ...' she trails off, looking over at Kiki who makes her way back towards Mark. They're elevated, so he can't see her.

Dom helps the waitress as she returns with a tray of cocktails, and Jaz sees Mark and Megan – what? – are they arguing? She looks more closely at them.

Megan is poking him in the chest, almost aggressively, and gesticulating. Mark isn't having any of it. He shakes his head. She wishes she could hear what they're saying.

Jaz sees Kiki turn the corner and spot the pair. She stops, watching them. They haven't seen her. Whatever they're saying, Kiki is clearly listening.

'Thanks,' Jaz says to Dom, taking a cocktail.

When she looks back, Megan has vanished and Kiki has wrapped her arms around Mark, kissing him on the mouth, her hand low on his back, the other wrapped up in his hair. He goes to stand upright, but she pulls him down again, pulling him in tighter.

He doesn't resist, Jaz notices. He glances around, to check no one's watching, but is more than happy to comply. Strangers glance their way, but Natasha has disappeared out of sight with Sam.

Mark is friendly enough, but Jaz thinks he's an idiot. Natasha was clearly going through something. No matter how hard she pushed her husband away, he should have just waited for her to work it through. Men are such assholes at times.

Jaz doesn't want to look any longer. She turns back to the table and laughs at something Theo says. When she looks back, Mark leads Kiki out of the shop, face flushed, eyes bright, hand tight on Kiki. He's a cat with cream. Kiki carries a bag in her hand, complete with expensive logo.

Megan starts down the same street but, seeing them, turns and steps into a nearby shop.

The tourist streets are busy, thick and woven with bodies. The temperature falling just a touch.

Jaz turns back to the group, losing interest in it all.

'Come on,' Dom says after their drinks. 'Let's get back to *Lulu*. I promised Stani we wouldn't stay much later.'

10

Tash

The gentle descent of darkness is like velvet on the water. In a bubble of soft light on *Lulu*, Stani steers them back towards the villa as Dom changes the music to songs they all recognise. Tash sings along to a soulful Adele track, as the air cools and is soft on her sun-exposed skin.

Megan sits up with Stani. The champagne has been free-flowing, and Megan has drunk her fair share. Tash can hear her laugh from up beside the captain's seat. This weekend could prove interesting.

'Feeling OK?' Sam says, sitting down next to her, where Megan had been. His blond hair falls forward over his sunglasses, and he lifts them up. His brown eyes are warm. He tops up her glass.

'Better than OK, surprisingly,' she says, smiling and reaching out to rub his arm quickly. 'And thanks for keeping an eye on Dom in Boston. He tells me you've been taking him out for regular lunches. Hope he's been behaving himself.'

'Ah, to be young. When life is full of drama and possibilities.' He laughs, and Tash wonders if there's something he's not saying: he didn't quite answer the question. But it's too late to probe, and she's had too much to drink to choose this moment for anything other than lying back. Even the blister of Kiki isn't rubbing as badly as it had earlier. Mark has clearly been trying to keep any displays of affection to a minimum.

'Theo, come down!' Becki calls out. She's halfway through tying up her hair as he leaps up onto the seat at the bow of the boat.

Instead, Theo grabs his glass and sings into it as the song reaches its chorus. It's another Adele belter, and Theo has a good voice and is an excellent mimic. He leans back over the water as he sings.

'Seriously!' Becki stands up now. 'Theo, you're pissed! Come down.'

Most of them are laughing, and Theo hams up his performance, throwing out his arm to perform the big line.

'Theo –' There's concern now in Becki's tone, and Tash looks at her, then back to Theo. What is she worried about? What does she know? Is it about his drinking – they'd all had some, but surely he'll just step down now. Does he seem drunker than the rest of them? Tash sits up straighter. If he's really pissed, then this is dangerous. Maybe this is more than just performative karaoke. She remembers his dad, Richard, blind drunk most evenings here last year.

'Theo!' she calls. 'Becki is right. Come down!'

As he strikes a pose, his arms flail a little and his head sways. He wobbles. The mood changes. The laughter slows.

'Enough!' Stani shouts. 'Come down from there now!'

Theo climbs, instead, closer to the front rails and tries to balance on the middle rail, reaching out precariously across the sea. 'King of the world!'

Sam stands. 'Enough mate. It's funny, but it's late and too dark. Come down.'

'Theo!' Tash shouts. She can't get to him – none of them can. He just needs to take a step back. If ... She can't think the worst. 'Theo!'

Undeterred, Theo stands, legs apart, in a full-on diva stance, leaning against the rails and tilting out over the water. He lifts both arms up, singing at top volume.

What happens next is both quick and painfully slow – Sam and Dom are already moving towards Theo, from two different directions, and Tash sees them both as though in slow motion. But there's no time.

Almost inevitably, he topples.

Tash isn't sure whether it's the boat's movement or if he slips on the rail, but one moment Theo is up, performing for them all, and the next, he's gone. Half a cry sounding out in the night air. Followed by a piercing scream from Becki and a torrent of Greek swear words from Stani.

Tash swallows hard, thinking of Emma, her own accident in the water. She can't move.

'Oh my God!' Becki screams, and Tash is frozen.

Theo is gone.

11

Tash

Dom is the first one to the edge.

'Don't jump!' Tash screams, fear for Dom spurring her into action. 'Wait!' *Lulu* hasn't slowed to a halt yet, although Stani has undoubtedly done all he can. They need to enter the water from the stern or they'll be hit. Her stomach is sick thinking about Theo down there.

But Dom knows enough about boats and instead throws in a buoyancy aid, shouting, 'I can't see him!'

Sam runs to the stern of the boat, followed by Dom. Stani has hit the lights, and bright white beams illuminate the area around *Lulu*. Tash feels sick as she hears a splash from the stern of the boat as someone dives in. Jaz is next, running along port side, she grabs another buoyancy aid and jumps into the water.

'I can't see him!' Sam shouts.

'Maybe here. Further back.' This is Jaz, and now Mark is in too. They swim back where they'd just been, as *Lulu* had covered water since Theo fell.

'I can't turn it around,' Stani says to Tash, 'or I'll hit him. I'll throw in the dinghy. Can you stay at the helm?'

She stares at him, the idea of another drowning freezing her to the spot.

'Tash!' Stani shouts, and he claps quickly in front of her.

She gives herself a shake, the task helping her focus. 'Of course. Go.'

Stani runs down the port side where the dinghy is strapped, used for shallow waters where the bigger boat can't go.

Tash climbs up to the wheel.

'You know where the searchlight is?' Stani shouts, as he lowers the dinghy.

'Yes.' She looks at the range of controls, forcing herself to think calmly. She's taken *Lulu* out before on her own. She's familiar with it. She finds the switch and spins the searchlight, swinging it back to where they'd just been.

Sam, Dom, Mark and Jaz are in the water now, and Stani powers the dinghy gently, back towards where they're all swimming.

'I see him!' Jaz shouts.

'Got him,' Dom says.

'Oh, thank God.' Megan is beside Tash, and she shivers.

'They'll need towels and hot drinks,' Tash says. 'Can you?' She nods down at the galley.

'On it,' Megan says.

Kiki leans out over the rails. 'Mark, are you OK?'

She sounds about sixteen, and she's clearly terrified.

'Can you help Megan? Towels and there's a first aid kit down there. Can you get it?' Tash asks her. Everyone needs a job.

Kiki nods, looking stunned, then steps towards the galley.

'Idiot,' Becki says, one hand on the rail, staring out over the water. 'He's such an idiot.'

'How much has he had to drink?' Tash asks.

Becki shakes her head. 'He's been drinking since the plane. If his dad knew –' She stops abruptly and shakes her head, pushing tears away from her eyes. 'Idiot,' she says again, angry.

Tash tracks Stani and Dom in the dinghy with Theo, as they make their way back to *Lulu*.

'Is he breathing?' she shouts.

Dom bends over him as Stani docks against *Lulu* and ties up the dinghy.

'Yes,' Dom says, lifting Theo's body up. He passes him to Stani, who has climbed up the rails. Becki and Stani pull him on board.

'He's conscious but seems a bit out of it. His head is bleeding.'

'Fucking idiot!' Becki shouts at him, then she starts to cry. 'I thought you'd died.'

Theo turns on his side and vomits, heaving out drink, sea water and whatever else he's consumed in the last few hours. There's blood on his face, and it's hard to tell with all the water, which dilutes and spread the redness, but it seems to be everywhere.

'Theo,' Becki kneels by him and blinks, looking at his head.

'I don't think it's as bad as it looks,' Sam says. He takes a cloth and wipes Theo's face gently. 'There's a cut on the side of his head. Can you pass me a dressing?'

Dom opens the first aid kit.

Sam works quickly and checks Theo's pulse. 'Is someone coming?'

'I've radioed for help,' Tash says.

Stani turns him, propping him so he doesn't collapse in his own sick.

'Right. I'll get the hose. Clean this up so it's safe for when the paramedics get here.' Stani stands, looking up at Tash. 'You OK?'

Relieved the worst is behind them, Tash nods, checking Dom, Mark and Sam are all back on board. Mark helps Megan hand out hot drinks. It's still warm, but shock can be chilling.

Tash's heart slows its frantic pounding. Seeing Theo in the water stirs up her worst nightmares about Emma – struggling at sea, all alone. She has to be right. Emma has to be alive. But where?

12

Tash

One year ago

Greece

'Richard is pissed,' Mark says, bending down over Tash and dropping a kiss on her upturned, unpuckered mouth. He lays a drink by her lounger – she hears the ting of ice in the glass.

'Again?' she answers, without opening her eyes. His lips are soft, and the sun has robbed her of all agency. It's all she can do to lie here. Even lifting an arm would be too much effort.

'Yup. And stone me if he hasn't taken something else as well. I know he snorted a bit back when we were young, but I wouldn't be surprised if he's gotten hold of something from somewhere.'

'Ugh. Why do we have him here again?' Tash still can't lift her eyelids. She can feel Mark settling on the lounger next to hers. The scrape of the feet of the chair as he pulls his closer. His legs lie alongside hers, and he traces a finger up and down her leg. It feels remarkably pleasant. A tingle buzzes gently in her stomach; she feels herself smile, despite the stupor the sun has sent her body into.

'Well,' Mark says, kissing her shoulder, then her stomach. 'Because he's trying to sweet-talk me into donating to his next campaign, and because he's smoothing the way for the deal we're trying to make some headway with. And he's my oldest friend.'

'Your oldest friend who you hadn't spoken to for years until the business started to take off? And are you going to donate?' Tash asks, as Mark's fingers move to her belly button, and there's a tightening in her stomach now as he draws ever decreasing circles, lightly, suggestively. He's very good at it.

'Probably. Anyway, Nancy was embarrassed, I think, about how clearly drunk or high he was, so she's taken him out in the car, ostensibly to watch the sunset from the top of the island.'

'Oh yes?' Tash murmurs, enjoying how Mark's lips have now reached her stomach.

'Oh yes. And Dom is out with Theo on *Lulu*. Megan and Emma have gone too. Stani is sailing them out to watch the sunset. The staff aren't coming back until dinner time.'

'So, what does this all mean?' Tash says; her eyes remain closed, but Mark has now slid down her bikini bottoms and slides his finger behind her neck to release her bikini top.

The sun warms her through, and there's the softness of shadow as she feels Mark climb across her, his lips now on her neck.

'It means, for the first time in days, we have the pool and villa to ourselves. We always used to do this out here at sunset. It's been too long.'

Mark's voice is thicker now, and Tash finally opens her eyes, slides her fingers into his hair.

God, but she loves her husband. She'd had wine with lunch, and she didn't think she'd be capable of movement until she'd slept it off in the sun. But she feels her body wake despite itself, her heartbeat quicken.

'Feel like it?' Mark asks, as he rises to kiss her, smiling in that slightly crooked way of his. Eyes dark. He's completely naked.

'Fuck yes,' she says. 'Yes please.'

Dinner is on the beach. The staff have moved the table down to the sand, candles send up a soft light.

Megan walks arm in arm down the final steps with Tash.

'Thanks for taking the kids out,' Tash says. 'Were they good?'

'Always' Megan says. She holds a glass of wine and pauses, looking out over the black of the water and then up at the stars. 'Richard Fowler is quite cute.'

'Megan!' Tash stares at her, mouth open. 'Richard Fowler has a wife and a son, and has been drunk since he got here.'

'But he's funny when he's drunk,' Megan says, still looking up at the sky, and almost refusing to look at Tash. 'He said he and his wife are separating.'

'I call bullshit,' Tash says. 'Because she's doing all she can to make him seem like less of a pisshead. He was fine on the first day, but it's like one drink and he can't stop.'

'He hasn't been drunk *all* the time. We had a swim on the beach after breakfast. He was telling me how hard it's been trying to be a good father and balance the job of running for senator. He's hoping to be in by the Fall. I think he's pretty sensitive. And undeniably attractive.' Megan looks at Tash now, eyebrows raised. Waiting.

What business is it of hers? She's not her sister's keeper. Tash is forever reminding herself of all that she has and tries so hard not to lecture Megan. She hears herself sometimes. Such a danger of being so sanctimonious. Dreary with it.

But still.

'Whatever he says, he's married, Megan. Be careful.'

'I'm not going to *do* anything. I mean his wife is here! If they weren't about to separate, I wouldn't even be thinking about it. You're being extra protective of whatever deal you're trying to do.' Megan's voice is a touch harder.

Tash can hear the others coming down the steps. She squeezes her sister's arm and shakes her head quickly. 'Not at all. I just worry about you. He's so much older, and he's –'

'You're only six years older than me. I don't think nine years is enough to get your knickers in such a twist. And yet here you are, lecturing me. Perfect husband, perfect family, perfect life. It gets a bit tiring, miss smarty pants.'

Tash winces at as Megan drops her arm and heads over to the table. She didn't handle that well.

'… not again with the ducks!'

Tash can hear Dom coming down the stone steps to the sand. He's laughing loudly, and he punches Sam on the arm.

'How many times have you told that joke!' Dom says, jumping the last step.

His eyes are bright, and Sam throws his hands up in a mock defence. 'You've heard that one before?'

'Like a million times, dude!'

Tash smiles. 'Is it the one with the duck?'

'Really, I've told that one?' Sam says, his face tanned and cracking in two. A flash of white teeth.

'Oh my God, Mum, tell him!'

'Drink?' Tash says, and she pours wine into a glass and hands it to Sam.

He smiles a thanks and follows Dom to the side table where silver trays are being laid, piled high with food.

Tash leans over to where Megan sits, fills her glass up as an apology and bites her lip as she says, 'Sorry.'

Megan takes the drink and nods, and it's done, smoothed over.

Sand underfoot. The stillness of the sea. Black sky, stars and candles.

Tash looks across at Sam, whispering to Megan. 'Sam's single.'

Megan rolls her eyes and shakes her head and hisses, 'Fucks sake, Tash. Leave it. I don't fancy him. Let me sort out my own life. Also, he's so much in love with you no one gets a look in.'

'What?' Tash rears back, stunned. She looks around quickly to make sure no one heard. 'What are you talking about?'

'So tuned in to my life you forget to look at your own? Mark's noticed. I don't think he cares, but don't play dumb.' Megan stands and heads towards the boys and Sam, who surround one of the caterers arriving with more hors d'oeuvres.

Emma bounces down the steps with Theo chasing her.

'Careful!' Tash calls to her sister and Theo. Then she stops herself. Emma is twenty-four. She can run down some steps if she wants. She needs to stop this constant mothering of everyone around her. She is suffocating them all.

'Sis,' Emma throws her arms around her, swinging off her as her pace pulls her round. 'Sorry. He was chasing me, but I won.' Her blond hair is loose in waves and her green eyes bright. She has a face full of freckles, which leap out in the sun.

'Oh, you did not,' Theo says.

Tash wonders if Theo has developed a crush on Emma. She's older than him. Old enough for her to think he's just a schoolboy. Not too old for Theo to think he stands a chance.

He's got no chance. Megan told her Emma has someone in the city, and she's head over heels.

Richard and Nancy are almost down the last few steps. Tash can't help but take another look at the man they all expect to be named senator in a few months. He wears a pale linen shirt, open at the collar. His hair is blond, almost silver in the light. It's thick. Pale blue eyes, ringed in black, startling. He's broad, and his shirt sleeves are rolled up. His forearms reflect all the tennis he plays, the gym he must go to. He courts his image, Tash thinks. Is he courting Megan?

Megan heads to them both and kisses Nancy on the cheek, before doing the same to Richard. He touches her waist during the greeting. He makes a joke. She laughs. Her head falls back a little and her neck is exposed in her dress – it's low cut and strapless. It falls below her knee. Megan is stunning and dresses like she's stepped out of a magazine.

Tash imagines wolf teeth springing out of his mouth, sinking into Megan's neck. Mentally adds pointed furry grey ears into the thick hair.

She needs to leave Megan alone. She can say don't press the red button as often as she wants. She knows her sister well enough to realise that, if anything, it will only make it seem more attractive.

Richard Fowler doesn't need any help to look more attractive.

Nancy crosses to Sam now and kisses his cheek in a greeting. It's like they all hadn't seen each other at breakfast. Is Sam flirting gently? His eyes flick back to Richard and Megan. Maybe he's being kind and distracting her from the hilarity of whatever Richard and Megan are saying to each other. There's laughter every few seconds.

Tash daren't look at them. She turns her back and heads to Emma, Dom and Theo. Richard's laughing again, and it's uncomfortable to hear, given what Megan has just said.

'What are you three on about,' Tash says, giving Dom a kiss on his head under which he squirms.

'Theo and I were diving this afternoon. Look, total wipe-out,' Dom says, showing Tash a video on his phone. 'Emma took the pics.'

'His was the worst,' Theo says, grinning.

'How can you say that – look at this!'

The two boys laugh, and Tash watches the video where the two of them hurl themselves from the side of their boat.

'Mine was perfect, but no one got the photo,' Emma says, sighing loudly for effect. 'Taught them everything they know.'

'Yeah, right, as if,' Theo says, and smiles at her. He doesn't take his eyes off her.

'You both feeling OK about university?' Tash says, without thinking, and instantly catches herself asking a mother-style question, too late to take it back.

Dom pulls a face. 'We've got a while. Thanks for letting me go, Ma, I know you'll be torn apart.' He drops a kiss on her head then snaps his fingers. 'Theo's suggesting we switch accommodation and go for the same halls. Do you think Harvard will let us do that? It would be unbelievable. What would you think?'

'Wow, good plan!' Tash feels on shaky ground with the idea of Dom going away but forces herself to sound positive. She's not ready for him to leave, but as Mark says, will she ever be? 'Yes, I mean that would be great if they can sort it. And just in case you forget about your parents, we're in New York often enough, and planning to make the trip up to Boston. The office there will be opening around Christmastime if everything goes to plan.'

'Well, just make sure you're not in Boston *all* the time.' Dom grins. 'You're not allowed to move in.'

'I'm coming though. You can take me out and show me how to party US-style.' Emma clinks her glass to Dom's.

'I'll take you out,' Theo says, and Tash sees him blush as Emma smiles at him.

'That would be lovely,' Emma says, then turns back to Dom. 'The girls better watch out once you arrive.'

'Urgh ... Stop! Leave me alone!'

Tash laughs.

'Did I see you dancing with someone at the club the other night?' she asks Emma.

'Did you?'

'Mark and I picked you up in Mykonos – remember? Megan had a headache and came home early. Said you'd met some friends.'

'Oh, yes.' Emma rubs her nose. 'Can't remember. I danced with a few people. Some mates were there from work. I didn't realise you'd got out of the car.'

'God, Mum, you just stalk us all the time,' Dom says, pulling a face then planting a kiss on her cheek. 'You can let go now.'

Tash laughs, feeling the tug of the cord she can't imagine ever letting go of. 'I get it. Don't worry. You can have your own space. What about you, Theo, what are you going to study?'

'Well, law. Dad wants me to have it under my belt. You know he was a lawyer for years. I'm thinking maybe looking into drama when I'm there. The Repertory Theatre is good. There's time yet.'

Theo is blond, like his father. He's got his father's looks too – the pale blue eyes with a ring of black stand out. But Tash will never think anyone more handsome than her son. He's dark-haired like her, and if anyone could look at Dom and not fall in love, she'd be amazed.

She watches the two boys. They've bonded quickly on this holiday. They'd met a few times before when they'd visited the Hamptons to stay with the Fowlers. After years of a half-remembered friendship, they'd been thick as thieves for the last few years. Mark likes spending time with Richard. There's a competitive edge that rises between the two that Mark thrives off. He's always loved to compete. Tennis, running, sailing.

Richard and Mark had met up again during a few promo events for the New York marathon. Friends in college when

Mark had completed his MBA with a year at university in the States, they'd bonded over ambition and competition. But apart from a few college reunions, Mark hadn't seen him in years. Then their business had started to take off, and Mark was a little more prominent. Richard was starting to gather some traction in the party.

Both had been running for the same charity. Then they ran Boston. There had been minutes in it.

A couple of days together as families, then Richard had helped them out with some hitch with a deal. Now this new deal is on the horizon, and if they can crack it, then their move into production in the US looks set. Richard Fowler had been elected as a temporary senator for Virginia recently but was expected to be elected in the Fall when the Senate elections took place. There didn't seem to be much opposition. He was very popular. He lived on the border of Washington DC and Virginia – he was a prominent figure.

'Tash, this food is delicious.' Nancy Fowler appears at Tash's elbow, flushed and glowing. Tash wonders if it's Sam working his magic. She doesn't seem at all on edge with Richard and Megan's laughter loud behind them.

'Emma, what a gorgeous dress,' Nancy says, touching the silver on the evening slip Emma wears.

Tash looks at her sister again. Dark blond hair, slightly taller than her. Some sparkle on her eyelids, but little make-up. Her slip is similar to something Tash wore in the 90s, and Tash reaches out, pulls her sister in. 'You need to tell me more about the mystery man,' she whispers when Nancy turns to say hello to the boys.

Emma had been staying at their apartment in New York, and Megan had told her there was someone, but she hasn't had a chance to speak to Emma about him yet.

'Oh, there's time for that, sis,' Emma says, squeezing her arm. 'Can I top you all up? The poor staff are busy replenishing all the hors d'oeuvres Sam keeps eating. She heads to the table, collects a bottle of wine and tops up Megan's glass and Richard's.

'Mom, you look beautiful,' Theo says, kissing Nancy's cheek.

'You see,' Tash says, swatting her son, 'not all sons duck their mother's attempts at affection.'

Dom laughs and slips his arm around Tash's shoulders. 'Aw, you know I love you. But be careful when you try to kiss me; I worry about you cricking your neck.'

'Cheeky!' Tash leans her head on his shoulder. He's over six foot now and loves to remind her.

'We just can't keep up with all the growing,' Nancy says. 'Can you believe, Tash, that they're planning to leave us in a few weeks' time?'

'Dom was just talking about it. Think we can keep them at home instead?'

'Emma's doing a good job of waitressing; do we need to pay her?' Mark says, crossing the sand towards them in a pale blue shirt and a pair of shorts. 'Hello, everyone. Dinner is looking excellent, I'm starving.'

Tash thinks of the afternoon and takes a sip of wine. This holiday has done them all some good. They'd been so busy recently. It's been good to see Mark unwind. And her sisters. Work and life really do get in the way.

'Dinner's ready?' she asks.

'Yes, Maria is up there and looks like she's done some of her best work. The staff will bring the food down. Emma, let me take over.' He reaches for another bottle of wine and tops up Tash's and Nancy's glasses.

'Dinner then,' Tash says. She lowers her voice to Mark. 'Megan and Richard. Can you keep an eye on them? I've got no idea what's happening there.'

He nods, his eyes flicking over her shoulder. 'I heard a rumour they're kind of broken up. Him and Nancy. They're staying together for the campaign. I haven't asked him about it; none of my business.' He speaks into her ear as he tops up her wine.

'Well, whatever the fuck they're doing, they're not doing it here, in front of the kids,' Tash says, quietly. 'Tell him to shove his dick back in his pants if he thinks he's getting it anywhere near Megan. My sister is out of bounds.'

'Loud and clear,' Mark says.

The nine of them move towards the table.

The night is warm, and the wine is free flowing.

Tash feels a twinge in her stomach.

Too much wine and dessert later, in bed, Tash climbs on top of Mark and kisses him, feeling drunk and almost ready for collapse.

'What did you think about Megan and Richard?' It burrows away like a worm. 'Did you see him touch her arm when she was speaking? He barely spoke to anyone else.'

'It's OK. I don't think Nancy noticed. Sam paid her enough attention. There might be something going on there.'

'With Sam and Nancy?' Tash stops kissing Mark's neck and sits up. 'No! What are you talking about?'

'Tash! You never think Sam is seeing anyone. Nancy is attractive. She laughed at all his jokes. She couldn't stop smiling at him.'

'But Sam – he was being nice to her.'

Mark laughs, rolling her and kissing her stomach. 'What, Sam is a boy scout and Richard a predator? Sam is a bloke, Tash. And Nancy is a good-looking woman. If they *are* living separate lives, what's wrong with Sam enjoying himself?'

'But still.' Tash has no idea why the idea appals her so much.

'Because Sam was married to your friend and shouldn't have anyone else?'

'No of course not! I want him to find someone but –'

'Someone you approve of. Not some hot sex behind doors on a holiday where you are present?' Mark sits up. 'Come on, Tash. We know he has a soft spot for you. I don't care because I trust you, and him come to that. But you have to be pleased for him if someone else wants him.'

'But –' Tash stops because she doesn't know what else to say. 'Theo ...'

'The boys were sneaking too much wine when they thought we weren't looking. They disappeared off halfway through dinner to go and play Xbox. They're out clubbing tomorrow. They're over eighteen. And dinner was civilised. It wasn't a sex romp. Theo is fine.'

'Yes, but –'

'Are you going to say *but* for the next half an hour? If so, I'll turn out the lights, and we may as well get some sleep.'

Mark is teasing her, but Tash hears something in his tone.

'Where were we?' she says, shaking her head a little, and trying to remove the words *Sam*, *Nancy* and *sex romp*.

'About here.' Mark kisses the inside of her elbow, and Tash lies back, swearing she'll leave Megan alone.

13

Tash

Friday night

Present day

Greece

'Senator?' Tash says, taking a breath and thinking the only way is to say it quickly and directly. The hospital is cold and it's late. Now that the doctors have updated her, she needs to make this call. 'Richard? It's Natasha Cadel. I'm afraid Theo was in an accident this evening. He's in hospital. He'll be fine, but he was knocked unconscious, so the hospital wants to keep him in for a few hours. He didn't want me to bother you but of course you need to know.'

She doesn't quote Theo. He'd been adamant she didn't call his father. The language would make a sailor blush, to paraphrase something her mum used to say. But when she thinks of Stani, she doubts anything would make him blush.

There's the briefest of silences – enough to imagine his face change. Then a sigh.

'Natasha – it's been a long time.' He pauses. 'Thank you for calling me. Look. I can get on a plane and come over. Don't worry – I won't impose. I'll have my secretary book me a room nearby. I'd like to check in with Theodore.'

'Of course. You're very welcome to –'

'No. It's kind of you but I'll arrange some other accommodation. Today is Friday – I guess it's late where you are. If I catch a flight tonight, I'll be near you Saturday. I'll call once I'm nearby.'

She doesn't want to for all sorts of reasons, but he's a parent, she reasons, offering, 'It's Dom's birthday party on Sunday. You're very welcome to attend. We're having a lunch. Join us for the weekend.'

'I'll see how I'm doing for time.' Richard Fowler is curt, and then he appears to catch himself. 'I didn't mean to be so blunt. It's a shock. Theodore and I are coming out the other side after Nancy ...'

'I'm so sorry. And I'm sorry I haven't seen you since the funeral,' Tash says, softly.

'Theodore has taken the ... harder route through his grief. I'm sorry for any trouble he's caused. You don't need it.'

'It will be nice to see you,' Tash says, though she doesn't mean it. She couldn't wish him away any more than she does.

'I'll be there as quick as I can. And thank you. For looking after him.'

The line goes dead, and there's no goodbye. Tash holds the phone and looks out at her reflection, mirrored back against the glass.

Her headache is back. She reaches for some pills and swallows two.

The day has stretched far longer than planned and sleep pulls at her eyelids and pushes up against her bruise.

14

Tash

Now

The hospital lights are dimmed now. The corridors quiet.

'Are you sure you want to go back to the villa tonight?' Tash asks Theo.

Sam glances at his watch.

Really, it's this morning, Tash thinks. But there's no need to point this out.

The doctor has finally finished with all the scans and everything has been checked. Theo has stitches. It's amazing really, she thinks. That he didn't injure himself more seriously. Some people seem to get away with everything.

The window nearby looks out across a dark Athens, lights bright from the city and the sky heavy with jewelled stars. With the dressing on his head, he looks very young. Beneath his tan there are rings around his eyes.

'I've spoken to your dad and he's flying out. He'll be here tomorrow.'

'Dad's coming?' He rolls his eyes.

'I had to call him, Theo.'

Theo stares at the wall.

Sam, sitting on the other side of the bed, picks up the fresh tray of snacks they'd brought Theo once they said it was OK to eat again. 'This doesn't look half bad. Sure you don't want some fancy food and your own room for another day? The hospital has recommended some rest.'

'They said I'm fine. It's just a superficial cut. You heard them.' Theo sounds almost rude then appears to collect himself. He nods. 'The food is good, but not as good as the villa's. If it's OK, I'd like to come back.'

Tash nods, glancing at Sam who shrugs. 'The helicopter is waiting. Would you like Becki to come with you? Sam and I will be there, and there's room for one more. The others will wait and get it on the return flight.'

'No, thank you.' He looks down. 'I'll see her when we get back.'

Tash nods, but she remembers how Becki had screamed at him when he'd been up on the rails and was the first to notice how dangerous his behaviour was becoming. How many times has she seen him act like this before?

'I'm not that happy about him coming back tonight,' she says quietly to Sam as they head to the café to tell the others the plan. 'I wish he'd just stay here. It happened so quickly, and it could have gone badly wrong. He's lucky he didn't drown. What if he takes a turn for the worse?'

'He's an adult – I mean, I know he's a kid, but legally he gets to decide, and you've spoken to Richard. There's nothing more to do. Becki seems sensible. I think she'll watch him. They said he's fine.'

'If you see him near the booze again this weekend, wrench it out of his hands, will you?' Tash says.

'Sure thing.' Sam stops. 'Look, go and get a coffee and sit down for five minutes. I'll go and tell Dom and the girls. You look exhausted.'

'Thanks, Sam.' She leans in, sagging against him for a second as the night hits her. 'Thanks for coming with me.'

'Sure thing. Mark was keen you know. He was worried about you.'

'Mark is a guest now. It's not his responsibility.' The words fly out short and sharp; she's pissed off.

More than that, she's bruised about Mark. This breakup business is like a wave. She minds; she doesn't mind. She's surprised she's coping so well; she's struggling to cope. She just hadn't been prepared for how beautiful Kiki is, how young. When they'd separated, it had been painful. But she'd hoped they'd stay friends. It was why she'd invited him. But Kiki was closer in age to Dom than Tash. She feels displaced, older than Mark even. Not just swapped but traded in. Redundant. She couldn't bear Mark to be too close to her now, to offer support. He'd been the first person she'd turned to once Theo was out of the water, but Kiki had been sobbing and hanging off him. She can't turn to him like that any more. She hadn't minded so much on the boat – maybe that was the glass of wine.

'I'll come with you,' he'd said, as the helicopter had landed near the villa to take Theo.

'No.' She'd been short. 'Go and look after your girlfriend. Sam will come with me.'

Mark's face had creased in something she didn't recognise.

'Fine,' he'd said and turned on his heel, before seeming to remember himself and look back to say, 'I'll ask Megan to get food ready in the kitchen. They'll need some sugar for the shock.'

As she'd watched him walk away, she'd almost sobbed out loud. He'd been hers for so long – leaning on Mark was something she'd taken for granted. The loss is new again.

Sam has been great. He's always great. When he finally settles down with someone else, she'll be lost. She knows she's been relying on him more than she should recently. It's not fair to him.

What Megan said last year has stayed with her. She doesn't see it – she doesn't believe he has any feelings for her beyond friendship. If something happened with him and Nancy, it must have been short because Nancy had died so quickly. She'd been so obsessed with her own marriage breakdown she'd never even noticed if Sam was upset about Nancy's death.

He's always been cagey if she mentioned Nancy, so she's never pushed it, but since Megan made that stupid remark, she'd been careful not to give out any signals.

He's dating again, and she's happy.

I'm really happy for him, really, she thinks, *really*.

She sips the hot coffee from the machine and leans back in a chair. She doesn't want Sam – not like that. And she's a mess. She doubts anyone sees her as desirable. Mark certainly doesn't any more. But Sam has been such a support to her – she's not ready to let him go just yet.

And she'll have to.

The blades of the helicopter are loud as they start up. The hot night air whips around her and her hair rises from her neck.

'OK?' Tash asks Theo.

He nods.

'Here, hold my arm. It'll be windier out there.' Sam takes Theo's arm, and they walk out onto the roof of the hospital. Medics flank them, making sure he gets in safely.

Tash is used to helicopters, and she feels a relief to be back out in the night air, reassuringly warm after the bite of the air con. She pauses for a second, as Sam and Theo climb in, and she looks up at the stars.

Richard Fowler could be in the air now. If not now, then soon. She had wished he wasn't coming. Not this weekend – she's got enough to cope with. But a thought had dawned on her. Maybe fate is on her side. If he's here, then maybe last year's invite list is as complete as it can be, without Nancy or Emma. If anything is going to emerge this weekend, to draw out the secrets of what happened last year, Richard Fowler's presence can only help.

'Ready?' Sam asks, extending a hand.

'Coming!' She takes his hand and lets him pull her in.

15

Jaz

Jaz shivers in the fancy hospital cafe. It had all happened so quickly, she'd not had time to change. Earlier, Sam had ducked out of the ward into the night market and come back with huge sweatshirts with *Athens* written across the centre, and she's never been more grateful for anything.

Becki is ashen.

'He's going to be fine,' Dom says.

He sits and drops a handful of chocolate bars on the table, and Jaz rips open a wrapper. European chocolate tastes weird. Good, but weird.

'Mum said he wants to come home tonight, so they'll fly first. It's just under thirty minutes. Back by two. I'm knackered.'

'Can you fly this late?' Jaz asks.

'I think you can do most things if you're Senator Fowler's son,' Becki says. Her voice is flat. Her eyes close. 'I want to go home. Not the villa. Actual home.'

'Oh, Becs, it's OK! He's going to be OK.' Jaz squeezes her hand.

'No. He didn't give a shit what he was doing tonight. He was so cagey earlier. We need to see what he bought in that shop. Something strange is going on this weekend.'

'Wait, what?' Dom stops biting into the chocolate bar and holds it still. 'What do you mean?'

'After we landed, when he got the car to stop by the shops, he picked something up. Wine for your mom, he said, but I found a bag – he went mad when he saw me with it. He said it's something he bought to go fishing with. He said to be careful – I might get hurt if I mishandle it. There's something in there that's worrying me.'

Dom blinks a few times. 'OK. We'll look when we're back.'

'Shouldn't we tell somebody how much he's been drinking? Your parents?' Jaz looks at him. 'He almost died tonight.'

'I'll talk to Sam.' Dom stares at his fingernails, bitten down and raw. 'We're going to leave my dad out of this. And Mum. I'll tell Sam. But nothing to my parents. I'm serious. You hear me?'

Jaz doesn't remember seeing this expression on Dom's face before.

Despite the sweatshirt, the cold creeps in. She wishes for her bed. And for a moment, like Becki, she wishes for home. The safety of the farmhouse. Her mom downstairs. Her sister in the next room. She's spent such a lot of time adjusting to life at Harvard, adjusting to life with Dom. She'd almost forgotten the relief of home.

She looks out of the window. The café is at the top of the private, top of its game hospital. Everything the best. Everything shiny.

But she's starting to realise that not everything shiny is as good as it looks.

16

Tash

Last summer

A year ago

Greece

Emma climbs out of the pool as Megan brings out a tray of drinks. It's almost 11 a.m. and everyone else is out.

'Is it too early for gin?' Tash says, applying sun cream to her arms.

'Nope. We need to take advantage of Mark taking them all to the black beach for the morning. They'll be back later,' Megan says. 'We're never on our own. Time for sister drinks.'

'I'm in,' Emma says, retying her hair up after her swim.

'Are you eating enough?' Tash says. 'You've lost weight.'

'And she looks amazing,' Megan says, throwing an olive at Tash. 'Leave her alone.'

Tash nods. 'You do look amazing. Tell us about this new man.'

Emma's eyes flick to Megan. 'You told?'

'No secrets!' Tash says. 'No leaving me out just because I'm old and boring.'

'Even I don't know who he is,' Megan says. 'Only that the sex is amazing.'

'Meg!' Emma says, hiding her face. 'God, did I say that?'

'Is it true?' Tash asks. Emma being twenty-four means she never normally gets the good gossip. Since their parents died, she's been more like a mum than a sister.

'I suppose it is. He's quite ... experienced.' Emma raises one eyebrow, then sips her drink. 'I mean, I blush sometimes, just thinking about ... his hands.'

The sisters all scream and Tash laughs so hard her belly hurts. 'When do we get to meet him?'

A tiny shadow crosses Emma's face, and her freckles crease in a frown. 'At some point.'

'He's not an alcoholic, is he?' Tash says, before she can stop herself. Emma had dated someone last year who was always pissed.

'Oh my God! Lay off her!' Megan throws another olive at Tash. 'Details – does he have his own place?'

'Yep.' Emma nods.

'Ooh – rich. I mean, property in New York is the bees' knees. How did you meet him?' Megan asks. 'I could do with some tips.'

'Enough about me!' Emma lies back on a lounger. 'You're always dating, you must have some gossip.'

'Always the bridesmaid,' Megan says easily. 'I'll let you know if anything ever gets serious. One day we'll all be old and boring like Tash.'

'It's all expensive creams and supplements at my age,' Tash says.

'Well, we know you're not past it. I get a bit sick of hearing you moaning out for Mark at night,' Megan says, looking at her, side eye on.

'No! Shut up!'

'*You* shut up. The walls aren't as thick as you might think they are. You're lucky it's just Emma and me in the rooms closest to you.'

Tash feels her face heat up.

'Speaking of men. You were flirting with Richard again last night?' Tash just can't help herself. Megan looks at her glass.

'I was being *friendly*,' Megan says. 'Sam was talking to Nancy for most of it. All above board.'

Emma places a hand on Tash's arm. 'How are you feeling about Harvard?' Tash knows she's changing the subject.

As always, Tash could cry and forces herself not to. 'I'm being strong!'

'You're going to blub like a baby, aren't you?' Megan says.

'Hopefully not where Dom can see me,' Tash says. 'I've made Mark promise to whisk me out of there if I start getting embarrassing.'

'What do you mean, *if you start*?' Megan says, and laughs. 'Come on, Tash, it's not like you don't mother everyone in a ten-minute radius. What will you do when Dom disappears?'

'Sod off! I need another drink. Who wants one?' Tash stands and heads to the kitchen with orders from Emma and Megan.

As she climbs the steps, a memory from last night flits across her brain. She'd woken for water in the middle of the night, and she'd heard a noise. She hadn't been able to make it out and she'd been half asleep, but now she thinks of it, she remembers what Megan had said about the walls being thinner than she thought.

What she had heard, had definitely been a moan. And it hadn't sounded like one of pain.

What does that mean? Was there more to Megan's flirting with Richard than she'd let on?

★

Tash sees *Lulu* before she docks near their beach.

'They're here!' she calls, running down the stairs and out to the patio, her arm lifted and her hand shading her eyes. All this talk of Dom leaving has made her long to get him back. She only has a few more days with him.

He and Theo are up on the deck helping Stani dock. She can see their two heads, one blond, one dark. They throw the rope, and then Theo leaps out to tie *Lulu* as Dom holds his hand out to help Nancy cross. Then, once everyone is off, they jump back on and help carry the picnic baskets.

Tash had decided early they weren't going to be overrun with staff, that Dom would learn to look after himself. She knows Nancy has a full staff at their house, bordering Washington DC and Virginia, but to give Theo credit, he's been bending over backwards to help out this week at the villa.

Richard strides ahead and Nancy walks up with Sam.

I wonder, Tash thinks. It's got nothing to do with her. She needs to stand back.

'Hello!' Richard calls as he walks past the pool and up toward the patio.

'How was the beach?'

'Excellent,' he says. 'And Mark took us to a superb restaurant for lunch. The food was incredible.'

Tash smiles. Richard is a very appreciative guest. Well-mannered to a fault.

But he's clearly had a few this afternoon. Megan and Emma are down by the pool with more drinks. He greets them with a kiss on the cheek and a hand on their lower back. He touches Emma first, and Tash's stomach turns. He's very careful about space when he's sober. Not so much this afternoon.

'Is he pissed?' she mouths at Mark who climbs the steps and kisses her.

'As a newt,' he says in her ear. 'Theo got upset. Richard spent ten minutes back at the restaurant talking to the waitress. He tipped her a hundred euros. It was embarrassing. Nancy left to go shopping – Sam whisked her away.'

'Poor Theo. Thank God the most embarrassing thing you do is sing bad karaoke. Dom should be more grateful.'

'Moi?' Mark looks shocked and clutches his heart. 'But my "Born to Run" is surely better than even Springsteen's?'

'Run to the kitchen and turn the oven on, like you were born to. I've had moussaka delivered. We just need to serve.'

'Mum!' Dom drops a kiss on her head as he passes. 'I'm going to shower.'

It's Tash's turn to touch her chest as she watches him fling an arm around Theo as they head upstairs. All too soon, he'll have left home. Time doesn't so much fly, as blink away. One moment it's there, and then it's passed.

Just her and Mark. Well at least she has him. She watches him jog into the kitchen.

Maybe it won't be so bad.

17

Tash

Greece
Now

'Morning, mother,' Dom swoops in and lands a kiss on Tash's cheek.

The breakfast table on the veranda is laid out for a feast. Just above the pool, it sits under the pergola whose roof blinds don't lift until later, as the sun hits the road side of the villa in the morning. It's Tash's favourite part of the day – cooler, fresh air – and Maria came in early to lay the breakfast. She's a distant relative of Stani's and helps out when they have guests and watches the villa when they're not here. She'll be back later to clear up.

It's the calm and the privacy that Tash loves. She's invited Richard Fowler to come immediately from the airport and stay for lunch. He'll want to see Theo. At least, she hopes he wants to see him. What she remembers most about Richard Fowler isn't overwhelming paternal affection. But since Nancy's death, Tash hopes that Richard and Theo have helped each other. She hopes Richard had been the father Nancy would have hoped he be.

Then they'll all be here, except Nancy – the only missing piece. Tash can use Dom's birthday as a way to gather everyone and try to work out why Emma ran away. *Definitely ran. Not dead*, she tells herself, again and again.

'Can I help with anything?' Jaz sits across from Tash and smiles. 'You must be exhausted. The beds are too comfy; I totally caught up on my sleep. I was like a log this morning.'

Dom pours orange juice into her glass and sits next to Jaz, his hand sitting lightly at her back.

Tash nods. 'Me too. I hit the pillow and that was it. I saw Becki earlier, by the way. I left a tray of breakfast bits outside their room, and she came down to get more toast. I think Theo must be feeling a lot better.'

'Sorry, Mum,' Dom says. 'He was behaving like a dick last night.'

'Has he been in trouble at school,' she asks, trying to slide the question in easily, as she pours coffee from the pot into her cup.

'What do you mean?'

'Oh, I don't know. Has he been drinking a fair bit? Becki seemed on edge with the amount he was knocking back on the boat.'

A look glides between Dom and Jaz so lightly that Tash almost doesn't see it. But no, it was there.

Jaz shrugs, reaching out for butter. 'I mean, he's a student. And there's *some* drinking.'

'Yeah, Mum,' Dom says, following it with a laugh, which almost sounds natural. 'You've been to uni. You know what goes on.'

Tash nods, knowing two things: if they aren't ready to tell her, they won't, and students' behaviour with booze and behaviour that is out of control aren't always indistinguishable. There's no point pushing.

'The hospital has recommended he stay off alcohol for a few days. You were all due to go to the restaurant on Mykonos later, and I've booked a table in the beach bar for you after. I can't imagine you'll want to cancel with the DJ they've got coming, but if you can try to steer him towards soft drinks, it would be a good idea.'

'Sure thing,' Dom says, like the conversation is over. He looks at Tash. 'Kiki is young. I know you said you were fine, but ... are you?'

Tash forces her face into position, hoping she doesn't look like The Joker on a bad day, and says, 'Yes of course. We've been split up for a while now. Kiki seems lovely.'

Dom bites into a croissant and watches her as he chews. 'Top marks for effort. Almost convincing, Mum. You know he'd be back in a second if you said the word.'

The world is a big place, Tash thinks, thoughts like arrows. *Life is short. All those emotions whizzing round constantly. It's amazing people aren't simply imploding on a daily basis.*

Her son is almost a grown-up. Does he wish they were together? Of course, he must. It's not rocket science. No matter how old the child is, it's never easy when their parents split. He is bound to believe that Mark would run back to her – does she think it's true? No. Mark has moved on. It's behind them. She has pushed him away. She had blamed him, though even now she's not sure for what. Once Emma had gone, she had too much of everything tight inside, and it leaked out of her, repelling anything trying to get in.

She had repelled Mark, been repelled by him. Any touch unwanted. She'd been so angry.

Finally, months later, she's calmer.

She's not sure he'd have waited around for her if she'd asked him to – if she'd let him.

'Your dad seems happy. I'm happy. We're all here. It works. And we both love you,' she says, watching Dom add butter to pastry and thinking that the part about them loving him is the truest thing she's said about her and Mark so far since they arrived. It's the glue really. That's why she needs to carry on with this path she's picked, as stupid and self-destructive as it is.

As if on cue, Mark and Kiki climb the steps up from the pool house.

'Morning, all!' Kiki carries the rosy glow of yesterday's sun. She wears a short yellow summer dress, and her hair is piled up in one of those knots that seem to spill hair and hold their shape all at the same time. She looks so *young*, and immediately Tash feels a hundred.

'Hi,' Mark says to everyone, looking straight at Tash.

Luckily Sam comes out of the villa at the same time, and Tash's throat, too full of something she can't express, has a moment to settle before she needs to speak, to greet, to host. She holds Mark's gaze and feels loss like a wound.

'What an evening!' Sam says, and then everyone is talking, and the others arrive.

'Theo, dude, how are you feeling?' Dom jumps up as Theo arrives, looking a little bruised but otherwise fine.

'Good. Sorry everyone.' His white-blond hair falls forward over his black eye, as he pulls at it. 'Don't worry, Dom. I'm still ready for the party. Mykonos later. Wouldn't miss it!'

The sun lights up the breakfast table as they all take their places and the sea is still, calm and blue stretched out in front of them. The panic of yesterday forgotten.

Something is off and with the party tomorrow, Tash is uneasy. She can't shift the worm of worry, burrowing deep. She pours more coffee. Tells herself she's just over-thinking.

18

Tash

'Mr Fowler has arrived.' Maria steps out onto the balcony. Tash pushes her chair back and stands, noticing as she does that Theo has gone rigid. She looks at Mark. He isn't the host here any more. But maybe she could let him take the lead.

Mark offers her the shortest of nods as though agreeing.

'Richard,' she says, as the senator steps through the kitchen doors to the balcony. He blinks a little in the sun, barely breaking stride, before opening his arms to Tash, dropping the newspaper he'd been carrying on a chair.

'Natasha, how lovely to see you. I can't thank you enough.'

'Richard,' Mark says, shaking his hand. 'Here's the invalid.'

'Theodore.' Richard covers ground quickly to his son, placing a hand to the side of his head without the bandage. 'Let me look at you. Does it hurt?'

'No. Sorry, Dad.' Theo looks a little warily at his father.

'At least you're OK. I spoke to the doctor at the hospital. He said you were very lucky. If the hull of the boat had struck a little more to the left, you might have been in real trouble.'

Theo still holds his frame stiffly; Tash wonders if Richard will have more to say to his son later. She hopes so. If Mark had flown out to see Dom after a boating accident, she imagines he'd scoop him up, crush him in a hug. Richard half tussles Theo's hair and it looks affectionate, but given the terror of last night, it seems lacking somehow. She's worried about Theo since the funeral, but her own life has been so changed she hasn't reached out. A flash of Richard after the funeral blinks in her head. Is he as cruel as he'd seemed?

'Richard,' Megan says, leaving her seat and leaning forward for two cheek kisses.

Very business-like, Tash thinks. Last summer, on a hot dark night, they'd both been drunk, and it had been different. Megan had been flirting outrageously.

She's keeping her distance now, Tash thinks. Megan had never really told Tash what had happened with Richard – if anything. Emma had vanished, and she'd forgotten to ask.

Megan returns to her seat at the far end of the table. The others begin to scrape at toast and clatter with cups, and the breakfast picks up pace again. The girls look at Richard with interest. Tash supposes it's not every day you get to meet a real-life senator. He's always in the media – so photogenic and talk of him as the next Vice President is rife. Kiki openly stares at him, before she catches Tash looking across at her and she looks away. Though not embarrassed, Tash thinks. In fact, for a second, the look had been calculating. Kiki looks at Theo before going back to her plate.

'Coffee? You must be exhausted.' Mark steps in and pulls out a chair next to Theo's for Richard. He takes the empty chair nearby. 'Theo managed to give us all a fright, but what's a holiday without a bit of excitement? And they're still planning to head over to the beach club in Mykonos later this afternoon. Oh, for the energy of youth.'

Richard appears on a charm offensive. 'Well, as a thank-you, I brought a case of champagne with me.' He waves his hand as Tash opens her mouth to thank him. 'It's the least I can do. I've left it with Maria in the kitchen. You know, I'd forgotten how amazing your food is. These pastries are incredible! Dominic, you must be looking forward to your birthday! I didn't bring a gift, but I've got tickets for you and your family to attend the White House Christmas carol concert. I know you all love to celebrate Christmas.'

'That's very kind of you, sir.'

'Not at all. Theodore and I will be there. It will be lovely to have some friends along.'

Tash had seen Richard last at Nancy's funeral where he had delivered the perfect eulogy. The President had been in attendance. Richard had grasped Tash's hand, firm and warm, as she'd filed out. *Thank you for coming.*

Light January snow had been falling, and the trees in the Washington church were dusted white as though the set had been designed. Photographers were held back at the gated entrance, so the church grounds were private. Long black cars had formed a line, security tight.

There had been a moment when grief escaped her, the realness, the ache, the sadness – 'Abide with Me' played as Tash had dropped her head, tears choking in her throat. *Fast falls the eventide.*

Dom, beside her, had been convulsed in silent sobs. He knew Nancy a little, but as she'd reached for a tissue in her bag, she realised she hadn't seen him cry like that since he was little, and she'd snaked her arm around his waist.

His head had landed on her shoulder, and his tears had soaked through the black silk blouse she'd worn. The same one she'd picked out for the memorial service they'd held for Emma.

'Oh, darling,' she whispered, and kissed his head. But his cries had carried on for minutes. His face pale and wan. She supposed coming so soon after losing Emma, grief was something he carried with him, waiting for it to slowly dissolve into the ether that everyone promises would, at some point, consume the pain. Carry it away. Lighten the load.

He'd been quiet for the rest of the day.

Tash looks at him now, laughing with his friends, making a joke about the DJ who was playing later.

He'd gone back to Harvard after the funeral, and she hadn't seen him until Easter. She'd been pleased when he'd come home. It had taken away the ache of missing Emma, and the look on Mark's face each time he'd tried to touch her, and her skin had crawled.

But she'd been so blind with her own grief, she hadn't stopped to wonder if there had been more to Dom's tears. But what could it have been?

Whatever seems to be going on with Theo – is Dom somehow involved? They'd been roommates that year. Dom had asked to switch halls in the second semester. Something about proximity to class. Again, she hadn't thought too much about it. Had she taken her eye off the ball?

Could it have anything to do with Emma vanishing? No, surely not everything has to do with Emma. As a family they seem to have been caught in a downward spiral and they must come out of it soon.

'Hey, Mum, do I need to speak to Stani about what time we're leaving?' he asks now, smiling at her as though he hasn't a care in the world.

Has she missed something in her son's life?

19

Jaz

Now

There are a few hours for sunbathing on the beach before they need to leave. Jaz can't wait to flop, and Dom grabs her hand as they head down the steps from the pool, through the rocky cliff path to their private bay.

Jaz hasn't had much to do with beaches. She's always thought of them through a Californian film filter – people rollerblading along the boardwalk, clusters of bronze bodies, surfers. They always seem busy in her head.

'Dom, this is gorgeous!' She'd seen it briefly last night as they'd boarded the boat, but as Dom pulls out a lounger for her, complete with shade and drinks already laid, the quiet and the calm sea are a blissful surprise.

He kisses her softly and takes his time. 'Are you having a good time?'

'Absolutely.' She rises on her toes to meet him. He's her first proper boyfriend, and she can't believe the gold she'd struck.

There had been a few boys in high school, but they were not anything like this. Dom is pretty perfect.

'Here.' He turns her, and rubs sun cream into her back, taking his time, rubbing the knots out of her shoulders. 'The others will be here in a second, but we should come down again, on our own,' he whispers, and she leans into the feel of his fingers on her neck.

'Oh my God! This is all yours?' Becki turns a cartwheel in the sand, landing like a cat on her feet.

'Love your suit!' Jaz says, taking in Becki's off the shoulder pink two-piece.

Jaz has gone for pale green, which always works with her hair. She's looped a Dutch braid around her head and added earrings and a few gold chains, which hang low on her chest. She'd been so nervous about what to wear on a beach she'd poured over Instagram looks, and she knew she'd nailed it when Dom had let out a slow whistle as she'd come out of the bathroom.

'Race you out to the buoy?' Theo says to Dom.

'Don't forget us!' Becki jumps up, and Jaz follows.

They splash into the water and, as soon as it's deep enough, dive beneath the cool blue.

Jaz opens her eyes, to see all the colours of the fish. The saltwater stings, but it doesn't bother her. It's like another world, under the sea, the sun glinting off the surface of the water. She's strong, and she stretches out in freestyle.

Theo wins the race. Theo wins at most things.

'I'll be dry in seconds,' Becki says, lying back on her lounger and closing her eyes.

'Water?' Dom opens a cooler chest he'd brought down and throws a few bottles in the sand by their chairs.

'I don't think I can leave,' Jaz says. 'Can we please move here?'

There's a splash from further up the beach, and Jaz sees Kiki climb out of the sea. She pauses, tying her hair back up on her head where it had come loose. She's in a pale bikini and her skin shimmers as the sun catches the water. Jaz sees the flash of a ring on her finger – the same one they'd bought the night before.

She's on the other side of the wooden promenade where two dinghies are tethered. *Lulu* is right at the end, where the sea gets deeper off a ledge.

'Kiki!' Theo calls.

They all turn.

'It's Kiki,' Theo says, like he hadn't already announced it.

She looks at them for a second then walks over. There's something guarded about her expression, Jaz thinks, as she looks at Theo. They'd been messing round in the water yesterday. Had he made a beeline for her then?

Theo stands quickly. He looks at Dom. 'I'll go and have a chat with her. Back in a minute.'

Jaz looks from Theo to Dom. There's something she can't quite put her finger on.

'Why do you want to speak to her?' Becki says, sitting up.

'I won't be long.' Theo walks quickly away from them, towards Kiki.

Jaz watches as they speak quietly, then Kiki shrugs and starts back up towards the pool house.

Theo follows.

'Theo?' Becki calls.

But he doesn't turn around.

20

Jaz

'We're looking now,' Becki says, running up the stairs ahead of Jaz, who follows with Dom, jogging to keep up.

'Are you sure he's not in his room?' Jaz says, breathing heavily. Becki had been quick once Theo had disappeared with Kiki.

'You mean *they* might be in our room?' Becki stops and spins, raising her eyebrows at Jaz. 'They better not be.'

'Fair,' Dom says, from behind. 'Look, I'll stay outside the room. You two head in. If I cough, he's on his way. I'll say you're trying outfits on for this afternoon.'

Jaz follows Becki to the wardrobe.

'It was in here,' Becki says, kneeling and pulling out bags and the suitcase.

Nothing.

'Where else could it be?' Jaz wonders aloud, looking round the room. It's like theirs – more of a rectangular space and smaller, but still big with a view of the pool and sea. The balcony is shorter, and there are a few plants under the shaded roof outside the window.

Becki looks under the bed, in drawers.

Dom coughs on the stairs and they freeze, looking at each other.

'Where are the girls?' Theo's voice drifts through the door.

'I think Becki wanted to show Jaz an outfit. I was just heading down to get a beer. Want to come?'

The sound of their footsteps can be heard on the stairs and Jaz breathes out again.

'I know I probably seem like I'm being stupid. It was probably nothing, but I was convinced there was something strange about it.' Becki pauses in the room, looking round and sounding like she's second guessing herself. 'I feel like I don't know where I am with him any more. Am I mad and hyper suspicious?'

Jaz shakes her head. 'Always go with your first answer. It's exactly like a pop quiz. Trust your instincts. Where else?' She scans the room.

There's an urn near the window. It's there for decorative purposes, a kind of clay pot, that complements the colours in the room and looks expensive and handmade. But the lid is ever so slightly off, as though it's been knocked.

She's there quickly, kneeling, and lifting the lid.

At the bottom of the pot is a paper bag.

'Here, help, hold the pot still while I pull this out,' she says to Becki.

Jaz eases out the bag, careful not to be too rough. Once it's out, she lays it on the floor and opens it up. Inside, there's a white bundle of linen. She unwraps the linen carefully, unrolling whatever the contents are.

Drugs? Her head spins at the thought. A present for Becki?

As the layers get thinner, the object feels hard under her hands.

She unrolls the bundle the final few times. A long wrap of linen lies on the floor, and she and Becki look up at each other.

'Not being paranoid then,' Becki says.

Jaz's mouth is dry.

Lying on the tiled floor of the room, is a knife.

21

Nancy

Last year

Boston in the Fall

Nancy pulls her scarf more snugly round her neck. She pats the knot quickly – symmetrical, good. The air is perfectly still, and the cold is crisp, like a fresh apple.

She'd been apple picking earlier in Washington that week. She'd tried to talk Theo into taking a break from his studies, but he hadn't been deterred. The greens, yellows and reds of the apples had been the same as those in the leaves, and the city is no different. Boston in the Fall is like a magic land. The Charles River reflects a blue sky, and leaves pass by, blown in the pull of the water, reds and golds of the season like a picture book.

It wasn't just that he hadn't been deterred. She hasn't seen him for more than five minutes in two months. He attends Richard's photo shoots. Then he's gone. He won't take her calls for more than thirty seconds.

She smooths out the gloves on her fingers, staring at the water. She knows there's some gossip swirling, thick and fast about their family. She knows what some of her friends are saying. She closes her eyes, the sting sharp.

The summer had been hard – Richard worse than ever. More than that – he'd been sloppy. He'd started drinking and his behaviour had slid out of his usual tight control – it had almost been catastrophic. But his eye remains on the campaign. She remains by his side.

She wants it as much as he does. The next step up. Their quiet campaign. Now that he is elected senator, Vice President and Second Lady is the next step. Higher office has always been their dream. It had been his ambition that first attracted her. The possibilities.

The current VP is older and looking to step down had been the whisper in the ears of those who counted. The time frame mentioned had been roughly a year or so. *Could Richard raise his profile in the party? Could he try to attract more of a swell of support in the media?*

He'd been tipped off. A word in his ear. He needs to be a clear choice.

She has played her part well – dutiful. But more than that – she had to pull him back after Greece. He'd lost his way with drink, and he'd occasionally slipped. She'd had to re-evaluate what she really wanted. Was it all worth it?

He really is focused now. She'd told him she wouldn't stay unless he sorted himself out. She'd tried to clean up his mess as much as possible. His eye is on the final prize, and maybe they can be saved in the process.

It's Theo she thinks about. It's affecting him.

Richard won't talk about Greece. It's like it didn't happen. Nancy hasn't spoken to Tash about it since, and she doesn't think Richard has spoken to Mark.

What else is there to say except how sorry they are?

The family losing Emma has been so sad. She shakes her head as she walks, checking her watch. She'll be late if she's not careful.

She'd kept up with the news, but Tash's sister seems to have vanished into the sea. Why she'd gone for a swim in the dark no one knows. No sighting of her.

'It's just a matter of time,' Richard had said, very matter-of-factly. 'They'll issue a presumption of death certificate. They'll have to. Emma had shares in the company. Mark will want them resolved. She had voting rights on the board.'

The last time Nancy had tried to reach out to Tash, she'd been faced with a blank wall. Tash had been hiring search and rescue teams for weeks after Emma had vanished. The evidence had pointed to a drowning. The lack of body was a stumbling block, but enough traces had been found to satisfy the police. So they'd stopped looking.

She turns the corner into the street where the café sits. Leaves dot the pavements like a mosaic. Even in this cold, a few people sit outside on wooden tables, steaming drinks in large coloured mugs in their hands. Plates piled with cake and muffins make Nancy feel hungry. She isn't eating cake at the moment. The photos for the campaign trail are brutal in their honesty. She's dropped a few pounds since the summer and needs to drop a few more.

She's been microdosing a new drug. The injections had been recommended by a friend. The weight is staying off easily. She lies to friends when they eat lunch or bring out treats – *oh I ate earlier; oh I've got a hangover, and I've lost my appetite; I ate so much cake with my coffee this morning, I can't face any more!*

The summer had been lovely to begin with. Tash had always been so good at organising. So much in love with her husband, loved her son so openly – always hugging, kissing. Nancy had tried to be more like that, but Richard likes a formal household. He doesn't like her to hold his hand, and he doesn't really hug Theo. In fact, since the campaign, he's taken to calling him Theodore which sends Nancy's heart sinking to her stomach. Their photos are picture perfect, but she worries what all the perfection is doing to them.

They'd always enjoyed Tash's company. She was always laughing and steering people together, introducing them with details. Well-dressed. Beautiful in a classic way. Dark hair and understated clothes. She'd had such a head for business – she'd been passionate about their projects, her mind all over the details. Mark had a head for numbers and a competitive streak she'd only ever seen matched in Richard.

Things have changed in the last couple of months. Tash looks colder. Little make-up. In the odd photo she's seen, Tash is dressed down, often in T-shirts, sweaters. Her hair is usually tied up. The last time Nancy had seen them all had been from a distance when they'd taken their respective boys out for lunch after the Parents' Day at Harvard, and they'd ended up in the same restaurant. Nancy had found herself looking across a few times. Tash had reached for her son throughout the meal – smoothing his hair, touching his arm. Never once had she reached for Mark, and Nancy doesn't think she'd ever seen such loneliness etched on any man's face.

The heat in the café forces her to unwind the scarf, and she looks for him.

There. He's early.

Inhaling, holding it, she lets it out in one long breath then raises a hand in greeting. He half rises.

'Sam,' she says, turning her cheek as he offers up two kisses. A very European greeting in this American city.

'Nancy. It's good to see you.'

Sitting, she lets Sam order a black coffee and watches him eat cake.

'You wanted my help?' he says, after they tell each other that they are well and comment on the changing weather.

'Yes, please. It's Theo. I think something is wrong.' She takes a drink of the coffee. She hasn't spoken to Richard about this, and she feels a pang of betrayal, but her son comes first. 'I know you meet up with Dom. Theo mentioned you'd taken him out for lunch too the last time. Thank you for that.'

Sam smiles. 'They're fun. They make me feel young.'

Nancy guesses that Sam does it because Dom has lost his aunt recently and his parents are in freefall, but there's no need to say this.

'Theo is quiet. I've been trying to get him to meet me, but he's always too busy. I also got a statement from his bank account recently.'

She pauses, taking a sip of coffee. 'I know I shouldn't open his mail, but I was worried. Please don't tell him – he'd be angry.'

Sam nods.

'There was quite a lot of money in there.' Nancy doesn't say how much. She'd cursed aloud as she'd read the statement. It can't mean anything good.

'He gets an allowance from us, but in the last six months, there have been quite significant deposits – looks like cash – made by Theo himself. I tried to talk to him about money, I asked if he had enough, or how was he coping, but he just made a joke and clammed up. He didn't come home for my birthday; I've seen him once since he went back to school. The odd photo shoot – he never misses those. He knows Richard wouldn't like it.' She grinds slowly to a halt and swallows the break in her voice that was threatening to rise. She forces herself to smile. 'I'm sure it's nothing, but I want to know what it *is*.'

Sam bites into the cake and a few crumbs of dark orange sponge drop to his plate. *Pumpkin flavour*, she thinks, and her stomach gnaws.

A passing waiter does a double take, looking at Nancy. She sees. She looks good, she knows this, but it's far more likely he recognises her from all the photos.

Nancy ignores the attention, turning back to Sam. She is silent. The confessional statements have drained her. She's been so worried, and Richard brushes off her concerns with annoyance – he's so busy.

Parents of Theo's friends from high school get together for glasses of wine and to express collective dismay about the fact they don't see their boys any more. Nancy organises these evenings and nods along with them, but she also knows that there's more to it with Theo. Even the way he held himself was different the last time she'd seen him at a recent photo shoot when he'd done a fly-by visit at Richard's request – demand, really. She can't put her finger on it. She will not stand back and watch him crumble. It's not who she is.

The clatter and hum in the café is busy. Someone drops a tray, and a few turn and look. Nancy has to squeeze her chair in as someone else passes.

'You'd like me to keep an eye on him?' Sam asks, as the volume settles.

'Yes please. I know it's a lot to ask. Maybe, discreetly? I haven't wanted to worry Richard, not with his work.'

'Not at all.' His smile is warm.

He's attractive, she thinks. Different to Richard. She puts them side by side in her head. Richard is classic and photo-ready. Tall, outdoorsy American, and the public love him. Pale blue eyes, dark-rimmed round the iris. Sam is shorter, always smiling, and so English. Blond too, but a darker, strawberry blond, and his hair is messier. It falls forward over his brown eyes. He is self-deprecating. She'd seen him hand a gift to Tash during the summer, and he'd been so throw-away: *It's nothing.*

Richard expands on his gifts: *I went to three stores to hunt this down; I knew exactly what I was looking for. I knew you'd love it.*

'Is there any news, about Emma?'

He shakes his head. A tiny crease appears in his forehead. 'I don't think there's going to be. But Tash won't rest. It's the not knowing. I think if there was some closure ...' He looks away, out of the window, then back to her. 'It will be hard for them to come to terms with. I miss her too. We all do.'

Nancy nods and reaches out, taking his hand. Then she finds herself feeling uncomfortable – is touching him too much? She pulls her hand back.

But Sam takes her fingers, holding them for a moment, reassuring her, before releasing them. Her hand feels hot where his skin had lain against hers. An image of Sam smiling at her, on the beach under the stars in Greece. Richard was drunk and flirting, and she'd enjoyed talking to Sam. She hadn't wanted it to stop.

'But I hear you about Theo. You must be worried sick. Let me try to find out.'

Nancy feels a buzz in her stomach.

She hasn't had sex with Richard for over eight months. The last time, they'd come back from a fundraiser, and she'd drunk too much on an empty stomach while a young aide had flirted with her. Richard had been busy all evening, and after she'd been on stage, the aide had brought her a drink and told her how brilliantly she'd spoken, how she'd held the audience in the palm of her hand. His open admiration had been wide-eyed. She'd been dressed well – she always dresses well. He'd made a joke, and his face had lit up when she laughed. He'd made another. Told her how clever she was, asked *had she thought of running herself?*

Richard had been whisked into the crowd, and she found herself drinking another drink, listening to the flattery of someone in their early thirties. Young. Not too young.

She'd thought about touching his arm, leading him upstairs from the hotel's huge function room. She's never done something like that in her life.

She likes Egyptian cotton sheets and scented candles and a slow burn. She'd had a one-night stand at college once, and she'd felt terrible afterwards. It had been too quick, and he'd blanked her the day after. After that, she made sure there was dinner and gifts before she offered herself up. Richard had begged in the end. She'd made him wait months. She knew her family's money may have had something to do with it. But they looked so good together. When he'd first asked her out, she'd just known. Dinners, movies, the theatre. He'd taken to going down on her in the absence of full sex after the first few months, and he'd taken his time. Sometimes the night would end with her calling his name, damp with sweat, before she kicked him out – wouldn't let him stay over.

At three months, she'd decided she could take the next step, and before he'd left one night, she'd pushed him down on the bed and put him in her mouth.

His groans had made her feel powerful. After all, he was likely a future candidate for President. She spat discreetly as she imagined herself as a First Lady, and Richard groaned loudly that he loved her, did she want to marry him?

Of course, she didn't reply straight away. He'd asked her again, in Venice. He'd called first to ask her father's permission.

But after Theo had been born, it had died off a bit, and she didn't miss it. He's stopped taking his time. She'd seen something on his credit card that had made her pause, but then he'd begged her forgiveness and paid her much more attention. A few years ago, it had all tailed off again.

Life is so busy, and she's so tired at night. She just didn't really miss it.

Eight months ago, the flirting with the aide had kick-started something inside her she hadn't felt for a while. When they'd got home, she'd lit a candle. It had been over pretty quickly, and she'd thought of the young aide as she'd climaxed. She'd imagined being straddled in a hotel room, with Richard downstairs, unknowing.

Whatever she'd felt for Richard in the past had withered. She's not sure it's died completely. And the dream of office is still real. But Richard had been less discreet and stopped apologising. Then the huge row about their future – after Greece – all that they've worked for.

Really, she's not sure she wants it *enough* any more.

The buzz is still there as she takes hold of her coffee, and Sam smiles at her reassuringly.

'I'll do what I can.'

'Thank you.' Nancy has done the right thing. 'If you don't mind, could you stay quiet about it? I know Richard would be uncomfortable if he knew I was talking about our family more widely.'

'Does he have any idea what's going on? Any theories?'

She looks down at the half-drunk coffee. 'I haven't told him anything. I know that sounds dreadful. But he's so busy with the campaign. I don't want to worry him.'

And he might react badly, she thinks. *He might be ... unkind.*

'I'll let you know if I discover anything.'

Nancy carries the smell of pumpkin, cinnamon and spiced apple with her as she steps out into the chilled Fall air, smoothing her gloves. She will protect Theo at all costs. She loves her son like she loves nothing else.

22

Tash

Greece

Now

Tash helps Maria clear the breakfast dishes.

'You'd like me to serve lunch?'

'Yes, please,' Tash says. 'I'm having food delivered. Once you serve it up, then you can finish. We're going to spend the afternoon on the beach after the kids head off. They're almost ready.'

Maria nods and smiles, busy in the kitchen, and Tash heads up to her room.

She hears her name called as she's halfway up the stairs.

'Natasha?'

It's Kiki.

Tash walks down the last few steps.

'I bought this for you, yesterday. I didn't get a chance to give it to you with everything. It's a scarf. I thought it would suit you.' Kiki hands her a paper bag with a logo Tash recognises.

'Thank you.' She realises she sounds a bit stilted. She wasn't expecting this.

'And there's a pair of earrings in there. It was kind of you to invite me.' Kiki smiles at her. Her blond hair is in tendrils round her face, and she is so very pretty.

Tash wants to hate her, but she can't. 'Thank you, that's kind.'

'You must be so tired after last night.'

Tash nods. 'Yes. I really am.' She tries her best to smile in gratitude.

'Right, I'll go and get changed. We're heading to the beach soon, aren't we? See you there.'

Tash watches Kiki turn and head out towards the pool house where she's staying with Mark. She picks up a newspaper dropped on a table in the kitchen as she leaves, tapping it on the door frame as she goes.

Unexpected, she thinks.

If she's honest with herself, she's dreading the afternoon on the beach. Mark had been great at talking to Richard. But once Richard had disappeared off to the hotel he'd booked to drop his bags and change, Kiki had sat next to Mark, and once again, Tash felt outplayed.

It wasn't anything out of order, not really. Mark had topped up her drinks; she'd touched his arm a few times. He'd cracked more jokes than usual; she'd laughed at them – even the ones that fell flat. At one point, when the table had been loud with chatter, and she'd been talking to Megan, Kiki had whispered something in Mark's ear, and he'd blushed.

Tash is aware of everything they do like it burns her skin. No matter who she's talking to, what's happening. If they're nearby, it's like needles. After thinking she was doing OK, for some reason she's started to mind more, and she has no idea why.

An afternoon of seeing Kiki making Mark happy, even just talking to him, isn't something she can face.

The problem is, she doesn't really hate Kiki.

Kiki had offered to help with the plates, bringing stacks into the kitchen with Tash once breakfast had finished. She'd complimented Tash on her home, thanked her for her hospitality. Tash had been doing the Sudoku from the paper, and when she'd put it down to make coffee, Kiki had glanced at it and suggested a few numbers. They'd all stacked up.

No, she doesn't hate her. Although help with a Sudoku is always annoying.

Tash changes into her own bikini, woefully aware of how she will look standing next to Kiki. She grabs some fake tan, the instant stuff, and rubs it in. She doesn't sunbathe, and she has a line where her running shorts begin and end. She hasn't looked at herself in a bikini like this in a long time.

She chooses a nail varnish and paints her toes. She thinks of Megan and her gold studs in her ears. She selects some jewellery. She's not worn her wedding rings for a long time. She pushes the drawer closed on those.

Lipstick, mascara. She finds a nicer bikini, with a little more support.

Hair. She pulls out her expensive air curlers she hasn't used in a while. Plugging them in, she has a flash of memory – she and Mark getting ready for events.

She shakes it out of her head. She'd asked him to go. She'd made him leave.

Curling her hair, she thinks that she's also no further forward in trying to work out what really happened to Emma. She must mention her a few more times, ask again what had been happening at the villa before she'd gone for a swim. Tash had stayed back at the Acropolis to show Nancy around. It had just been the two of them by the end.

Megan, Emma, the boys and Richard had all come back to the villa earlier, at different points in the day.

By the time she'd come back, it had been too late.

23

Tash

'Are you sure you don't mind? They can take the helicopter,' Tash asks Stani.

'I can take them to Mykonos. It's only just over an hour by boat. Too nice a day to pollute the skies.' Stani's face creases into a smile.

Tash laughs. He hates helicopters. 'If you're sure.'

'It will be fun on the water. I'll wait and sail them back tomorrow. They're staying overnight, yes?'

'Yes.'

Tash feels a knot in her stomach. 'Keep an eye on them?'

'I'll keep an eye on that one. He's trouble. I've told him. Any messing around and it's —' Stani draws a line across his throat with his finger. 'On my boat, he will behave himself.'

'Thank you.' She doesn't really want Dom to go. Last night had scared her. He's been distant this morning. She'd asked him again about Theo – if there was something going on, and Dom had waved her away – 'Mum, it's my birthday weekend; lighten up!' Then he'd bent down to kiss her and hug her tight, before patting her on the head and racing up the stairs to get ready. It's all passing affection – tap and go. She wishes she could sit down with him for a good hour with no one else around.

'Tash, can I take my curling iron on the boat, in case my hair gets frizzy?' Becki is at her side.

'Yes. There's a shower on there too if you need it. The trick with it is to keep it short in case the water runs out. You don't want it to go dry with soap in your hair.'

'Oh, thank God. I mean, I know photos aren't the main reason for going, but I need them to look right!'

'Of course. Hair is everything.' Tash parrots this line, smiling at the blue eyes on the young blonde woman, who makes her think of Emma.

'Absolutely!'

'Thanks, Tash.' It's Jaz now, wearing Tash's perfume.

'Of course!'

They all collect in the kitchen and troop towards the doors out to the patio, heading for the steps that lead down to the beach and the short private jetty where *Lulu* is moored.

'Remember what the doctors said,' Tash says as Theo passes.

He clips his forehead in a mock salute. *Very West Point*, she thinks, which is where Richard had threatened to send him if he didn't behave. 'I think your father is on the beach. We're having lunch down there soon.' How they've ended up entertaining Richard even though Theo won't be here ... she's put it down to an unfortunate twist of fate.

In dribs, drabs, shouts, return trips to collect something forgotten, trailing toast and coffee cups, they depart.

Tash waves them off from the beach. Sam joins her. He is quiet as the boat diminishes on the horizon.

'Think they'll be OK?' Tash says, not entirely sure why she's so worried. Theo isn't even supposed to be drinking today, so the exuberance of yesterday should be a one off.

'Sure,' Sam says. But his tone isn't convincing.

Once again, she can't put her finger on it. His face gives him away.

'What do you know, Sam? Is there something I'm missing?'

'No. Dom's sensible. You've done a good job.' Sam's confidence sounds forced.

What have I missed? In all the grief over Emma vanishing, she's missed a change in her son, under her nose.

Lulu becomes smaller as she heads out to sea. Further and further. Tash puts a hand on her stomach, quietening the wrench.

24

Nancy

Winter, last year

Nancy scans the hotel bar for Sam. He had called yesterday with some news about Theo, had started speaking to her on the phone, but she said *I'm in Boston tomorrow night. Did you want to meet for a drink?*

She hadn't been due to be in Boston, but coming here gives her an excuse to drop in on Theo. She'd called him – really wanting to see him. She thought she could legitimately say she was there for another reason. It would make her seem less clingy. Theo sniffs out clingy in seconds. She doesn't want him to start despising her.

But he'd let her call go unanswered. She messaged him to ask him out to lunch today. His reply was brief – *too busy*.

Still, there's Sam. When she thinks about seeing Sam, she thinks of the buzz she'd felt last time.

Richard has someone new. She's sure of it. He hasn't come home in Washington before midnight for the last five nights.

He'd presented her with a diamond necklace last week. She'd oohed and aahed and assumed it was some kind of guilt pay-off. As long as he's discreet, she supposes. It's the embarrassment that breaks her. It threatens everything.

There. Strawberry-blond hair, messy. No tie. Clean-shaven. Jeans and casual shirt.

'Sam!' She lifts her hand.

'Nancy.' He drops two kisses on her cheeks, as has become their custom, and looks at her half-empty glass of wine. 'Can I get you another?'

They settle into two armchairs by the fire. The early December bar is covered in wreaths, and the tall Christmas tree is nearby. The light from the candles flickers on his face as he smiles at her.

He is handsome. More so tonight for some reason. In a similar vein, the more she loses respect for Richard, the uglier he becomes. His all-American good looks tilt and skew.

'Any news?'

'Yes. And no. I took Dom and Theo out to lunch last week. Theo had to leave early. I'm not sure how much use it is, but I tried to quiz Dom after he'd gone, and he rolled his eyes a bit about Theo's drinking.' Sam holds the stem of his wine glass lightly, swirls the dark red liquid. He breathes it in before taking a sip. Nancy can feel his hesitancy. 'Theo ordered shots for lunch, and paid for them. Gold tequila. I know you're well off, so it's not surprising he'd choose the expensive stuff. But it's not how I lived as a student. I didn't drink mine – I had work later – so he had both. It's not much, but Dom wasn't really into it; he seemed disapproving. They were quite ... wired.'

Nancy shakes her head. 'The drinking is worrying. How did he look?'

'I don't know really. Thinner, maybe? Really, it was Dom that made me think. He was biting his nails, and there was tension when the drinks came. It seemed like Theo's drinking was causing some issues – has something happened with him?' Sam's forehead creases a little. 'The summer must have affected both of them – Theo was there when Emma went missing, and he seemed fond of her.'

'I'll drop in on him tomorrow.' Nancy takes a sip of wine. 'When he's not expecting me.' She looks out of the window the Christmas tree is positioned next to. It's a huge, ceiling-high Crittall window and the black-edged panes look out onto the lamp-lit street. The cold weather has finally brought the promised white.

'Oh, snow!' She leans forward.

'Really? I heard it was due. I love it.' Sam turns to look.

The firelight adds shades and shadows to his profile.

That buzz.

She won't have to explain about the state of her marriage. He'd been there this summer. He'd seen Richard drunk. He'd been witness to her husband's flirting with Tash's sister.

Nancy settles back in her chair and crosses her legs. She'd chosen her clothes carefully. A black dress, resting just above the knee. Casual enough to slip into a hotel bar without looking as though she'd made an effort. Diamonds – the ones Richard had given her. But she always dresses carefully. She looks good; she knows she does.

Worry for Theo burrows away. She will see him tomorrow. She will settle it – whatever it is – once and for all.

Tonight could go either way. But she knows how she'd like it to end. She's sure of it.

Lifting her hand, she gestures at the wine glasses, catching the eye of the waiter.

This is one of the hotels that Richard uses. She's seen it on the credit card statements. He doesn't think she checks the financial side of things, but she goes over everything. She knows it's a discreet hotel. It will be why he chooses it. It gives her a certain amount of pleasure to think that she could behave here – as he has likely done. That he will know nothing.

'Oh, not for me. I brought the car,' Sam says, as the wine arrives. He pushes the glass laid out for him towards her.

'No, don't worry.' She slides the glass slowly back to his side of the small, polished table. 'If you drink too much, they have rooms.' She accompanies this with a laugh. 'It's the least I can do. To thank you for looking after Theo. Unless you've got somewhere to be?'

Sam opens his mouth a little, then closes it. He taps his phone and glances down at the screen.

Nancy forces herself to breathe, to look back out at the snow. She hasn't committed herself. There's enough room to wriggle out of this with grace if he's busy – if he declines. She's given him enough of an out. But the meaning is clear. The man is not an idiot.

It feels like minutes pass before he replies, but it must be faster. Her heart races.

'I can do another glass,' he says, lightly, smiling at her. 'I haven't got much on this week.'

Nancy pushes the door open to her suite. It's the top floor, and the curtains lie open at the side of the windows. The city is painted white. Fat flakes fall from the sky, and her head is fuzzy from wine. Just enough.

'The view!' she says. 'Come look.'

Sam follows her to the window, the Boston landscape slick and white.

Nothing has been said. She'd talked about a book she'd been reading, and he'd said it had sounded good. Then she'd mentioned it was in her room – did he want to get it now?

In the elevator ride up they had discussed Christmas plans. 'We're holding the annual drinks party,' she'd said. 'I've invited Tash and Mark. They came last year too. Most of Richard's colleagues attend. It's become quite the thing.' Her laugh had sounded natural. Then she asked if he was heading back to England.

'I usually do, for Christmas Eve. But I'm back in Boston for New Year.'

'You must come. We host the party two nights before Christmas Eve, as so many people travel the day after.'

Now they stand and look out at the city.

Sam won't make the first move. She knows this. She's married. They've had wine. Not too much.

It's up to her.

She places a hand on the windowpane, looks out at the bright lights of the city. Thinks of Theo and feels a stab of fear.

'I'm really worried about him,' she says, turning to Sam, forgetting everything else. 'What if something's really wrong? What if I've missed something serious?'

'Oh, Nancy. Look, if there is something. Then you can help him. I mean, students get in trouble all the time.'

'Richard won't be forgiving,' she says. Her husband can be cruel.

Sam takes a small step back, and she realises she's ruining the mood. The unspoken act they are about to take part in is losing momentum, but she doesn't care. Not this second. 'You really think it's not too late?'

Sam nods. 'I'm sure. He's clever. Dom is a good friend – he's got support. And you're a great mom.'

Nancy smiles. She likes how he's Americanised the word for her.

'Look, it's late. I'll get a cab from downstairs. I've had a lovely –'

'No.' Nancy puts her hand on his arm. She does want this. She can't do anything for Theo tonight. 'Stay.'

Sam looks hesitant. But, she reasons, he wouldn't have come to her room if it was a no.

'Look, Nancy, you're upset. I don't want to –'

She takes a step towards him, puts a hand on his cheek. Lifting to her tiptoes, she kisses him on the mouth. God, he tastes good.

Holding herself up, his skin soft to her touch, she slips her tongue between his lips and lets the buzz in her stomach take hold.

It's been eight months. Enough of a slow burn, even for her.

His fingers fall to her lower back, and she reaches round, undoing the top of her zip. Her mouth still on his, she pushes herself closer to him.

She breathes him in, and she waits. As she'd hoped, his fingers touch the zip she'd pulled a fraction.

He slides it down, and she pushes down the silk of the dress which rests on her hips, letting it fall. Then she pulls back, climbs out of it and she unhooks her bra. It lands on the floor.

Sam swallows and shakes his head a little. 'Are you sure? Really?'

'Absolutely.' She turns to look out of the window. They are so high up. Cars are like dots of light below them. The city spreads out before her. She places both her palms flat on the glass, her forehead touching the cool windowpane.

She leans her head to the side, and Sam kisses her neck. She takes his hands and lifts them to her chest. She's impatient.

Richard, miles away. Out there, in Washington, with someone else?

Screw Richard, she thinks, whispering to Sam. *Screw him.*

25

Nancy

Boston

Winter, last year

The campus grounds are dark, but the old-fashioned streetlights hang from buildings and cast an amber glow down onto the snow. It's almost midnight.

Nancy had been on her own when the message arrived. She'd stayed an extra night partly because she had barely slept the night before. Partly because she wanted to mark the time between Sam and going home to Richard. To savour. To transition.

After not having time to meet her yesterday, and being out when she'd dropped round this afternoon, she'd been surprised when Theo's name had flashed up.

'Mom, are you still in Boston? I'm in trouble. Can you come?'

She'd been dressed in a flash.

Sam had left after brunch in bed that morning. It had been everything she'd hoped and more. She'll see him at the Christmas party, and there are butterflies in her stomach thinking of it.

But she'd come to Boston mainly to see Theo. And now he's in trouble. She speeds up, walking more quickly, snow crunching under foot. The cold has iced the top layer of the fresh fall from that afternoon. Few footsteps scatter before her. There's something satisfying about the crunch, and she speeds up still, the sound working like a drum beating her there, faster and faster.

She managed to gain entrance by mentioning a drink with a dean who knows Richard. *No need to phone ahead, he knows I'm coming* … she can't remember what she said.

This way. She's sure Theo's dorm is this way.

A group of students pass by, laughing. A runner comes up behind her, the crunching snow giving her warning, and she flinches. A beanie and gloves. She barely sees their face.

Here. This is it.

She needs to speak to her son. It's only a month since the coffee with Sam. Strange how things can gather pace. The early December air is sharp on her chest, and the snow had begun relentlessly again this afternoon.

Theo has never gone dark on her before, refusing to answer any calls. Now this message.

Someone is on their way out as she approaches the door to his dorm. She lets her posture, her good hair, and her handbag speak for her as she nods to them and they hold the door.

Running up the stairs, her boots *clip clip* on the wood. Theo shares a dorm room with Dom.

Knocking, she hears a shout and then quiet. No one answers. She knocks again, calling, 'Theo? It's me, Mom.'

No answer, but there is shuffling and scraping behind the door. She bangs her hand in a fist on the door now. 'Theo!'

Shouting will get his attention. He will need to silence her if nothing else. He hates it when she's loud. *Karen*, he calls her.

The door swings open.

She's unprepared for what awaits her.

The room is the same, mostly, as the last time she was here. It isn't huge. There's a shared living space – a sofa, a TV. She's sat and had coffee here before. Not often, but before the fancy lunch on Parents' Day. The hardwood floors are the same.

The sofa, however, is upturned.

The TV is smashed.

Theo stands by the window. And his face, she can't …

There are more people. A girl with long pink hair. Older than him? She bends over on the floor, child's pose, kneeling near something. A mound.

Dom stands by Nancy at the door – shell-shocked. He'd let her in, and she sees his hand tremble.

And the blood. The blood everywhere. Over Theo's face. The girl's hair. Dom's arms.

The girl is howling, quietly, her body wracked with sobs, and she has her arms wrapped around the mound on the hardwood floor.

A man. A boy.

Oh my God, she thinks. *He must be dead*.

Instinct takes over. She pulls the door from Dom's hand and slams it behind her. She wants to scream. It sticks in her throat, sharp like glass.

The room swims a little. She puts out her hand, and it finds Dom's shoulder. He rocks as she touches him. He's never seemed more like a child.

No one says anything. Theo is white beneath the blood. The lights are off in the room, but the curtains are wide open, and the snow outside has bounced the light of the moon back up at the redbrick and the glass.

Swallowing hard, Nancy knows they're in freefall. It's up to her. Whatever this is. The first thing to do, is to protect her son.

Crossing to the curtains, she glances down through the thick glass panes. Is there someone on the lawn, looking up?

She pulls the curtains tight, making sure there's no way anyone could see in. Then she spins and faces the two boys, looks again at the girl on the floor, moaning now.

Pressing the light switch, she recoils as the electric light paints the colour of the blood even darker. Theo looks as though he might pass out. Dom has his fist half in his mouth, biting down on his knuckles, tears in his eyes.

There has been no movement from the mound on the floor, but Nancy can't ignore it any longer.

She touches the shoulder of the girl, who screams, and shrinks back, arms wrapped around herself. She pulls herself up against the wall, pulling in her knees.

Below where she had been lying, there is a young man. A student? Blood is everywhere, but she doesn't need to touch him to know. His head falls backward, the angle all wrong.

If she turned his head, she knows how his eyes will look – blank, staring. No blinking. Unseeing.

He's dead. But he can't be. She will not have these boys believe he's dead.

'He's still alive,' she hears herself say.

'Is he?' The hope in Theo's voice tugs at her heart.

'Yes. Absolutely. I need to get him to a hospital. He's just unconscious, but he has a very weak pulse. He looks like he's lost a lot of blood.' Her mind works quickly as she rearranges the body into a semblance of someone asleep. 'Theo, you can help with me getting him to the car. Dom, can you run to the janitor closet in the halls and get some cleaning stuff. Once we've left, come back and clean up. You boys can't be involved in whatever this is. I'll take him to the hospital, and I'll quieten it down. Dom cleans, Theo and,' Nancy looks at the woman on the floor. She's a bit older than the boys. 'And you. You come with me.'

The girl's face is frightened, and she shakes her head.

'You will come with me,' Nancy says. She imbues her years of breeding and authority into her words – lifts her head, sweeps her arm determinedly.

The girl half nods. She's definitely a bit older than the boys. Maybe a postgrad.

Sucking up air, Nancy sets her face, not allowing the terror to show. She closes the boy's eyes deftly as his head turns upwards, without seeming to do so, and loops her arms beneath his shoulders. 'Theo, the wheelchair we bought you, for your ankle at the start of term. Is it still here? In a closet?'

Theo stares at her.

'Is it?' She speaks louder this time.

He nods. 'I think so. The cupboard outside, by our room. With the suitcases.'

'Go now, get it.'

Dom follows him out of the door, and Nancy hears the girl behind her crying. 'Go get your coat. That must be yours on the floor.'

Without speaking, the girl rises and then Theo comes back, as Nancy has managed to get the boy up and sitting in a chair. His body is heavy and hangs, limbs askew.

'Are you sure he's alive?' Theo whispers.

'Absolutely. And I'll be able to get him the best treatment. Help me lift him. I'll look after his head.'

Nancy swallows a burst of bile as she lifts the body. She can't remember ever touching a dead body before.

Once he's in the chair, she grabs a blanket from the bed, and wraps it round him, pulling a woolly hat over his head and wrapping a scarf tight round his neck. There's barely anything of him visible. She wraps another scarf round his body, strapping him to the chair. 'We don't want him falling in the snow.'

'Theo, what happened?' she whispers. She reaches out and grasps his wrist, needing to feel the blood pounding his veins, the life force strong in him. 'What was this?'

Theo blinks, tears in his eyes. 'A fraternity thing.' He stumbles over his own words; they fall like glass, sounding sharp and dangerous as they land. 'It was fraternity pledge night. But...' He doesn't finish.

Nancy knows he's lying. He's grasping at anything – he's lost. She needs to believe him for now. They need to get through this somehow.

Dom returns with a mop and a bucket. He shrinks into himself, stares at the floor.

'Dom, you need to clean properly. Everything. I don't know what happened here, but there needs to be no trace of it. I'll come back and help once I've finished at the hospital. Don't leave the room.'

He's crying. She takes his hand. 'Dom, I need to know you can do this.'

A nod. He blinks.

'Just before we leave, could anyone tell me,' she says, as calmly as she can, her heart racing, chugging in her chest, heavy and painful, 'if there's anything else I need to know?'

26

Tash

Greece

Now, Saturday afternoon

Megan arranges herself on the lounger next to her. They settled on the beach after lunch. The water is still and clear. Fish of all colours dart and flock.

'You've been quiet this morning.' Tash watches her sister pull out a book.

'Is Richard Fowler staying at the villa?' Megan asks.

Tash shakes her head. 'No. He's at a hotel on the other side of the island. I had to invite him to lunch. I guess he'll hang out here today. God, speak of the devil.'

There's noise and chatter on the steps as Mark, Kiki, Richard and Sam descend to the sand.

Kiki laughs loudly at something one of them said, presumably Mark, who's never been more hilarious apparently.

Sun cream is pulled out and applied (Tash doesn't allow herself to see Mark apply Kiki's). Drinks orders are taken from the staff who are working for another hour or so. Tash had hired a few more hands for today and tomorrow over the lunch period and afternoon.

Once settled, the unrest is clear.

'Mark, fancy a race?' Richard eyes the sea. 'I could do with cooling down.'

Mark is off the lounger in a flash. 'Where to?'

Tash lays her head back against the striped cushion. This is what she remembers from them both. The need to compete. The need to win. The need to try.

It's not like she's never been like that. When Dom was born, she'd whispered a promise to him that she would give him everything he'd ever need. She'd built the business up with Mark with Dom in mind, and she'd fought and fought to make it a success.

'Out to the buoy, round it and back?' Richard stretches his arms high in the air.

Tash closes her eyes. She'll swim later when there's less posturing.

'I'll watch,' Kiki announces to Mark. 'Want a kiss for luck?'

Pleased her eyes are already closed, Tash tries not to wince.

Three races later, and more cocktails, Kiki sits up.

'I might go for a swim,' she says. 'I'm getting tan lines.' She adjusts the straps on her shoulders.

Tash sees Richard watching her. He's been drinking heavily. He's had at least four cocktails and has started on the wine. An empty bottle lies in the sand by his lounger. She remembers this from last year. The sun and booze don't mix well for him. All his charm seems to mutate into something less savoury. She doesn't know why he started drinking so heavily last summer. He seems so controlled in public life back in the States. But there seems to be some kind of release switch for him. Or more a low tolerance level. Once he goes past a certain point, he seems to abandon all restraint.

'Mark, give me a hand, I need this retied.' Kiki angles back towards him and hold the straps up.

Mark flushes a little with a glance at Tash, who puts her head down and stares at her book.

Richard takes another drink from one of the young staff Maria is overseeing. He drinks it down in one. He looks at Kiki again, then stands and stretches. He turns to Megan and Tash.

'Megan, that's a great suit,' he says. His eyes linger for a second too long.

He's pissed, Tash thinks. *So pissed*.

Beside Tash, Megan's intake of breath is quick and sharp. 'Thanks,' she says, her voice and smile neutral.

'I might join you, actually,' Richard says, almost lazily, turning from Megan to Kiki, swinging his arms and nodding to the sea.

Kiki stands, suit sorted, and starts towards the water. 'Sure, Senator.'

Tash glances at Mark. He looks from Richard to Kiki.

'I bet you're a great swimmer,' Richard says, walking away from the group, falling in line with Kiki. He walks next to her, almost right next to her.

Kiki blows a kiss over her shoulder, sending it to Mark, and he settles back down, watching them. His face is knitted in a frown.

'Anyone for a snack?' Sam says, leaping up. 'I fancy some crisps. Tash, want a packet?'

'Thank you,' she says, pleased to have something to do.

Megan looks uncomfortable. Richard's roving eyes can't feel good for anyone.

'Think this will be a car crash?' Megan whispers, not very quietly, as Kiki heads into the water and Richard starts to splash water at her.

She nods out to the buoy, and her voice carries across the beach. 'I'll race you.'

Mark half sits up to follow them. Then looks across at Tash and sits back down. He fidgets.

Tash isn't sure who she hates more: Mark for bringing his girlfriend and all this shit, or herself for agreeing to it. Why did she think this would be OK?

There's always going to be Mark. Having distance from him up to now had created a kind of mythology around them as exes. How grown up they were being. How mature. How she'd moved on.

Him arriving had blown that up in her face.

So much feeling, woven into an afternoon of sun, wine and beachwear. It's not how she ever thought being in her forties would play out.

'Let's go!' Richard calls, diving back under the water, his strokes long and quick. After a few seconds, he rises from the water, more than waist deep. He shouts, 'Sure you don't want to join us, Mark?'

'Go ahead, Richard,' Mark says, sounding like he'd rather say anything else.

'What the fuck is happening right now?' Megan whispers, and they watch Richard dive back in the water after Kiki.

More drinks arrive. Tash swallows wine like it's water.

Sam begins reading aloud select news items from the paper.

The sun burns, and Tash shifts into the shade.

For the millionth time, Tash wants to ask Megan if anything ever happened with Richard last summer.

Mark stares out at the water, sitting up and looking around. Richard and Kiki have disappeared far out, even further than the buoy. They seem to be happy out there, floating and splashing.

Mark fidgets again.

'Book good?' Sam asks him, and Mark nods, though he holds it upside down.

'Come on, let's play beach tennis.' Sam stands and throws Mark a racket.

Reluctantly, glancing out to sea, Mark hits the ball back and forth, missing far more shots than he would usually do.

Megan watches the sea, sitting very still. She sips occasionally from her drink.

'Meg,' Tash asks, very quietly, not able to stay silent any longer. 'Did something ever happen with you and Richard last summer?'

'What?' Megan's eyes dart to her then back to the sea. 'Why do you ask that?'

'Meg, he just gave you a slow once over. That's the kind of the thing you do to someone you're either involved with or you have been. Then he very deliberately followed Kiki out for a swim. He was messing with you. He's such a shit. I'd ask him to leave but I had to call because of Theo. I'll have a word with him later. But seriously, did something happen?'

Megan shakes her head, sharply, not looking at Tash. 'No. Don't ask me again. I'm going to play tennis.'

Tash sighs. This is torture. Her sister is never this cagey. It's as good as an admission. Why won't she just tell her? Something must have gone badly wrong. She looks back out to the sea where Richard flirts with Kiki.

What had he done?

*

After some tennis, Megan seems to have recovered her good mood, but forcibly. She puts her arm around Sam, poking him in his stomach. 'OK, Sam, let's see if this new physique is able to beat me. Here, Mark, hand me that racket.'

Mark passes it over and returns to his lounger, looking out at the sea, then sits up, swinging his legs to face Tash.

'I'm sorry,' he says to her. He looks subdued and speaks quietly. Megan and Sam have moved a bit away with the tennis. There's just the two of them within earshot. 'I'm sorry I brought her.'

'What, are you sorry because Senator Fowler seems to be trying to beat you at more than a swimming race?' Tash raises her eyebrows.

'Don't be stupid, Tash. I'm trying to apologise.'

'Don't call me stupid.' She opens her book and, finishing the wine in her glass, waves at one of the servers, who stand over by the beach steps. They're only working for another half an hour. 'Could you fill all our drinks up, please?'

Mark sighs and lies back down.

Finally, there is laughter as Kiki steps on the sand, shaking her wet hair back. Richard follows. He grabs her and lifts her, half off the ground, before swinging her round.

Interesting, Tash thinks. There's a flash of something that crosses Kiki's face that looks like she's having anything other than fun. She recoils at his touch. It passes quickly.

Why would she stay out in the water with him, alone, if she finds him so repellent?

Kiki laughs, but it doesn't sound very natural. Mark stands up.

'Put her down, Richard,' he says.

Richard grins and lowers her. 'Of course. Just a bit of fun.'

'Oh, cocktails!' Kiki exclaims, sitting on her lounger, squeezing up next to Mark. She gives him a kiss on the mouth. 'You taste of strawberries.'

'I'll go for a swim,' Sam announces.

Tash is just about to go with him, to get away, when Megan stands and follows him. 'Me too. How do *you* feel about a race?'

Sam laughs, 'OK, OK, but you can declare victory now. I can't be bothered to try to win.'

'What?' She pokes him in the chest. 'Oh, try, why don't you.'

Is Megan flirting? Tash wonders. This afternoon can go fuck itself.

She wants nothing more than to go up to the house.

Another hour or so stretches long. Megan and Sam swim and end up at the far end of the beach. Tash can see them diving into the sea from the ledge. She dozes.

Tash wakes to the feel of burn on her skin.

Megan and Sam are heading back towards them.

'I'll go and get some more drinks,' she says.

Tash runs up the beach steps, enjoying the trip to the small unoccupied beach house, where they keep towels, a shower, a small kitchen with a huge fridge. She holds the fridge door open, the relief of the cold as much a balm as the silence. The noise of the beach had been loud in so many ways, not least her own voice screaming inside of her head. All the questions about Mark raising themselves again, despite how firmly she thought she'd silenced them.

It's an effort to head back down the steps to the beach.

Kiki's talking as she puts down the drinks. 'Volleyball?'

'I'll play,' Richard says.

'I think it could be time to head up to the house.' Mark stands.

'Mark, you've never turned down a challenge before,' Richard says. 'Come on. I'll take both of you on.'

Tash looks at them all. She could turn tail. But she still hasn't had a chance to speak to Richard about last summer. He's as drunk as she's seen him, so this is the perfect time. This is, after all, her main focus for the weekend. To pick at the threads of what happened, to unravel and sort out, arrange. To create a picture she's craved – the truth.

'I'll play,' she says, heading over to Richard, closer to the water.

'Natasha, you look great!' Kiki says, smiling at her. 'That's a great bikini.'

'It is,' Richard nods.

His appreciative glance makes Tash feel a bit sick. His eyes are bloodshot, and his words slur every now and again.

'You be on my team,' he says to her, standing close.

'I've been meaning to ask you. Last summer,' she says, as they walk back to take their first shot. 'Did you see Emma, before she went for the swim?'

'Emma?' Richard looks at her quickly, confused. He seems to think, but he's so drunk, it takes him a while.

Tash can almost see thought bubbles appearing and popping over his head.

'Emma. I'm sorry about her. Really sorry.'

'Did you talk to her?'

He shrugs a little. 'I think she got the wrong end of the stick.'

A shot of cold into Tash's chest. 'What do you mean?'

'Here we come!' Richard throws the ball into the air, and manages to punch it, sending it high. Too high, and she squints in the sun, watching it fly.

'Richard, what do you mean, the wrong end of the stick?'

'Sorry?' He looks back to Tash.

'Emma,' she repeats.

'She was lovely,' he says, looking sad and shaking his head. 'I think Nancy sorted it.'

'What?' Tash feels sick. She takes a step closer, takes hold of his hand and pulls him towards her, leaning in. She doesn't want the others to hear. She can see Megan and Sam walking up the beach. 'What?'

Richard is quite close to her, and he blinks a few times. But his red eyes spark a little. 'I enjoyed last summer. But Nancy was cross.'

'What did Nancy do?' Tash asks.

Richard stumbles a little, as she pulls his hand. 'Nancy ... managed it. She took it the wrong way.'

'Sam, be on my team?' Megan is saying.

'Richard, what –'

He runs, staggering a little, to get the ball; it's rolling down the beach. He trips as he goes, and Sam jogs to help him up.

The moment is gone. Brief and transformative. Like a small match in a box of fireworks.

'Here, you playing?' Mark has got the ball now and throws it to Tash.

She lets it fall and takes a step backwards. 'I'm out.' She feels sick.

Mark looks over at her. 'You OK?' he mouths.

'Marky!' Kiki calls.

Mark takes a step towards Tash. She wonders for a second if she will throw up.

Kiki runs to the ball and looks from Tash to Mark and back again.

She throws it at Mark, hard.

'Come on!' she calls. 'Come and play.'

Tash is angry with herself. She should have asked Richard sooner. She should have gone for a swim with him, taken advantage.

It's too late now. He's drunk enough to let things slip but too drunk to make any sense. She'll have to try to catch him again soon.

She forces a smile onto her face. 'Going to check about dinner!'

'Tash!' It's Mark, calling her, but she keeps on going.

She'll leave Mark to his new girlfriend, Megan to flirt with single Sam. She'll get Richard on his own again later.

What does he mean? What happened last year?

'Tash.' A hand on her arm. Mark.

'What?' She snaps at him. She still can't look at him. It's too much.

'Mark!' Kiki shouts.

The air bites, the sun burns.

'Tash,' he says. Then nothing.

She stares at him.

His hand holds her arm, tight. 'It was you who told me to go, Tash. I thought …' But he doesn't finish. He just looks at her.

'Mark!' Kiki calls.

Tash looks at him, standing on the sand, part puppy and part bulldog. Words that say half a story, hanging in the air, unfinished. Never wanting to lose.

'Oh, for fuck's sake, Mark.' She leaves.

It had felt like this before, she realises. Last year. The same weekend last summer. Richard had been flirting with Megan. Nancy had watched them, unguarded for a moment, and Tash had wanted to scream at them. But then it had been Nancy she had felt for.

Sam had saved Nancy. He'd crossed to talk to her, made her laugh.

Is he saving Megan now? Is something going on? She knows she's leant on Sam this weekend. If he and Megan get together, then she is alone. Good and proper.

The pain she feels for Mark is eating her up. She'd wanted to grab him, make him hers again. This afternoon is the loneliest she's felt since she told him to go. All the questions and doubt hound her. She's drunk too much to think straight.

And Emma. What had Emma got the wrong end of the stick about? What had happened?

What did Nancy do?

27

Jaz

Saturday afternoon

Mykonos

The heat is oppressive on the boat and Jaz curls up under the deck sunshade.

'Another drink?' Dom asks, his shirt flapping open and the recent tattoo he'd had done just peeking out below his sleeve.

He hands her a glass of champagne with a strawberry on the rim. She laughs. 'You don't do half measures.'

'Never for you.' He wraps an arm around her, and she leans her head on his shoulder as he flops back on the deck sofa.

'How long?' she asks, and wonders if she should ask him if he's spoken to his mum about Harvard yet.

'About fifteen minutes,' he says, tipping his hat forward and putting his legs up on the coffee table. 'Stani will drop anchor a little further out and we'll take the dinghy in. You'll be able to see the restaurant when we're closer. It's up on the cliff.'

Jaz looks out at the prow where Theo and Becki lie drenched in sun.

'He's had a few beers,' Dom says. 'I told Mum I wouldn't let him drink, but I'm not his keeper.'

That tone again. Jaz has noticed it since before Christmas, when he said he was moving dorms. He's had some kind of falling out with Theo. They're still mates, still row together – their team is flying. But until recently Dom had drawn a line between him and Theo – they weren't the friends they had been. After Easter it seemed to change, but now, there's tension again.

'Why did you let him come here if he's bothering you?' Sipping the champagne, she stretches out her newly painted toes. She'd never really understood what had happened between them.

'He's not bothering me. His mum hasn't been dead long; I'm not going to drop him. The invitation was made last year, and Mum has been worried about him. I'm not sure she likes his dad very much. He was a bit of a dick last year. And what was he planning to do with that knife? Should I say something?'

'We could mention it to his dad?'

Dom looks across at Theo then shrugs. 'Oh, boring!' Dom slides his arm around her stomach and pulls her up closer, kissing her neck. 'His dad drank too much and flirted with both my aunts last year. He's a dick. Too focused on his job, on himself. And Theo did say to Becki it was something to do with fishing. I'll cling to that. Let's change the topic?' He kisses her neck again and butterflies dance around her stomach. 'Let's just enjoy tonight.'

'OK, birthday boy.' Jaz wriggles round so she's facing him, looping her arms around his neck and lying on his chest. 'I doubt Theo can ruin tonight. Even he must be feeling shit about last night. It's time,' she kisses him, 'to celebrate.'

She won't ask Dom if he's told his mum about Harvard. He can do it in his own time.

She snuggles into Dom. She's worrying too much.

★

'Another drink?'

The beat in the bar is loud. The sun is beginning to dip and they'd eaten a long late lunch in the open-air restaurant, covered with shady bamboo, and washed their hands in a small waterfall on the black shiny rocks that replaced a sink in the bathrooms. Jaz had spotted two Hollywood A-listers here, one of whom had come over to Dom and Theo to say hello.

'Hey, buddy – I'll get them.' Theo fist bumps Dom and heads toward the bar.

The boys had got on well this afternoon. Theo has been on his best behaviour, and he's spooled out stories of the last few years. *Remember when...*

At one point, Dom had snorted wine down his nose laughing. The vibe is good.

'Happy birthday!' Theo says moments later, lifting drinks from the tray that a woman in sand-coloured robes with braided hair carries. He nods at Dom. 'No better friend than you. You know it. Thanks, man. For everything.' He leans in and hugs Dom with one arm. Jaz could swear there was the glimmer of tears in his bright blue eyes.

'Let's party!' A shout from the DJ and the beat from the song of the summer kicks in, as whoops and cries rise in the air.

Little Jasmine from the mid-west is long gone, Jaz thinks, and she wonders if she's changing. Will her parents see a difference in her when she goes back for Christmas? Will her sister? Last Christmas, Harvard had been new and exciting to them. But her mother had been upset to hear she wasn't going to be at the farm for much of the summer. *Why don't you bring Dominic back here for a few weeks?* she'd said, and Jaz had been cross with herself for worrying what he would make of the old, hand-stitched patchwork quilt on the spare bed and the wooden kitchen, unchanged since she was young.

A man dressed in a robe brings a tray of drinks to the bar table they'd moved to. The DJ plays the beat loud and strong.

'Come on!' Theo gets up from the table and pulls Becki towards him. People are beginning to cluster round the DJ and dance. The view from the bar spills down over the beach club where sunbeds scatter across the sand, and the dress code seems to be part undressed – beachwear covered by throws, or mini dresses, crotchet tops.

Jaz downs the drink put in front of her. She needs a bit more Dutch courage to start dancing here. Dom sees her down hers, so he taps his glass against the side of hers and then knocks his back. He puts it on his head upside down.

'What are you doing?' she laughs, the rush of warmth in her veins fizzling as the shot lands.

'What the rugby boys used to do at my school.' He grins. He's almost shouting now over the music. What he says next he says in her ear, leaning in. His breath tickles, and the butterflies that have been dancing all afternoon start jiving.

'Come on!' He pulls her up, and they join the throng of people in their bikini tops and expensive dresses, and she snakes her arms up and wraps them around his neck, swaying with him.

28

Tash

Saturday evening

The wine is warm in Tash's veins as she puts the book down, lying on her bed. At least Dom will be having a good time on Mykonos. Here in hell, it's not so much fun.

The sunburn is tight on her skin, and her blood is up. She gets up and brushes her teeth. She picks up the book she's reading again but the words blur. She can't settle.

Should she try to find Richard? No, it's too late right now. Chances are he's passed out somewhere with everything he'd drunk. But first thing in the morning, she's going to get the answers she needs. *Wrong end of the stick*.

Oh, Emma.

She'll speak to Megan tomorrow too and tell her what Richard said. Finally, there's something else that could lead to answers – whatever Nancy had *sorted*; whatever the wrong end of the stick was – none of it sounds good. Maybe they could find a reason Emma might have run away.

What is going on with Megan? Why is she flirting with Sam? She's sure she wasn't misreading it. And Kiki. When she'd climbed out of the sea earlier, even Megan had done a double take. Mid-twenties. She'd forgotten what that could look like to a man who's allowed to stare. And Mark had obviously enjoyed staring. When Richard was winding him up, he bit, good and proper.

Mostly, she thinks, he brought her here to piss her off. But Kiki seems to like him. What's really going on she has no idea. He gives out a signal of one thing then is back to kissing Kiki the next.

I don't even want him any more, she thinks.

She throws the book down on the bed and climbs out, going to pour herself some water. In her pants and an old T-shirt, she looks out of the window across the sea.

After Emma, she had needed Mark gone. She needed space. She blames herself for Emma's disappearance. She missed something. She knows she did.

Now, again, she's missed something with Dom.

Lights out at sea blink in the dark. Somewhere out there ...

Emptiness touches her edges, closing in cold and hard. She fights it all the time. When Mark had first left, the solitude had been a blessing. The noise of someone else in the house had been too much – he had needed her, and she had nothing left to give. The business had needed her, so she'd asked him to buy her out. Dom had needed her, and she'd done her best. He had been all she had capacity for.

Yesterday, for the first time in a year, the emptiness had started to ebb away. Her feelings for Mark ...

She can't deny it. She's not felt like this for a while. What is it – Dom turning twenty-one? Seeing Kiki here?

Sam had been her rock. She's lent on him, and he's never asked for anything. And he didn't live with her. She could just head home when company became too much.

Yet today, when Megan had touched Sam's arm as she'd laughed at the joke he's cracked one hundred times before, a flash of loneliness had hit her like a blade.

The windows are usually closed at night for the air con, but she pushes hers open and breathes in the warm night air. Her balcony turns the corner of the house – road and sea – and she pushes open the door and leans out across the rail, looking back across the years.

She'd let this happen. She'd wanted to punish everyone. Including herself.

'Mark!' There's a shriek from the pool, then a laugh. The voice is soft on the night air and reaches up to her balcony.

Oh my God.

'Mark! Stop!' Laughter again.

'Tash can see two figures climb out of the pool in the soft glow of the night-time pool lights, which shimmer upwards from the water. She can't see who it is, but she doesn't need to.

One stumbles, and they laugh again. The clink of a bottle. They head down to the pool house.

Tash feels the bottom of her stomach drop away. They're all drunk. They've been drinking all afternoon. None of them willing to step down. It had been a power play, and she hadn't even noticed it starting. Just known she couldn't leave once she'd recognised it. She'd had to stay there, feeling like shit … just to save face.

All of them, not a single one of them willing to break first.

She considers lying down on the bed and howling, but that will not do. Her blood boils even more.

Out of nowhere, she remembers the smell of Mark up close. How he'd held her up so many times here. She'd called his name out here once. Her husband.

Tash closes the window.

She leaves her bedroom, not even bothering to pull the door closed.

Sam sleeps down the corridor. She pauses outside his door.
Am I sure?

She closes her eyes for one brief moment. Then walks in.

He's in bed, but not asleep. He's staring at his phone. For an awful second, she worries Megan is in the bathroom, and she looks at his en suite, but no, there is no light.

'Tash!' He sits up in bed quickly, rubbing his eyes. He wears thick rimmed reading glasses in bed. They're tortoiseshell, which catches the darker strands of his blond hair. His chest is bare, and she sees his arms again – tanned, defined. He's the Sam she knows and this new Sam all at once.

'Is everything OK?' he asks.

It's quiet in here. The sound from the pool house won't reach. She's safe from the noise. She has a moment to back out.

Surprisingly, she finds she doesn't want to.

Unsure of the reception she'll get, she decides there's no point in half measures. She pulls off her T-shirt.

He stares at her.

She holds his gaze, then grabs a blanket, trailing it behind her. She walks to his balcony door and pushes it open. The warm night air is soft on her skin, and she throws the blanket down over the lounger by the coffee table. His balcony is just round from the pool. They're not overlooked. They look out across the sea.

The light from the moon is clear. The sea stretches flat and black.

The spell of silence and warmth is quick to work its magic.

In the moment of peace out here she almost forgets Sam. There's no sign of Mark and Kiki. Whatever they'd been wanting to prove, if that's why they were in the pool so late, is carved in stone. There's no taking it back. The glove is down.

Checking in with herself, she still feels the heat. Rage sex. Anger. Or lust for the man she's lost. She has no idea. But she's come to find Sam.

'Tash?'

Turning, he stands in the doorway behind her. In boxers, he's hesitant, and looks uncertain. He takes the smallest step back as she takes one step towards him.

'We've all been drinking,' he says.

She takes his face in both her hands. His skin is warm and there's a touch of stubble to his cheeks. She leans her forehead to his, pulling his face down to meet hers. Their noses touch, and she takes a step towards him. Her chest touches his chest. Her legs meet his.

She needs to give him an out. She doesn't want him to feel obliged. 'Sam, you don't have to. You don't need to give me pity sex. You can say no.'

She whispers this with the sea behind her and the sound of water rippling against the sand.

The feel of his stubble lights a tiny fire inside her. The rage she'd felt moments ago fades. Lust snakes its way up into her belly. The aim of coming here the same – but she realises the motivation is different. She does want Sam. She really wants him.

She'd always thought – in moments when she'd given it any idle consideration – that sex with Sam might give her the ick. He's like a brother.

But his stubble is rough as his face moves in her hands, and she feels his mouth close down on hers. His lips are soft at first.

Thank Christ, she thinks for a second. How embarrassing if he'd turned her down.

Then she feels his hand touch her lower back.

His tongue slips between her lips, just a flicker.

The hesitancy out of the way, Tash needs to make this count. This burning inside her needs to be silenced. *Fuck* Mark. *Fuck* Kiki. *Fuck* Richard.

For a second, she will be whole again.

Wrapping her arms around Sam, she gasps as the feel of his skin on hers is hot and welcome. She jumps up, wrapping her legs around him, and she clings to his neck, feeling his legs stumble for a second, as he regains his balance.

'Are you really sure?' he says, his breath hot in her ear.

It's her fucking house after all. What right do they have to claim the night?

'Sam,' she whispers.

He sits down on the lounger. The moonlight is bright enough for her to notice that Sam doesn't really look like Sam tonight. There's a look in his eye she hasn't seen before.

He kisses her lips, her neck, lower.

The burning is stronger now. She wonders if his name will stick in her throat – will Mark be holding on in there, will it come out wrong? She tests out *Sam*, a little louder, and it becomes easier as he kisses her lower still.

She finds she can't say his name for a moment. A hot flush of pleasure.

'Are you OK? Are you really sure?' he says in her ear.

'You want me?' she asks.

'I've always fucking wanted you,' he says, gruffly. His fingers touch her gently as their faces meet. He kisses her. 'I've wanted you for so long it's almost broken me.'

'Then tell me,' she says, looking at him. She didn't think she'd be able to look him in the eye. Not during. She was sure on her way here she'd see Mark's face. She's lost track of whether she's rage shagging because of Mark or how much she really wants Sam – she'd been sure of something a moment ago but her thoughts fall away from her. He's never felt like this. She's never felt like this. Not about him.

'Tell me,' she says again.

'Oh, Tash,' he says, and it comes out loud and clean.

He calls her name again. And she lets herself go, rocking up and feeling the sweat between them make their skin slippery and the night vibrate. The wine sings in her blood and she doesn't think of anyone else in the house at all now. It's just her and him. And she's ready to claim this moment.

When she feels it, she lets herself call out, across the pool, the sea, and she slides down, collapsing on Sam, his broad chest, the blond hairs, tickling her face, the sound of his breathing steadying in her ear.

'Tash,' he whispers, as she lets herself drift off into sleep, out here on the balcony of her own home, after taking something that she's half known was always hers if she wanted.

Aware that giving it back might be much harder.

29

Jaz

Mykonos

Darkness knits the dancers closer. The glow from hanging lights and fairy lights of the bar mark out their space. The blackness of the sea is vast. Jaz shakes her hair back and airs the back of her neck – hot and damp.

The music is louder now if that's possible. They have drunk even more. Even Theo, but as Dom said, they're not his keeper. If he wants to ignore the doctor's advice, he can go right ahead.

'Heading to the beach for a breather!' Theo shouts, close by. 'Wanna come?'

Jaz nods and looks at Dom. 'What about you?'

'I'm good! See you in a bit. I'll stay with Becki!'

As Jaz follows Theo down the stone steps to the beach club area of the bar, the music fades behind her and her ears ring.

'Come on, let's get some water.' He jumps the last few steps and lands with a spring on the sand.

The bar on the beach is lit with a string of bulb lights offering a soft glow, shabby chic, with wooden stools and a hand painted sign, but a glass of wine starts at thirty euros – there's nothing shabby about that.

'Go and grab a seat. I'll get water and some snacks. I'm starving.'

Jaz nods and heads down to the gentle lap of the water. She can see the stars down here, and the odd flash of light from a boat far out at sea. She knows Mykonos is quite close to a few islands, but it feels so far away from everything.

She flops in the sand by the edge of the water and waits for Theo.

Taking his time, she thinks, looking round for him. *How long can water take?*

Squinting past a few others sitting on loungers and the sand, she sees him up at the bar. He's talking to a blonde woman who wears a pale dress. He has his hand on her arm.

Jaz tries to take more notice. The alcohol has made her head fuzzy, and she can't really make out what's going on.

The woman shakes her head at something, and Theo takes her hand, and takes a step back towards the steps. She can't see the woman's face. Just blonde hair, in this pale light.

Is he leaving without me? Jaz wonders. She half stands, crouching in the sand and trying to look without looking. Trying to stay discreet.

The woman shakes her head again, pulls away and turns. Now Theo takes a step towards her and takes her hand again. Then he pulls her towards him, wrapping his arms around her.

What the fuck?

Jaz stands now, taking a step towards the bar. The woman turns on her heel and runs down the beach, out of the reach of the lights of the bar.

Theo follows, kicking up sand and not looking back once for Jaz.

30

Jaz

Mykonos

Jaz tugs on Dom's shirt. He's dancing with his arms up in the air, as the song crescendos.

'Babe!' Seeing her, he lands a kiss close to the mouth, his aim slightly out, and she can smell beer on his breath. He looks so happy.

She can't tell him.

Looking for Becki, she sees her dancing with a group of girls they'd been chatting to earlier.

Fuck Theo, she thinks. *He doesn't get to ruin two nights in a row.*

Jaz jumps up and down with the crowd in time to the music, lifting her arms high.

Dom whoops, and Jaz forces herself to forget Theo. No, she's definitely not his keeper. Right now, she doesn't even like him that much.

*

An hour or so later, when Dom collapses on a low sofa round the bamboo coffee table they'd reserved, Becki finds them and grabs at the jug of water on the table.

'So thirsty! God, I love this place!' She necks the water and then looks at them both. 'Where's Theo?'

Dom shakes his head. His hair is damp, and his shirt falls either side of his chest as he lies back on the cushions. 'No clue. He was at the beach, wasn't he?' He looks at Jaz.

'Oh, I lost him, so I came back up here,' Jaz says lightly.

'I might go and look for him. I could do with a breather.' When Becki stands, she wobbles for a second. 'I've had too many shots. I'm calling it – water only from now.'

Jaz feels the pull of girl-code and should offer to go, but who knows where Theo is. She can't face being drawn into a drama any sooner than she has to. She's certain one is coming. But maybe Theo sorted himself out and is around somewhere, just enjoying his friend's birthday night out like the rest of them. It shouldn't be too hard. Not here. Not with all this luxury and privilege.

'I love you,' Dom says, his eyes closed. 'This is the best. Thanks for coming out here with me.'

'Wouldn't have missed it,' she says.

'Drinks?' A member of the waiting staff appears.

'Couple of bottles of water and I'll sign now. We'll head off soon. That OK with you?' he asks Jaz.

'Yes. I'm exhausted. We're staying here?'

'Yes – there's a hotel nearby. Theo knows where it is. They might want to stay longer.'

As Dom signs the bill produced, Jaz's eyes are wide-eyed at the amount. With lunch too, it's over six thousand euros. For one evening.

'Right,' Dom drinks the water, necking almost a half of the glass bottle. 'Have some water, and I'll leave the rest for the other two.'

As they stand, Jaz feels a prickle of discomfort. If Theo is still AWOL, then Becki will be left here alone.

'I'll run down and just let them know we're heading off,' she says.

'Fine. I've messaged him so he'll know, but I'll head to the bathroom. Meet you by the main desk?'

Running down the steps, Jaz's stomach is tight. She prays she finds them both.

Shit, she thinks, running out to the beach. Becki is sitting by the bar, a bottle of wine in her hand, and she's chugging it.

'What's going on?'

Becki looks at her. 'You said you lost him earlier?'

Jaz nods, dread heavy in her stomach.

'Apparently, he left with a blonde woman and hasn't been seen since. The bartender told me. He recognised him.'

Jaz shoots a look at the bartender who is busy wiping glasses. He studiously ignores them until Jaz says, 'He hasn't been back?'

'I haven't seen him.' His face is expressionless, and Jaz doesn't want to drag out their drama in public.

'Come on,' she says to Becki. 'Let's head down the beach and see if we can find him. He might be catching up with a friend.'

Becki swigs from the bottle again and goes to take it, but the bartender shakes his head. 'No glass on the beach. Here.' He tips the remaining white wine in a plastic pint glass, and Jaz wishes he'd just kept it.

Becki can barely stand as they head down the beach.

'I –' But whatever Becki says is lost as she double over and vomits on the sand. Once done, she lifts her head. 'It must be Kiki.'

'What?'

'You saw him earlier, running over to speak to her. You should have seen his face when she got here – his jaw dropped. I don't know what's going on, but it must be her. *Something* is going on. I think he's cheating on me. I think –' She bends again, retching.

Fuck, Jaz thinks. This is a train wreck.

'I mean, the knife too! Thank fuck we got rid of it. But what's he doing? He's such a –' But whatever Becki had been about to say is lost as she heaves. Becki half stands again. 'Let's tell Dom.'

Jaz doesn't want Dom to get involved so makes a quick decision.

'Look, you've had too much to drink. Theo knows where the hotel is. Come on, come back with Dom and me. We'll go now.'

Dom is dozing in a bamboo armchair with huge cushions as they arrive.

'What took you so long?' He rubs his eyes. 'Oh, you found Becki.'

'But not Theo,' Becki slurs. 'He's gone off with someone else.'

Dom looks to Jaz, eyebrows raised.

She shrugs. 'Look, wherever he is, he's not a child.'

'Theo,' Dom says, closing his eyes. 'He's pissed and the doctor said he had to be careful. I can't just leave him. I mean, if he's collapsed somewhere …'

Becki clamps her hand over her mouth and the woman at the reception desk points out of the building, over by the car park. 'Take her.'

Jaz gets Becki to the thin grass, behind a string of waiting four-by-four taxis. All sleek and shiny.

Becki retches and Jaz looks back to the club into which Dom has disappeared.

She looks at her watch. It's 1 a.m. and the drinks have given her a headache; all she wants is her bed.

It feels a long way off.

It must be almost an hour later as, mute and grimacing, Dom drags Theo out.

'I'll just stay! You can't make me!'

'Get in the fucking car.' Dom opens the sliding door on the sleek black van which has waited for them the whole time.

'We can go,' he says to the driver, naming the beach their boat is moored off.

'We're not going to the hotel?' Jaz is surprised. Becki is almost unconscious in her arms, and she reeks of vomit.

'No. We're going home. I've woken Stani. He's waiting for us. Then I'm handing Theo over to his dad. He can be responsible for him. I'm done. I'm not sitting up tonight next to him to make sure he doesn't overdose, or her, to make sure she doesn't gag on her sick. This night is a fucking shitshow.' Dom stares out the window and his jaw is tight, his head up straight and his fists clenched.

'You don't understand,' Theo says. 'It wasn't what you think.'

'Then tell me what it was,' Dom says, still staring out of the window.

'I can't ... You'll just have to trust me.' Theo's pupils are wide and dilated. His speech is quick.

'Like fuck I will. I'm sick of it all. I'm sick of *you*!'

Theo looks down at the floor then over at Becki. 'How is she?' he says quietly to Jaz.

'She's upset and she drank to compensate,' Jaz says. 'I saw you go off with someone. The bartender told her. We couldn't find you.'

Theo doesn't reply. He looks at Becki, then lifts a damp strand of hair from her face and sweeps it right, hooking it behind her ear.

'I'm sorry,' he says, so quietly Jaz has so strain to hear him. But she's not sure to whom he's talking, or to what he's referring.

The cab curls the bends quickly, the roads thin and winding. The air con is cool and welcome.

The battery on Jaz's phone and smart watch have both given up. She has no idea what time it is, but it must be gone 2 a.m., and the last hour has erased the whole afternoon and evening. It had been the best time. Now it's the worst.

Whatever happened tonight has killed whatever was left of their friendship.

31

Tash

Early hours of Sunday morning

At some point, and Tash doesn't bother to look at the clock, she wakes and she's thirsty. Sam lies on the lounger, and his nakedness is disarming. She touches his chest lightly, almost afraid. She knows him so well. And not really at all – not like this.

Giving herself a shake, she heads into his bedroom and pulls on the robe hanging by the door. She pads down to the kitchen and pulls out a sparkling water from the fridge. The cold and bubbles bring some life back into her veins. Her throat is wine sore, and she winces a little as she remembers the few hours before. The clock is a gentle companion. It's 2.30 a.m.

'Natasha? Sorry, I didn't think ...'

Kiki stands in the doorway; she looks embarrassed.

'Thirsty?' Tash says, making sure her voice is calm and even. 'Here, have a water.' She pulls out another bottle and pushes it over the counter. Once again, she will not run. She sits up on a stool at the breakfast bar and forces herself to smile at the young woman before her, who's dressed in some silk pyjama shorts with a matching top.

Kiki hovers for a moment, looking over her shoulder, back at the safety of the pool house and Mark.

Tash drinks, waiting it out. Letting Kiki speak first will bring her a feeling of control. She doesn't want to fill the silence.

'I'm sorry, about the afternoon,' Kiki says, staring down at the granite worktop. 'It wasn't cool of us, I guess. To be so ... affectionate. I knew that ... I knew that and I didn't stop.'

Tash looks at her, Kiki's head bowed. This afternoon, she'd felt threatened. Like something she'd had within her grasp was slipping away. It had scared her. She knows what it's like to lose something she loves.

'Is it really over, with you and Mark?' Kiki looks up at her. She doesn't seem embarrassed now, but a tiny bit fearful. 'I think one of the reasons ... I want him to choose me. When you're around ...' She closes her eyes for a moment, wincing, then opens them and makes herself continue.

Tash can see the effort it takes.

'Mark told me before we came here that it was fully over. But I've seen how he looks at you. You curl a finger, and he looks over. I know he likes me. I know I can –' she swallows, 'I know we're good together. We laugh, and I know he wants me. I feel I should apologise for that – but I won't.' She shoots a defiant look at Tash. Then she continues, 'But his expression when he looks at you is pretty fucking tell-tale. And I feel like it's a sham. I feel like I might have been brought here as a test. I'm no one's pawn, Natasha. I don't have the money you both have; I don't have the history. But I don't deserve to be treated like a flag, waved to see if the other side is ready to stand down. Maybe I should have just gone home. But if you want him, you need to tell him. Because I want him. I really want him.'

The clock on the wall ticks so softly it's impossible to hear it during the day, but Tash listens now as she thinks of her answer. She wants to be honest. She owes Kiki nothing, but the question is a good one. It's one she's not sure she really has the answer to.

'When Emma – left,' Tash pauses, allowing the knot in her throat to tighten then release. 'We changed. I don't blame Mark. I pushed him away. I had nothing left to give. It just broke us.' She looks up at Kiki. 'I will always love Mark, and I want him to be happy. I can't tell you I don't want him back. I can't tell you I'm not planning to ask him to come back.' It's true. For the first time in a while, she's started to think of Mark. Kiki coming here has stirred that up. If Mark brought her to make Tash jealous, then it's worked. She is. She hates seeing them together. Does that mean she wants him back? She doesn't know.

She takes a drink, glances out, but the sea is black, and the soft evening pool light casts an amber haze between the ocean and her. 'My sister is out there somewhere, I'm sure of it.' She doesn't really speak to Kiki and thinks of the early morning heat at the Acropolis. The flash of blonde hair.

Kiki slams her glass down. Her frustration clearly bubbling over. 'Look, I get it, and I'm really sorry. But I don't know Emma. Mark told me your sister went missing, but we've all lost people. You don't get to rule the world because of it. Grow the fuck up. It isn't my concern. I want to know if I have a future with your ex-husband. I'm not really here to counsel you or try to help you work out how you feel. I saw you look at him this afternoon, and I bothered you. I could see that you were jealous. I played up to it. I wanted to drive it home – to test him out. You and he doing your married couple thing – that's not OK. He's with me now.' Kiki's voice rises. She shakes her head, and her eyes flash, catching the low lights of the kitchen. 'You either want him back or you don't. I need to know. Is that what this weekend is about? Bringing your blond fit partner here to flash at Mark, so that he can see what he's missing? I got together with him for other reasons, nothing to do with you, or his money. But he's a good guy. Now I'm with him, I want to keep him.'

Tash wonders how it feels to really ask for what you want. On purpose. To decide to really stir it up. And is that how others see Sam – blond and fit? It's never really occurred to her.

Other reasons, bounces round in her head. What *other* reasons could Kiki have to be with Mark – money? Mark has a lot of money, and that's hard to ignore, even if Kiki declares there are other reasons.

Maybe it's time Tash asked for what she wanted.

This is her house. Kiki wants to *keep him*?

'He's not a toy,' Tash says, forcing herself to sound calm. 'As you asked so nicely, all I can tell you is that I haven't made up my mind. He, as you point out, was my husband. Maybe he does want me. Maybe I'll ask him to come back. And I probably don't need to stage a parade. I don't need a circus to do it. This weekend is about my son. Not about trying to win back a husband. As you so calmly point out, if I want him, I just need to say.'

Does saying that out loud give her a thrill?

No, she decides. It doesn't. It just makes her sad. This isn't her. This stupid, pointless battle. She's forty-two. She cast Mark adrift because she couldn't be with someone when sadness had settled in and taken root.

That's the truth of it.

Kiki slams her glass down one more time. It shatters on the granite. Kiki pays it no attention. She stands up.

'I don't think it's very nice of you to invite someone here, then try to steal their boyfriend. For all your fancy houses and money, you don't know much about actual manners.'

Her face changes. She looks older, a flash of pain vivid in her eyes.

'You think you know about your son, your blond man, the senator, those kids. You know nothing. You've got no fucking idea what's going on under your nose. Sitting there with your money, your perfect fucking life, thinking it's all happening because you've organised this. You're in control of *nothing*. It's going to bite you in your ass. Watch out.'

She turns and flounces, stamping her bare feet on the marble tiled floor. She cries out, touching her foot, and Tash sees a flash of glass.

Then she's gone.

Cold to her stomach, the words have winded her.

It's going to bite you in your ass.

What? *Your blond man.* Does Sam know what she's talking about?

Tash sighs. She grabs the dustpan and brush and sweeps the breakfast bar and the floor around the bar stool. She wipes the blood and sprays disinfectant on the floor.

Emptying it all into the trash, she aches to be back in her own bed. This is not going well. Her head hurts.

Just as she's about to climb the stairs, there's clatter at the door. Glancing at the clock, she sees it's almost 3.30 a.m.; who is arriving at this hour?

32

Tash

'Will you just fuck off!' The door slams and Becki strides in. Her mascara streaks down her face, and Theo follows, mute and radiating rage. He leaves the door open, and Jaz enters, white and exhausted.

'Cheers,' Dom says outside, and Stani's soft goodnight falls away.

Becki hugs her arms around her shoulders and stares at the floor. It's Theo who sees Tash and makes a visible effort to calm down. He forces a smile.

'I'm so sorry, Natasha. Did we wake you? I know it's late.'

'Not the night you planned?' Tash looks to all three of them and then Dom when he enters. They stand, shifting their weight to each foot.

'Not quite,' Theo mutters, and he glares at Becki who hasn't taken her eyes from the floor.

It's Jaz who breaks the stand-off. Tash likes her more and more.

'Right, I'm making tea. Natasha, would you like one, or are you on your way to bed?'

Torn between leaving them to sort out whatever is going on and wanting to check Dom is OK, Tash glances at them all and then turns back to the kitchen, tightening her robe. 'I'll put the kettle on. And toast. There is cake too if anyone wants anything sweeter.'

She leaves them in the dining room, adjacent to the kitchen, to sort themselves out, ears perked and listening for a hint of what has happened. They weren't due back until tomorrow after lunch. The big birthday party was due to begin with drinks on the beach late afternoon.

The hissed whispers start immediately, and Tash can't tell who is speaking.

'Do you want to just go to bed? I'll bring up –'

'If anyone is going to bed, it should be –'

'Look, it's done now. We've all apologised. Can't we –'

'Apologise? That's it? I was humiliated! I think –'

'Come. Drink tea. Mum's right. Toast will help too. Then we'll all go to bed. There's a spare room if you want it, Becki.' This is Dom. Thank God for Dom.

Jaz comes in first, pulling out milk from the fridge and getting the sugar. 'Let me make them. Would you like one?'

Tash nods and sits back down on the bar stool. This is proving quite a night.

Theo is still barely talking. He stomps in, his mouth twisted tight, and it's only good manners, Tash thinks, that is holding him together. Years of his mother telling him to be polite to the host. She wonders how much of an effort he'd make if she wasn't here.

She raises her eyebrows at Dom who rolls his eyes.

'Fun?' Tash asks.

'It was great,' Jaz says, smiling. 'Thanks for booking.'

'Yeah, Mum, it was brilliant. We had a really long lunch. Drank way too much, then moved to the bar. They had this amazing DJ,' Dom says, pulling a quick dance move. 'I mean, dancing, a proper vibe. Great sunset.'

Even Theo nods now. 'Yes, loads of faces there too.'

'Here.' Jaz hands a cup of tea to Becki who takes it and has a sip. Moments later she pushes her hand to her mouth and runs from the room.

'Oh, fuck,' Theo says, rolling his eyes. 'She's so drunk.'

'Yes,' Jaz says pointedly. 'Maybe you could go and see how she is this time?'

Theo huffs and leaves.

Dom and Jaz visibly relax.

'OK, give. What happened?' Tash asks, her voice hushed.

Dom rolls his eyes again. 'It was awful. Theo disappeared. Too many shots. The music was loud. Becki had drunk too much and puked. I can't be responsible for him. So we came home. His dad can have him.'

Jaz shakes her head. 'Yeah, he didn't exactly do anything, but he disappeared off with another woman and Becki lost it.'

Dom takes a drink of his tea and looks as though he's considering how much to say next.

'Go on,' Tash says.

'He headed away on the beach. Left the club.'

'Ah,' Tash says. She supresses a yawn, the night is catching up with her.

'Theo screamed at me when I made him leave. The club kicked us all out.'

'Even you?'

Jaz looks at Dom. 'Dom didn't want to leave him on his own. They were both out of it.'

Tash looks at Dom. 'Did you come back on *Lulu*?'

'Yeah. Sorry, Mum. I just wanted to get us back. I woke Stani up.'

'I'm sure he won't mind the overtime. Will you apologise tomorrow?' Tash remembers what Kiki had said. 'Dom, is there something else going on? Kiki hinted you and Theo and even his dad were ...' She struggles to remember exactly had been said.

Dom's face has turned a shade or two paler.

'What did she say?'

Tash looks at him and goes for hedging her bets in the conversation. 'Kiki knows more than she's letting on.'

Dom turns even paler. He sniffs and wipes the back of his hand against his nose. *Playing for time*, Tash thinks. He's trying to work out what she knows.

Wait for it.

The clock ticks out the waited time again. 'Dom, don't you think it's time you told me the whole story?' Tash smiles at him, trying to offer reassurance. 'You know I'm on your side, right?'

Tonight has tied itself up in a web of knots and string.

'I ...?' Dom's eyes give him away – wider now and they blink rapidly. Tash can taste his fear.

Becki comes back in. 'Sorry,' she says to Tash, wiping her mouth with tissue. 'You must think I'm dreadful.'

'I think you're all young and I'm older, so I'm going to bed,' Tash says, standing up. She saw the way Dom's eyes had darted to Becki and back to her. She won't get anything out of him now. 'There is paracetamol in the cupboard by the fridge. I don't know what Theo has taken, but he didn't take it here and he's over twenty-one. Can you tell him I don't want anything in the villa? He can sober up and apologise to Stani in the morning.

And he should phone the club and apologise if you want to stand a chance of ever getting back in. Dom, come up and find me once you've sorted Theo out.'

'Is Theo with you?' Dom says to Becki.

Becki shakes her head. 'I haven't seen him.'

Jaz comes back in. 'Theo? I'll look for him. Idiot.'

Tash kisses Dom on the head on the way past, smelling his hair, worried. 'Don't forget to find me. Wake me up if needed. Let's talk.'

'Jaz, you walk Becki to bed. I'll head out to the pool, see if he's there,' Dom says, his voice becoming distant as Tash climbs the stairs.

It's the last thing she hears, before sleep and rest.

What will the consequences be, she wonders, *to tonight?*

Mark, Kiki; Sam; Theo and Becki. She just hopes in the morning, when they all wake, that they don't find the sun has burnt a hole in the fragile peace of the weekend, setting it all aflame. Razing it all to the ground.

33

Jaz

3 a.m.

Dom's mom hands out tea and toast. 'I'm off to bed.'

The expression on Tash's face is the same as Jaz has seen on her own mom's before – worried but prepared to leave it be for the greater good. There's nothing like parents trying to fix something to ensure the opposite reaction. She is suddenly homesick. Desperate for her old comforter and the sounds of the farm in the morning, and for rolling her eyes at her mother who made kind suggestions and knew when to leave it well alone to let Jaz figure it out for herself.

All this money, this luxury doesn't seem to have made Theo happy. And whatever is going on with him has seeped into the weekend and poisoned it.

The knife. How poisoned was he? Had he been planning something so crazy they should have spoken to the adults? She hopes they don't regret thinking throwing it away was enough.

'Is Richard here?' Dom asks, just as Tash turns.

'Somewhere,' she says, looking back over her shoulder. 'Maybe in the beach house, maybe in the empty top guest bedroom. I left it to your dad to sort out. I'm going to bed. Wake me when you need a hangover cure in the morning. I've got bacon in.'

When they're alone, Dom's eyebrows knit and he stares into his mug of tea.

'Fine. If his dad is here, then he's on his own. Ready for bed?'

'Look, you head up, and I'll check on Becki. This isn't really her fault. She told him he can't stay with her tonight. I guess he can sleep on the sofa if nothing else. It's not cold out – even a lounger by the pool. I'll make sure she's got some water and a bowl by her bed. See you in ten.'

Carrying a glass of water up the stairs, Jaz opens the door to Becki's room. It's dark and there's a mound in the bed.

She can see a bottle of water near the pillow – the housekeeper replaces them each day and it looks from the doorway like Becki has opened it.

Rather than disturb her, Jaz closes the door gently and heads to their room. Passing a huge arch window that overlooks the pool and the sea, she looks down. There are two figures outside, and they're shouting. A muffled rumble rises up through the window, but any words are indistinct.

Theo is down there, with Richard.

Interested, Jaz pauses to watch. She can't make out what they're saying, but from the gesticulating and the volume of their voices, they're clearly arguing.

The moon glows bright – a passing cloud releasing its rays – Theo's face is lit for a second, and he's looking at his father like he doesn't recognise him.

Jaz is spellbound; two blond heads equal in height, poised as though they're about to exchange blows. Theo lifts his hand in the air and Richard bats it down, stepping close to his son and taking him briefly round the neck with one hand.

She blinks, and they're apart again.

Richard Fowler turns and strides down the steps towards the beach, and Theo screams in rage after him.

Flinching, Jaz takes a step back.

It's time for bed. She has no idea what they're arguing about – probably Theo's drinking. But Richard seemed pretty angry. She can't imagine Mark ever taking Dom by the neck. She'd be surprised if Theo and his father are still here in the morning. Hopefully they'll be long gone, and the rest of them can try and enjoy what is left of the weekend, a skeleton of the planned celebration.

34

Nancy

December, two days before Christmas

Nine months ago

Nancy is lightheaded as she zips up the dress. She'd eaten breakfast hours ago. Had no lunch. The dress fits perfectly. *Yes*, she thinks, turning side on. *This will do.*

Half the party are coming tonight – senators and their partners. Their house, on the edge of Washington DC and Virginia, is lit up tastefully. Staff have been hired and have been working all afternoon to get things ready. The President can't make it, but the VP is coming.

If she doesn't end up First Lady, she'd take Second.

All the work. The campaigning, the dinners. It must surely come to something.

What she'd done a few weeks ago ...

She looks at herself, briefly not recognising the woman she sees. Bile is quick on her tongue, and she waits for it to pass. She's not who she thought she was.

Blinking, she forces herself to focus. There she is – herself again. Polished, elegant.

They've worked too long and too hard to give up now.

Theo had come home for Christmas, just in time for the party.

'Darling,' she'd said, and tried to hug him. The rebuff of empty arms stung. He ducked under and stepped back. *Given her air*, as he'd describe it. He's thinner. She'd tried not to let the disappointment show on her face.

Since that night, he won't take her calls. She'd visited a few times, but it was like he had a radar set to tell him when she was coming, and he'd never been in.

'I'm tired, Mom. End of semester is a killer. Look, I'll go and take a shower. I'll come and find you in a bit.'

He hadn't though.

She'd been so busy organising. Richard had been doing a reading at a local church – she had joined him. The church was packed; gloves, the smell of incense, the choir shuffling as they stood. But she'd slipped out once he was done. She's barely seen either of them all afternoon.

The snow has been falling, and a winter wonderland sits outside. Candles are lit, and carols are being sung. A choir had been round their neighbourhood already. Festive songs play downstairs. It's the whitest of white Christmases.

'Darling, are you ready? They'll be arriving.' Richard comes out of the bathroom and pauses before her.

She straightens his black tie. It's habit, more than anything.

'You look good,' he says, smiling. He drops a kiss in her hair, close to her ear. 'Don't want to disturb the make-up.'

She nods. 'If it goes well tonight, it will help position us. I've heard he's stepping down sooner than planned.' She means the VP, but she doesn't need to say this aloud. They've been on red alert since they heard the rumours. Second Lady has such a ring to it.

'Where did you hear that?'

'I have my spies.' She taps her nose.

'What would I do without you?' His eyes gleam. 'It hasn't even been announced.'

Nancy shakes her head. 'The diagnosis is real. He wants to take some time with his grandkids. They're looking for someone younger, I heard. The tennis tournament you won – that will help.'

'As will having you by my side.' He steps back and produces a blue velvet bag. It's tied up with ribbon. 'I know I don't always live up to my side of the deal like I should.'

'You think?' she says; it pops out before she can stop it.

Richard laughs. He's in a good mood.

'I'm grateful for all you do,' he says. 'Honestly. I'd be nowhere without you. I love you, Nancy.'

He kisses her on the mouth this time.

'You were one of my best decisions,' he says, holding her gaze.

Of course the public vote for him, with a face like that, she thinks. He drips sincerity. Good looking. Intelligent. Well-dressed. Youthful for office.

'I really think we can do it,' she says, thinking of the White House. The Christmas tree she'd choose. The charity events she'd hold.

'Here. For you.' He hands the bag to her.

Pulling the ribbon, she gasps. A string of grey South Sea pearls lie at the bottom of a velvet-lined jewellery box.

'You've earned them,' he says, lifting them out and fastening them round her neck, turning her to see them on in the mirror. He bends and kisses her neck.

'Earned them?' she says. 'Is this a bonus or a Christmas gift from a husband to his wife?' She laughs, but it's hollow in her mouth. What a life she has settled for.

Out of nowhere, the taste of Sam is on her tongue, and she imagines it's his lips on her neck. When he'd said her name, he'd sounded like he enjoyed the taste of it. Richard's touch brings the lightest brush of loneliness, like a feather, running from her neck down her spine.

She closes her eyes and imagines Theo on the bed, chatting to them like he used to when he was small. Her doing her make-up. Him trying to put the lipstick on for her. He drew outside the lines, and then they'd laughed as they both looked in the mirror.

What had happened a few weeks ago has taken something from her. She'd been trying to protect him, but he's further away than ever. She can't remember the last time she heard him laugh.

'An early Christmas gift for my wife. Whom I love,' Richard says. 'I love you, Nancy. I know I'm not perfect. You deserve more, and I will be better. You put up with a lot from me. So, it's a gift, but it's also something you deserve. You deserve no less than the very best.'

He kisses her neck once more, and she holds his gaze in the mirror.

'To work,' he says.

The feeling of his lips on her neck tingles, and she rubs at the spot, cleaning it.

Work. It's been more than work recently. Covering up the ... she can't even think it. But what it took to protect Theo and the campaign has been something that's cracked her soul. She can't tell Richard. But she's nervous.

These things will out.

'Nancy, darling, you look incredible!' Praise and kisses land near her ear for the next hour. It's not fake praise – the house looks amazing. They'd invested everything they had at the time into the huge ivory house, with its curved drive and tennis courts beyond the lawn. Tonight, fairy lights decorate the trees. Snow is thick across the ground. The gardeners had put up lit reindeers. The evergreen to the side of the sweeping drive is dressed like a Christmas tree, and she's wrapped presents in all-weather paper, piled high beneath the branches.

'Virginia, your hair! I love it.' Nancy remembers details about the guests. She's checked who's talking to whom. Checked anything that could throw the party off.

Champagne fizzes in coupes on trays, circulated by smartly dressed waiting staff. Mistletoe hangs to create the necessary buzz and laughter. Canapes take the edge off hunger and the alcohol.

She spots Theo over behind the tree. He talks to a member of the waiting staff, who hands him something. He looks around the room before taking it.

Nancy wants to go to him, but guests stand in her way, and she greets Senator McDonald, who wears a kilt despite being four generations in the US.

'Nancy! Gorgeous as usual. Come here.'

He's drunk, and his sweaty palms slip a little low on her back as he greets her. She shuffles to the side, seeing his wife spot the roving hands, and she pulls back as his lips head towards her, too closely aimed near her mouth. She brushes them off with a 'Gosh, you both look wonderful!'

His wife wears a black dress with the family tartan edges. Everyone else says plaid. Senator McDonald insists on *tartan*.

Family tartan my ass, Richard always says. *Got it online from Tartans R Us. Thinks he's Mel Gibson on a horse. He'll paint his face blue given half the chance.*

Nancy sees Theo duck out of the French door to the patio.

'I must talk to you!' She grasps Alice Cruickshank by the hands as she passes, not stopping to say another word.

Out in the cold, the air tightens further all the pores she'd had closed earlier this week in her facial. She shivers.

'Theo?' she whispers.

Light from the house softens the darkness, the snow landing silently, disappearing in the dark beyond the halo.

'Theo?' She takes a step further.

There. Just beyond the shadows.

His hands are cupped around his mouth, and there's the flash of a spark.

'Smoking?' she says, lightly, kissing his cheek. 'I had a few of those back in college.'

The scent is muskier than a cigarette. Her stomach tightens. Richard would lose his shit if he knew Theo was smoking weed here. Security dogs prowl the perimeter with the Secret Service.

'Theo. Not tonight.' She takes it out of his mouth and bends, dipping it in the snow to extinguish the burning. 'You don't want the FBI picking you up.'

He shrugs.

He hasn't looked directly at me once, she thinks. At the ground, in the distance. Never into her eyes. The last time had been that night, when his eyes had pleaded with her.

'Is everything OK?' she asks, reaching for his arm.

At this, he looks at her.

'Who have you become, Mom?'

'What?'

'How could you ... Ryan. She came to see me.'

Nancy's stomach tightens. 'Who?' Although she guesses.

'Ryan's friend – girlfriend, I think. You said you'd taken him to a hospital.'

'I did.'

He laughs, digs his hands in his pockets and looks out at the snow. 'She said he never came home. She asked me to find out what happened to him. She was upset.'

'Look, if I was him, I'd have left and not come back. He probably had PTSD from whatever happened that night. I gave him some money and paid the hospital bills. Once he was discharged, I imagine he ran. I doubt she'll see him for dust.'

She pushes him further on that night. 'How did the fraternity pledge go so wrong? Was he a student? I haven't seen any press on it or heard any rumours.'

He narrows his eyes as he looks back at her. 'Didn't you stay with him? Didn't they tell you what was wrong with him? Did they not find his parents and call them? You must know more.'

'I had to get back to Dom. I made sure he was safe with a nurse, then I left. You remember, I got Dom over to you a few hours after I left you.'

His look has a trace of Richard now. The curl of the lip; one eyebrow lifted.

The difference is, she long ago fell out of love with Richard. Theo breaks her heart. She'd lie down and die for him. She'd commit any sin.

'You were supposed to be the one I could turn to,' he says, and his eyes drop down.

'Theo.' Tears line her throat. 'I'll always be there for you. I will do anything.'

'Yeah, Mom, but you weren't supposed to do *anything*. You're supposed to do the *right* thing. Dad covers his shit up. I thought with you, it would be …' He trails away to nothing.

The cold, the snow, the music behind them. It's like another world, eating at the edges of reality – the brutality of the truth is out here in the snow, not back in the laughing room.

'Mom, I can't live with myself. I have nightmares.' He sounds about five years old.

'Oh, Theo.' She grasps his hand, squeezes it. She doesn't mention the nightmares she has. How she feels sick. The pack of cigarettes she keeps in her car for when the smell of the blood hits her again – she can't seem to make it disappear.

A torch flickers across the lawn. The protection detail is doing their rounds. They need to get out of here.

'Come,' she says, tugging his hand.

Should she have called the police? Should she not have washed the blood from the floor? Not paid off the girl? Had she gone about it all wrong?

And as for the hospital.

He won't be going home. When she'd stopped at the edge of the bridge overlooking the Charles River, Ryan's body was already stiffening under her fingers.

There was no welcome return home for him. She couldn't let the kids go to jail. She has no idea what happened, but he is dead, and that kind of scandal is bigger than all of them; Theo didn't deserve to be mixed up in something like that, whatever it is. She might have nightmares now, but the idea of Theo in jail makes her heart race and her mouth paper dry.

She pulls his hand, like he's a toddler again, heading back into the house via a door near the kitchen, nowhere near the guests.

She can never tell Theo what she'd done.

She'd vomited as the body had plummeted like a stone, down towards the water. The icy river will have consumed him by now. She's sure there'll be no sign of him. Even if the memory stops her in her tracks at moments. Makes her freeze.

Whoever Ryan was, the last trace of him had disappeared into the current weeks ago. She's sorry for his parents, whoever they are. But she's here to protect her own son.

At any cost.

35

Nancy

The Christmas party

Nine months ago

'Nancy, what a wonderful party!' Tash takes both Nancy's hands and holds them, smiling. 'Every year you pull it off, but this year is the best one yet.'

'Tash.' Nancy hugs her. She whispers in her ear. 'Not now, I have to do a speech with Richard, but we need to talk. Find me later?'

'Is everything alright?' Tash sounds worried. Her face creases into a frown and she glances back at Mark, who is shaking Richard's hand. 'You can tell me now.'

'Not now. There's no time. Later. Don't leave early. Promise me.'

'Of course.' Tash's head tilts a little, her expression concerned. 'You know you can talk to me, Nancy.'

'Tash!' Richard is loud as he swoops in to greet Tash, and Nancy stands back.

They need to do the speeches, then she'll head back upstairs to check on Theo. She'd left him in his room, made him promise to stay there.

She's thought it through, and she's decided to tell Tash most of it. Not all of it – but Dom's involved, so it's only fair she knows. Tash deserves the truth.

'Darling, shall we?' Richard calls.

'Of course. Let's go.' Nancy weaves through the throng of diamonds and perfume, her head lifted and a smile as bright as anything in the room.

'Evening, and Merry Christmas!' The room applauds as she beams and lifts her glass.

'Ms Fowler, there's a problem in the kitchen.' A member of the waiting staff is at her elbow. He holds himself stiffly as she watches Richard tell a joke about a mishap on the tennis court.

'You need me? Can't you deal with it?'

'If you could come with me.' He's jumpy. He looks left and right then walks quickly towards the kitchen.

Irritated, she follows discreetly. They enter the kitchen, and the staff look efficient and busy.

'I don't know what the problem …'

A shout of rage, over by the door. 'Get your hands off me!'

The member of the waiting staff steps back.

Nancy's heart skips a beat. A butterfly in her chest.

Dressed in a black slip that hugs her body gently, hair up and curled, and looking so unlike the girl whose cheek she'd held so firmly, warning her about what could happen next, is Ryan's girlfriend; the girl who she'd thrust half a million dollars at and hoped never to see again.

'I said, get your hands off me!' A member of the secret service restrains her.

'Hello,' Nancy says, striding over. She needs to get her out of here quickly. 'What's going on?'

'Ma'am, we found this woman coming in at the kitchen doors. She's not on the list. She says she's a guest, but I can't let her in.'

Nancy sees his gun flash as his jacket moves. This could escalate quickly.

'I told you she'd let me in.' The girl stares at Nancy, hard and cold. 'You will, won't you? I'm a friend of her son's. I'm Theodore's friend. From Harvard.'

She'd shopped well, Nancy thinks. The dress looks expensive, and the jewellery is discreet. It's the voice that gives her away – the need, the desperation covered by bravado. There's no ease to this girl, this woman. There's something about her that screams *lie* about being a Harvard student. Nancy can see it plain on the face of the security detail.

'If you're a friend of Theo's, then let me take you to him,' Nancy says, hoping her voice doesn't sound as tight and terrified as she feels. 'He's not in the party, so there's no need to go in there.'

'Thank you, ma'am. I can't let anyone in who hasn't been checked. Not with the VP in there.'

'Of course,' Nancy says.

'The Vice President is in there?' The girl's mouth falls open.

The look the dark-haired security detail gives her is blank. He stands up straighter.

'Look, why don't you put someone on the door to the room the party is in. I'll keep Theo's friend in the snug at the back. I can ask Theo to come down. You can put someone on there if you like, to make sure everything's contained.' Nancy tries to smooth the way for everything. The party, at all costs, must not be disturbed. This girl looks like she'll cause a scene – Nancy can't have any secrets spilt out here in the kitchen, with a bunch of waiting staff and presidential levels of surveillance.

'Come with me,' Nancy says, tucking her arm through the girl's, keeping her close by. 'Now, who shall I tell Theo is here?'

'Camilla,' the girl says, standing taller than Nancy and looking, as she straightens and lifts her chin, like a million dollars. 'Kiki to my friends. Don't you recognise me?'

36

Tash

Greece

Present, Sunday morning

The scream wakes her. The morning light is bright in Tash's room. Her head aches as her eyes fly open too quickly. Little sleep and far too much wine have built a road in her head and trucks seem to be driving up and down.

'Oh my God!' Now it's a shout, and there are footsteps running and doors bang.

Emma, Tash thinks, and pulls on shorts and a sweatshirt.

She takes the last few steps in one bound and almost crashes into Sam.

'Tash!' About three different expressions cross his face.

'Emma? Is she back?' It's a year to the day since she'd gone missing.

He looks surprised. 'I don't think so,' he says, shaking his head. 'It's coming from outside.'

They both run through the kitchen and down the steps, grinding to a halt at the pool.

Becki is on the phone, crying.

'What is it?' Tash says. 'What's happened?'

Becki looks up at them, face tear-stained and mascara streaked. Tash notices she's in last night's clothes. 'In the water. Someone's in the water, in the sea. I'm phoning the police.'

Tash runs. Barefoot, the stone steps are hard and cold as the sun hasn't lifted high enough for this side of the house. It has hit the beach though. The light is bright on the water and Tash can make out splashing.

'Shit,' Sam says, running past her.

Thinking of Emma out there stalls Tash, but only for a second. She splashes out into the shallows, chest tight.

'Help me out here,' Megan calls. She's in shorts and a T-shirt and is soaked through.

Sam reaches Megan first, and Tash hears him say, 'Fucking hell.'

Stani is at the other end of the body.

A dead body, by the looks of it.

Tash's chest is tight. Blond hair.

Stani cradles the head as Megan pulls her towards the beach.

'It's not Emma,' Megan says, in case Tash can't see.

'Then who?'

Light-headed, Tash watches the sun flash off the water, as she makes out Kiki's face, hair soaked, body lifeless.

37

Tash

Present

'It's Kiki.' Sam looks at Mark, walking towards him, but his shorts and T-shirt are soaked from the sea. He drips water on the tiled floor.

'Kiki? What's she done?' Mark is heavy-eyed and working the coffee machine. 'Mate, you're all wet!'

Tash has no idea how the screams have passed him by, but Mark's hair is damp, and the commotion of an hour ago must have happened when his head was under water in the shower.

'Mark, she's dead.' Tash's voice breaks when she speaks. She swallows hard.

'What?' Mark looks from Sam to Tash. 'What are you talking about? Is this some sick joke?'

'She's dead,' Sam says. He says it quietly, like he's trying to soften a blow. The shock is still raw in his voice, and he rubs his brow with the base of his hand. 'Stani found her. In the sea, just out from the beach. The authorities are on their way.'

'Where is she?' He stands, looking out towards the beach. 'I should go to her. I mean – I should see her ... What –'

'Don't. Not now. We should leave the scene for the police.'

'But I want –'

Sam holds his arm. 'Mark, you don't want your DNA down there. Just in case there are problems. Stay here. They'll let you see her in the hospital. You'll want to say goodbye.'

'Shit!' Mark sits on a bar stool, his hand reaching for the granite surface of the island. He's pale.

Jaz enters with Becki. Both are crying.

'Becki told me,' Jaz says. Her hands shake. 'But I can't believe it. How did it happen?'

'Is Dom up?' Tash asks, thinking of her son. Another tragic event here, so soon after Emma. The same weekend a year later after Emma went missing. 'Does he know?'

'I said I'd bring coffee up,' Jaz says. 'I'll tell him.'

Tash goes to them and wraps an arm around each of them. 'It's a lot. Look, we'll get together in a few minutes. There's fresh coffee here. Or you can have something stronger. We'll meet in the lounge. Go and tell Dom, and I'll come and find you in a second.' She pulls the girls to her before letting them go. 'Here.' She fills three coffee cups.

'Is Theo awake? Does he know?'

Becki shakes her head. 'I don't know. I didn't stay with him last night. Shall I go and find him?'

Tash nods. 'I think we all need to get ready. The police will be here soon. Go and splash some water on your face. Let me speak to Mark.'

Jaz's eyes widen, as she looks across at Mark. 'Oh, I didn't see ... Yes, we'll wait in the lounge. I'll get Dom.'

The girls back out, Jaz leading Becki. Jaz smells fresh, Tash thinks, but Becki is clearly unchanged since last night. Cigarette smoke and stale beer are her morning perfume. Where did she sleep? Tash half wonders, but a sob behind her makes her turn.

'Megan's with her now. Stani pulled her in from the sea and laid her on the beach. Kiki's not on her own. You can go down in a minute. The police and an ambulance should be here soon.' Sam is talking quietly.

'Mark.' Tash walks over to her ex-husband and wraps her arms around him, tight.

'Oh, fuck. Tash. I can't believe it.' Mark falls on her shoulder, his arms wrap around her, and he cries, quickly and angrily. He's quiet almost immediately, but he doesn't move. The warmth of his head nestles deeper into her.

Feeling him close, his smell and the sound of his tears, tugs at her heart. She strokes his back.

'Mark, I'm so sorry,' she whispers.

Comforting her husband for the loss of his new girlfriend is weird. She probably shouldn't be doing this. But all she can think about is Mark in pain. And Kiki was so young. Even if, after what she said last night, she might not have been who Mark thought she was.

A cough catches her attention, and she glances up. Sam is looking at her, with an expression she can't read. He says, 'The police – I can hear a car. I'll take them to the beach.'

'I should go.' Mark lifts his head. 'Dom – I should speak to him. Tash, will you stay here? Look after them? They shouldn't see her – the body.' Mark pulls himself upright and clears his throat. He wipes his arm across his face, then he forces his face into the passing resemblance of composure. 'I'll take care of it. Look, you all need to eat something.'

'I'll come,' Sam says, walking past Tash without looking at her.

Sam will have woken and found her gone, Tash thinks. Rage sex last night, and then she'd just vanished. He will have known why she'd been there. Kiki, all over Mark on the beach yesterday – Sam had seen it all.

He'll think she used him.

Has she?

He'd told her in no uncertain terms how he'd felt last night. He'd been exactly what she'd needed. It had been him she'd wanted. Once he'd kissed her, she was all in last night, and he had been ... lovely.

But today? Today she's barely drawn a breath.

He – it seems – had wanted her for so long.

What has she done?

She heads to the stairs.

There's no thinking about today, or tomorrow. Her mind is a blank. Kiki drowned. The police here. Dom to look after.

This time last year races at her and will take her down.

She must stay busy. She'll speak to Sam later. Last night just won't process in her head this morning.

Running upstairs, she knocks on Dom's door.

'Come in.'

Pushing the door open, Dom is pulling a T-shirt over his head. 'Mum, Jaz just told me. I can't believe it.'

'I know.' Wrapping her arms around him, his body is tight and trembling. 'It's awful, just so sad.'

'But what happened?'

Tash shakes her head. She hasn't thought through the details. 'I suppose she went for a swim early.'

But had she? The picture of Kiki in the water comes into Tash's mind. She'd been wearing the silk PJs she'd had on in the kitchen last night. It must show on her face, as Dom takes another step back.

She has a flashback to him withholding something last night. Something to do with Kiki. Kiki had held quite a few secrets it seems. And Dom had been scared last night – he wouldn't tell. 'Dom,' she starts.

'Something's happened, hasn't it? It wasn't just swimming.' His words fall out, sharp and hard. His pitch rises. 'Mum, what happened?'

'I don't know.'

'Did she drown? Was it something else?' He sounds almost hysterical. He is pale again.

Tash feels a tightening in her stomach at the idea of the boys being involved. Dom clearly doesn't know what happened to her. But what if he'd gone to find Theo? Tash had intimated that Kiki spilled some secrets. What if Theo had been nervous about her giving something away?

And what Richard said about Emma getting the wrong end of the stick – was Richard behind this? Was last year's history unfolding again now?

'Dom, did you tell anyone what I said – about Kiki telling me something last night?'

His head rears back. His eyes blinking quickly. 'I did see Theo –' He starts but he stops.

'Did you tell him?'

'Mum, how did she die? Please, tell me.'

'I suppose it was drowning.' Tash feels fear creep into her belly, cold and hard. 'I saw her in the night when I came down for water, and she was in the kitchen. She was in her pyjamas, but she was wearing them in the sea. Maybe she went for a night swim?'

'Mum, that's bullshit. I can see it on your face.'

Tash shakes her head. She speaks slowly, watching his face. 'What else could it be?'

Dom sits down on the bed. Jaz had been at the side of the room, but she crawls across the bed to sit next to Dom.

'There's some stuff you don't know. What we were talking about last night.' Dom's eyes squeeze tight. He shrinks under her gaze. 'Kiki wasn't who ... I mean she wasn't just Dad's girlfriend or Theo's friend. Look, I don't know what she told you. But I've ... met her, before.'

'You know her from Harvard?' she asks.

Jaz is very still. She's looking confused.

'Yes. Dad told you she was a counsellor there.'

'But she wasn't, was she?' Tash says. She's making it up as she goes along, but she's always had good instincts, and she knows her son.

Dom shakes his head, quick and short. 'No. I mean, you can tell Dad if you want. I bumped into her once ... on campus ... but I don't think she ever worked there. I didn't know it was her until she arrived. I don't think any of us did.'

His voice is hoarse.

The clock ticks in the silence that follows. Tash needs to tread carefully.

'You didn't want to tell him who she really was.' Tash speaks gently, hoping this pays off.

Dom's mouth opens and then he closes it again. His eyes are wide, and he doesn't blink for a good few seconds. Jaz looks to him and then back to Tash.

'Who is she?' Jaz asks after the silence stretches long and taut.

Dom looks at Tash as he answers. 'She might be a friend of Theo's. I think maybe he met her at a party.'

Jaz looks confused. 'I saw someone on campus around Easter, looking for Theo. Your dad met her too – that must have been her. I didn't remember her face that well.'

'I don't know why she said she was a counsellor there, but I didn't want to embarrass her and say it wasn't true.'

'But she's dating your dad – didn't you want to tell him?' Jaz shakes her head a little.

Tash forces herself not to say anything. Jaz is doing an excellent job here.

'I only knew it was her once we were here. Like since Friday. There was no point,' he says. His voice is tight now, and Jaz's eyebrows rise and fall.

'What else?' Tash asks, quietly.

'She's known Theo for a while. I met her a few times when I roomed with him. Last winter, just before Christmas …'

'When Nancy died?'

'A few weeks before. She came to our rooms. Nancy too.'

'What?' Tash is confused. 'But Dad met her three months ago? What do you mean she came to your rooms before Christmas? You've known her that long?'

'Mum, I can't go into it all now.'

Tash sees him glance at Jaz.

'Jaz, could you give us a minute?'

Jaz nods, looking from Dom to Tash and back again. 'I'll go and see if anyone needs anything.'

Tash waits until the door closes behind her. 'What can you tell me?'

'Just be careful with the police. If they find out who she is, things could get tricky.' He stares at the floor as he speaks.

'Tricky for who? Are you saying someone might have killed her? Do you mean it could be murder?' Tash thinks hard. 'Is this to do with the bar last night?' This all sounds ridiculous. He's so young. 'Dom!' Tash squats in front of him, looking up at him. 'I can't believe it's anything like that. It'll be an accident. Honestly, I know it's so soon after Auntie Emma. I know it's a lot to take in. It's so hard when someone young dies.' She reaches for his hand on his knee and takes it, squeezing it tight.

But the image of Nancy in their rooms before Christmas comes hurtling back. 'Nancy met Kiki? Did Kiki know Richard? What happened?'

Dom stiffens, and his hands cover his face. 'Don't ask me now. Not now she's just died. Oh God, Mum, I can't cope. I just can't …'

Her thoughts pile up, come out in a tumble. 'It's the saddest thing. There can't have been anyone else here. The cameras would have picked it up on the drive. There was just us. They might have argued, but it's Theo we're talking about.'

'What if it's more than that, Mum?' His dark eyes look at her, red rimmed and scared.

'It won't be. I won't let it. It's going to be OK.' Tash hugs her son and stands. 'Come on. The police are here, and they'll tell you it was a drowning. We'll feel better after food. I'll make bacon sandwiches.' *We'll have to cancel the staff*, she thinks. They'll have to keep the house at a minimum. If it's anything like last year, the police will be busy for a while.

'Downstairs. Have a shower first and wake yourself up. You'll feel better.'

But the words settle in her brain as she heads down the stairs. *Murder*. Surely not? But why had Kiki been in her PJs? And Nancy. Nancy again.

What has gone on?

38

Tash

Tash slices open a packet of bacon, and the sizzle and smell fill the kitchen quickly.

The bang of the ambulance door can be heard from the kitchen, and an officer enters.

'We'd like to speak to everyone at once, just to explain the situation and what happens next. We need everyone to stay off the beach and out of the pool house where she was staying. We also need to search the house. Is there a room where we can talk to you all and that you can remain in while we search?'

Tash opens her mouth, but Mark has come in and is everywhere all at once.

'The lounge,' he says. 'There's enough seating. I'll take you. Becki?' He looks at Theo's girlfriend who enters with wet hair. She'd gone to get showered and dressed. 'Can you let Theo, Dom and Jaz know where we are?'

Mark leads the way towards the lounge and Tash puts the bacon in the oven on a low heat, then follows. The wide pale sofas stretch out into a three-sided square. A low coffee table has books and candles artfully arranged at the centre. There's enough seating for about twelve.

'Tash, I'll go and get Sam and Megan. They're with Stani, helping him secure the boat. He dived in when he saw the body. It had drifted out. I put Richard in the beach guest house last night. I haven't seen him this morning. Maybe he's still passed out after all the booze. I'll go and wake him. Though I can't imagine how he's slept through all this.'

It's just Tash and the officer.

'Did she drown?' Tash asks.

The officer doesn't answer right away. He looks at her. He has dark hair and is tall and thin. His radio buzzes, and he answers it in Greek, before pocketing it and then looking back at Tash.

'Do you have any reason to think something else happened?'

'No, of course not. But she was in her pyjamas.' Tash stops.

'Had you been drinking yesterday?'

'Yes, it's a weekend party. My son's birthday.'

'What time did you all go to bed?'

'I don't know.' Tash thinks that there was the time she went to her bedroom, but sleep had come much later. And not much of it. She'd seen Kiki again, that must have been around 3 a.m., then more sleep.

'We will ask everyone questions. Our investigating officers are still busy on the beach.'

The bacon. 'I'll go and bring in sandwiches. Would you like one?'

'No. Coffee. Black.'

Tash almost runs from the room. It's so like last year. The police had come when Emma had disappeared. She'd been distraught that day. She remembers them being kind but impassive. She can't fall apart. Whatever grief is stirring and threatening to paralyse her, she needs to stay in control today.

Whatever the police thought, they were giving nothing away. *Had they been drinking?* She winces at the amount of booze they'd got through yesterday. All the bottles wait near the bins. It had been like a frat party. And to think she'd warned Theo not to overdo it.

Theo – and Richard. She hadn't spoken to either of them all morning. She'd just seen the back of Richard's head. She can't even remember him leaving last night. She'd given up and gone to her room. She couldn't take it any more. Kiki had been calling for shots, and Richard had been like glue at her side. Mark's competitive edge had been riled. It had been too much.

But Richard had stayed here. And Megan had been with Stani this morning on the beach. Had she spent the night with him?

Tash had been with Sam; then she'd seen Kiki in the kitchen. The kids had come back. After that Tash had collapsed in her own bed.

Kiki must have died between then and this morning. Anyone could have been anywhere. Theo and Becki had slept in different rooms. Richard had stayed somewhere. Kiki had left Mark in the pool house – had she gone back in there? Megan was maybe with Stani. Dom and Jaz were the only two who had definitely been in the same room. If the police declared the death a suspicious one, then most of them didn't have an alibi.

39

Nancy

The Christmas party

Nine months ago

Outside is a winter wonderland with a dangerous edge. The snow on the trees is heavy on branches, and they bend under the weight. The windows are lined with banked snow, and there has been discussion from a few about heading home early because the roads are getting bad. But no one has moved. A buzz radiates from the room. The champagne is fast-flowing and the string quartet plays Christmas carols. The VP has done a turn on the piano and Senator McDonald's wife sang with him. This party is even better than last year.

All this would usually bring a punch of success, like a shot straight to Nancy's veins.

Except Kiki is in the house, and whatever agenda she's come here with has to mean bad news.

Nancy must stick to her story. She paid her boyfriend off. He's left with the cash.

She nods to the serviceman on the door of the snug.

Pushing open the door, she scans the room.

Theo is curled up on the sofa, knees pulled in, and there's a half empty bottle of champagne in his hand. As she approaches, he takes another swig.

'Where is she?' Nancy can hear the tightness to her voice. 'Theo, look at me, where did she go?'

'No, *Are you alright my darling boy*? No, *Is everything OK*?'

'This is serious.' She sits by him and stops herself from taking the bottle from his hands. 'Where did she go?'

'Dad came in.'

'What?'

'Oh yeah. Daddy dearest came in looking for me. He wanted to introduce me to someone. She stood up and pulled a whole Senator Fowler routine. You know what he's like. She's only a few years older than me. About the perfect age for him.'

'Theo!'

'Oh, fuck off, Mother! You think I don't know he plays around?'

'What do you mean?' The words are a slap to Nancy's powdered cheek.

'You must know. It's not like you and him spend any time together. I wonder sometimes if you even care. Anyway, he rocked up in the last half hour and she asked if she could see his office, and he took her out the back, so the detail on the door didn't see. They must have gone back into the house by a different door. He seemed drunk. You know what he's like when he's drunk.'

'Oh my God.' Nancy puts a hand to her chest. There's a fluttering in there that she can't quite get a handle on. She takes short quick breaths.

'Did you kill him?' Theo asks, his eyes red-rimmed. 'Ryan. Did you take him away and kill him?'

'Oh, darling.' She closes her eyes briefly before she speaks. 'He was already dead. I was trying to protect you.'

Theo nods, then takes another swig of champagne. 'So, you think I killed him. That's what you think of me?'

There's no way to answer this. 'Did you?' Her voice is barely a whisper.

'Fuck you, Mom. Fuck you.'

Nancy's hands are shaking as she pushes the door to Richard's office open. He's definitely drunk. Once the speech had been delivered, he'd let himself slide from sobriety. A public face of bonhomie, often anger behind the scenes. He rarely embarrasses himself in public, but occasionally the drinking gets so bad he almost ruins it all.

She's surprised the door opens.

Nothing. It's empty. The curtains are wide open, and the winter is a blanket outside. She shivers. The room is filled with a fragile, ghostly haze from the Christmas lights bouncing off the white of the snow.

Listening as hard as she can, separating the strains of 'Silent Night' from the strings below from a sound she can't place, she closes the door and explores.

A guest room. To the right.

The door is locked, but they're easy locks. She takes a ring off, slots it in the lock and turns.

There's no light turned on, but the same ethereal quality casts an almost cinematic glow to what she sees. Later, she will wish it had been more obscured.

Richard has his pants down, around his ankles. He's kneeling on all fours, and his face is creased – eyes closed, mouth open. The sounds he makes are guttural.

Behind him, Kiki's arm is raised high, and she lashes down what looks like the cord from a lamp. She's in her underwear. No bra.

Nancy takes a step back, her eyes blinking fast.

Richard lets out a groan as the cord lashes against his flesh.

'No.' Nancy can't help it. Her hands press to her mouth. Her yelp leaks through her fingers. Kiki sees her. Her arm pauses. A green light flashes from the fireplace. It's a familiar light she can't place.

Richard takes a second to notice her.

The expression on his face is not one she's seen before.

He's so deep in, he can't pull himself out. Lust drunk. Eyes almost rolling in his head. The first flash of anger beginning, but not fast enough. He can't yet move.

Time spins itself long and slow. What must take only seconds, seems like hours, as Richard pulls himself together. Stands.

She's frozen, watching him try to gather himself, turn towards her.

He takes one step in her direction.

Nancy turns and runs.

40

Nancy

Washington

Last Christmas

Nancy crashes into Tash as she heads down the wide and wreath decorated staircase.

'Wait...' Tash grabs her arm as she reels and pulls back. 'I was coming to find you.'

'I can't –' Nancy looks up behind her. The shame of Richard ... in their house. With guests downstairs. He must be so drunk. He will be rough later.

'What did you want to tell me?' Tash is kind and it makes Nancy's eyes sting with tears.

She pulls herself up straighter. She is still the hostess.

'Are you in trouble?' Tash says, worriedly. Looking over Nancy's shoulder. Her tone is hushed and concerned. 'Is it Richard?'

A sob betrays Nancy as she opens her mouth to say anything. She does not cry. She forces it back down.

Tash waits. She touches a tear on Nancy's cheek and brushes it away with her thumb, the green silk on the sleeves sliding down her arm and revealing diamonds at her wrist. Tash carries the scent of discreet, expensive perfume. 'Come on. I can make you a cup of tea, and we'll sit down. Away from the others.'

'A cup of tea?' Nancy laughs, her voice rising in near hysteria. 'What will that solve? My husband is upstairs with someone young enough to be his child! The political world is downstairs in our house, and Theo –' She pulls up short.

'Go on. What is it about Theo?' Tash is more urgent now. 'What about Theo and Dom?'

'Oh, Tash. I just can't.' Nancy pulls her arm free and runs. Tears blind her eyes, and she stumbles on the last step. The fringes of party leak from the closed door to the reception room and a security detail officer she doesn't recognise takes a step forwards.

'Is everything OK, Ma'am?'

'I'm just stepping outside.' Nancy turns on her heel and tries to maintain her dignity as her cheeks sting and her heart breaks. She pulls a long wool coat from the cupboard and wraps a scarf around her neck.

She needs some air.

The door swings back with force as she pulls it. A blast of the night, icy and sharp, takes her breath away.

'Mom?'

Theo stands across the hallway. He looks younger than he's seemed for some time.

'I just need a few minutes.' Then she crosses the wooden floors quickly and wraps her arms around him, tight and desperate.

'My baby,' she whispers. Maybe she's being silly. Where does she think she's going in this weather?

'Nancy!' The shout from up the staircase is loud, and she looks up, past Tash, to Richard. 'Nancy, wait!'

She squeezes Theo's hand tightly. 'I'll be back later.'

Out in the cold, she searches for her car parked to the side. The guests' cars had been parked by the tennis court. Hers is here, just out of sight of the main drive of the house.

She scrabbles with the door handle. 'Open, for fuck's sake,' she mutters, as the snow whips down her neck like needles.

Once in, the windscreen wipers start up, and scratch at the frost and ice on the glass. She puts the car into reverse, and it spins out as she puts her foot down. The flash of the bent tree, laden with snow; the swirl of flakes in the air.

As she changes gear, and the car's wheel spin in the snow, she swears. She manages to get some traction as she changes gear.

There's a knock on the glass of the passenger door.

The door opens.

41

Tash

Greece

Now

The sun's rays soften as the police gather them all.

'We'd like you all to remain in the villa. The left-hand side of the beach and the pool house are out of bounds until we say so. For the moment, while we do a preliminary search of the house, we'd like you to stay downstairs, in these allocated rooms.'

Tash nods, sick and redundant. She usually thrives off busyness. And she can't seem to get through to Dom. Since he spoke of Nancy coming to their rooms before Christmas, he's retreated – gone inwards.

Mark has launched into an organiser, father and host on overdrive, riding on adrenalin and, maybe, grief? How sad *is* he?

Tash has no idea what his relationship with Kiki really was, how serious they really were.

She can't process any of it. She's numb.

Sam has barely spoken to her above the basics – tea, coffee, toast.

Megan has been with the police for some time, giving her statement. They took Stani to the station.

The officer with the neatly trimmed beard waits to speak to everyone.

Tash's mind is like Swiss cheese with questions. And her ache for Emma has sharpened into something like the end of an icicle – it was a year ago. And it's like it's all happening again. Cold drips down the back of her neck at regular intervals, despite the heat of the day.

'Mum?' Dom sits next to her and takes her hand, speaking quietly. 'Are you OK?'

She nods out of habit but forces herself to stop. There's no point offering platitudes that mean nothing. Dom knows her better than that, and he can't have two parents acting like they've been injected with amphetamine.

'I have no idea what happened,' she whispers, as the officer is called to the edge of the room, and nods to an older man not in uniform.

Dom shakes his head and seems to have regained some of his composure. He sounds almost normal. Anyone else, Tash thinks, wouldn't notice the tremor in his hand, the swallow before he speaks. Has it been there the whole time? Has she just missed the signs?

He says, 'I mean, it was just another night, right? Once we got back, we just went to bed. I thought all the drama was finished.'

'Dom, I know it went wrong at Mykonos – but did it go badly wrong? Did Theo do something?'

Dom looks at the sofa opposite. Jaz sits next to Becki, arms linked. Both of them are pale and have clearly been crying.

'I'll talk to you later. But I was going ask you to send Theo and his dad away today. I mean, that's not going to happen now. But he's not good, Mum. It's worse than you thought. I know he was stupid on the boat, and we ended up with him in hospital, but he was high last night. He went missing. I think he and Becki have split. There's no way back. I'm done with him. And Becki,' he shakes his head and rubs at his face, 'Becki thinks he met Kiki on the beach last night, in Mykonos.'

'Kiki!'

'Shhh.' Dom looks worriedly around but no one seems to have heard. 'I mean, I don't know. He met a blonde woman, and Jaz didn't see her properly. But he had a long chat with Kiki on the beach in the morning yesterday. He went to speak to her, and they disappeared off. He didn't come back for an hour.'

Tash thinks of Nancy, not in her grave a year. She'll be turning in it if she's watching over Theo right now. She must speak to him later.

Why did Kiki go into the sea so late? Surely there was no time for her to get to Mykonos. Tash had been in her room by, what, 8 p.m.? She'd taken some food up there and left them all to it. But she'd seen Kiki and Mark in the pool about 10 p.m.

They'd been drunk. If Mark had fallen asleep, there was time. It was an hour by boat. Kiki would have had to organise one. But there'd be CCTV to confirm that.

Even if she hadn't gone, why was she wearing her pyjamas in the sea?

The time waiting for the house search to be complete stretches long.

42

Tash

'Suspicious death?' Megan says, sounding sceptical but not incredulous – the practised lawyer tone in her voice keeping her reasonable.

Tash thinks she could cry.

'What the fuck?' Mark half stands but a look from the officer makes him sit back down.

The tone in the police has changed. When they thought it had been an accidental drowning, there had been an air of sympathy. Now they are sharp. Their movements swift.

The officer looks at them all, his tone unchanged. 'It's too early to say anything else – all I can say right now is that the death initially does not appear to be of natural causes, and we're asking all of you to remain here a little longer. The autopsy will take place later. We've almost finished the search of the bedrooms. You will be able to use the rest of the villa soon. But can you all please remain at the property. The scene of death remains cordoned off.'

Two officers had introduced themselves to Tash when they'd arrived. The younger, in uniform, stands before her now, talking to them. Mainly expressionless.

The other, salt-and-pepper hair, tanned face, blue eyes and an open-necked shirt with no tie, had shaken her hand, smiled, and said he would survey the scene and speak to her later. Both his entrance and exit to the room had felt like a jolt of the law – she'd smoothed her hair, pushed down the impulse to declare she had nothing to do with any of it.

The younger officer with the clipped goatee glances in Richard's direction, and she can only imagine how the Greek police will have had pressure applied to ensure the investigation *moves smoothly* – read *quickly* – and how the details will surely stay out of the press for as long as possible. She'd seen Richard speaking to the older man with the clear authority earlier.

Richard had then made a phone call. Within half an hour the team had doubled.

'Do let us know if we can help in any way possible,' Richard says now. He sits upright, and Theo is sitting on the opposite side of the room, eyes ringed in dark circles, chewing on a nail and staring at his father blankly.

'But why would someone want to hurt Kiki?' Mark says.

Tash glances at Dom. He's pale and quiet. Whatever the story is with Kiki, she still doesn't know the half of it yet.

Mark seems oblivious to it all – most of the time with Kiki his expression is one of either excited teen or guilt. Tash will have to tell him when she gets the chance. It will all come out, and it's not fair he doesn't know first.

Megan can have no way of knowing anything about this. Does Richard have something to do with it? If Theo knew her, then Richard maybe also did. The truth is a mystery that scares the shit out of her.

Then Tash looks at Sam – the colour in his cheeks has heightened.

Who had been where? she thinks. Tash had assumed Kiki had gone back to bed with Mark after she'd cut her foot and left the kitchen – but what if she hadn't?

She feels sick.

'When did she die?' she asks; her throat is dry, and her voice sounds tight.

The officer looks at her. His eyes narrow a little, as though he's thinking about how much to reveal. His dark hair is thick and swept off his face, as coiffed as his beard. He must be in his early thirties. His English is excellent, with a touch of an American lilt like he's practised his English watching films or visiting the States.

There's a collective pause – Tash can't hear anyone even breathe.

'According to her smart watch, her heart stopped beating at 4.23 this morning.' The officer speaks slowly, watching them all as he delivers his line.

His audience hang on his every word. Some gasp, some hold their breath.

'We'd like to ask you all to give statements now. We'll gather information about the evening. No one is to leave this room without permission until we've completed a search of the bedrooms. We'll leave an officer in here with you, in case of any issues.'

'Surely you should be looking at passing boats?' Mark says, his voice gaining volume, almost hysterical. 'If she's been killed then someone passing must have seen her and docked at the beach?'

The group look back to the officer.

'No, we don't think this is an option.'

'But why not? Surely it's the obvious answer?'

Eyes back to Mark.

The officer appraises Mark, and the gaze of the room swivels.

'We've looked at the security footage. As we understand it, there is surveillance just beyond your bay and the perimeters of the property.' He looks to Tash who nods.

They'd had cameras outside their bay fitted after Emma had gone missing. One of the earlier theories, later discounted, had been that she'd been snatched for ransom. No one had wanted CCTV on the villa or beach itself – too intrusive.

'There was no one else. We have your boat arriving back just before 3 a.m., but nothing after. If Miss Sanderson's death involved a third party, then it has to be someone in the villa.'

Tash gasps at this point. Eyes dart round the room.

'One of us?' Jaz says, her voice quiet, disbelieving.

The officer says nothing.

'That's exactly what he means,' Megan says.

43

Tash

Now

'Please, call me Natasha.'

After giving her statement about where she was, how she'd talked to Kiki, Tash needs some normality.

They'd been sitting in the room for over two hours while the police had searched all the bedrooms. An officer had sat in the corner of the room the whole time, and one by one, they'd been taken out to give statements.

It had been implied that they were being allowed to stay at the property to minimise press intrusion. They had been told directly that they had all available officers completing the search in order to expedite the investigation.

Having a senator, who was in the running for the next Vice President of the United States (if the rumours were to be believed), was helping. They were now allowed back into the whole house but not allowed to leave the grounds of the villa.

The officer taps his pen on the desk and closes the book he's been making notes in. They sit in the office, with its neat wooden desk, the pale washed chair.

She feels sick, and she needs to get a handle on it all and break this mood of fear. She's good at relations. Her networking skills and ability to connect with people are one of the reasons their business was so successful.

'Christos,' he says, his smile disarming. He must want them on side too if he's to get the truth out of them all.

The day is sticky with heat and lies. She has been honest with Christos about her talk with Kiki. She'd relayed it, almost word for word, skipping the part about Kiki saying Tash had no idea what was really going on.

She must keep them on side so they carry on keeping it quiet. This could easily get out of hand – the public would smell it a mile away. Richard being so high profile. Their wealth. Nancy's recent death. Emma vanishing at the same time and place last year.

She shakes his hand. 'Can I bring you some coffee, Christos?'

'You could ask Theo Fowler to come in?'

Tash nods. 'Of course.'

'Oh, I wonder, when was the last time you saw Richard Fowler and his son before this holiday?'

Tash furrows her brow for a moment. 'It would have been at Nancy's funeral, Richard's wife. Let me go and tell Theo now.'

She and Mark had split very quickly after the funeral. She'd asked him to leave, and then time had sped up and slowed down. She'd come here, to their villa, to look again for Emma and try to wait for the pain to stop.

Days had been eaten up with looking at how they'd divide their lives. Then visiting Dom. Finalising her role in the company.

She'd remembered her resolve to bring Theo to the villa when they were organising Dom's birthday before the summer. And one trip to A&E later, Richard is here too. Not something she'd planned or even wanted.

Now Kiki is dead. She has all the questions and none of the answers. What had been the issue with Dom and Theo? How was Sam involved? What happened to Kiki? Emma?

She feels, somehow, if she could answer one of the questions, then maybe the rest would unravel. She just needs to find the right piece of thread to pull.

Theo is in the kitchen, making toast.

'The officer would like to speak to you. Are you OK? Would you like me to come in with you? Or I could get your dad?' An image of Richard, his hand raised to his son – that had been after the funeral. Tash had thought she'd seen it – Richard was always so charming, he made you disbelieve things you could see with your own eyes. How had she forgotten that? Or rather, why had she assumed it was a one-off. Why on earth would Theo want his father around if he could be like that?

'I'll be fine.' He speaks without looking at her, exiting the room quickly.

It's time to ask some serious questions. But who to ask? She doesn't want to frighten Dom into clamming up. If he was ready to tell her, he'd have told her already.

She pours a coffee, lifting the handmade cup, delicate and bought on the island. She touches the expensive top of the kitchen island, thinking of when she and Mark had picked it all out together, building this home. And she watches as Christos opens the door of the study, across the hall from the kitchen, his face neutral as Theo enters the room.

Richard is at the heart of this somehow. *The wrong end of the stick*. What had he meant? Did he have anything to do with Kiki, and if so, how? So many questions. This weekend will not last forever. She needs to act.

44

Tash

The funeral
Late January, earlier that year

'Theo!' Tash calls as she sees him disappear up the stairs.

The reception is almost over, and she hadn't managed to find him, but she wants to say how sorry she is. She wants to tell him he can always talk to her. Nancy had been worried about Theo and with Nancy gone, he will need people in his corner.

He doesn't even turn, and wondering if she's overstepping the mark, she pauses for a moment. Then she thinks of Nancy's face as she'd come down these stairs the night of the party. When she had said Richard was upstairs with another woman, a much younger woman, and she had run out into the snow only to be found dead.

Nancy would want someone to keep an eye on her son, Tash decides. Someone must keep an eye on him. She runs up after him. 'Theo!'

He disappears into what must be his bedroom, and she follows him, pushing open the door.

He stands at the window, and he turns, angry – mouth in a tight line, brow furrowed. But when he sees who it is, he softens. Almost haltingly, almost waiting.

'How are you doing?' she asks. She doesn't want to close the heavy door behind her. He might feel cornered. The rooms are wide and the furnishings plush. Sound surely can't travel too far.

She leaves it ajar and takes a step into the room. 'I'm so sorry about your mom.'

Still silent, he watches her. There's something he's expecting her to say, she thinks. Nancy had been going to tell her something about Dom and Theo the night of the party. She had never had the chance.

In for a penny. 'Your mom was worried about you. About you and Dom,' she says, beginning gently.

There's a flicker of an eyebrow, a twitch of an eyelid.

'She spoke to me the night she died.'

Still, nothing. He's pale. Paler since she started speaking?

'You can talk to me, if you want. If you ever need anything. Please, come and talk to me.'

'What did she say to you?' he asks. Another twitch of an eyelid.

What should she say? She knows none of it.

'She told me how worried she was about you both. She hadn't had much of a chance to talk to you leading up to Christmas.'

'Did Sam send you up?'

Sam? What has Sam got to do with this?

'No. Is he here?' She hasn't seen him.

Theo nods. He appraises her, then he seems to make up his mind. 'There wasn't anything. She was just worried, like moms get.'

'No,' Tash tries again, 'she was worried in particular, and she told me –'

'No, she didn't,' Theo says. 'She didn't say anything. You're winging it. She was just worrying. Dad was screwing around, and she was upset. She died because he was screwing around. She ran away from him and his wandering dick. He's the reason she's dead.'

The words slide out rough and heavy.

He's not telling her the whole truth. Something did happen before Christmas, and he's not going to let it slip. Richard was with someone the night of the Christmas party – Nancy had told her.

Wrought with the desire to comfort Theo and the desire to shake the truth out of him, Tash tries one more time. Even if she's getting this wrong, she can't ignore it. She needs to show one of her hands in order to get him to trust her. If nothing else, Dom is involved. But more than that, Theo has lost his mom and he's on his own. She wants to help him.

'I know about the affairs. I knew about the woman at the party.'

'You knew about her?' Theo's head rears up in shock. 'She told you?'

'She confided in me.' Tash takes a step forward and offers what she hopes is a reassuring smile. 'She started telling me about everything else, because although it affected you, it involved Dom as well. She wanted me to know.'

Theo starts to cry. He sinks to a chair by the window and leans his head forward on his knees. 'It wasn't my fault,' he says, his voice muffled and broken. 'It wasn't my fault.'

Tash crosses the room and kneels at his feet, placing a hand on his arm. 'None of it was your fault.'

But he won't say anything else. His tears bring Richard who must have been nearby.

Tash barely hears his footsteps on the deep carpet, but the door touches the table as it swings open wider, and then Richard is here, placing his hand on Theo's shoulder, and Theo's eyes dry up immediately.

Tash can't ask anything else.

'Thank you, Natasha,' Richard says, stately and gracious. 'Theodore and I have got it from here.'

She nods. There's nothing else to say. 'Well, if you ever need to talk.' She backs out of the room and closes the door.

Then she leans back against the wall and strains to hear.

It's almost impossible. But after a few moments, voices rise.

'You tell anyone and …' This is Richard.

'… the money! Just a dirty pay off …' This is Theo.

Tash is tense. There's silence for a moment and then Theo screams. 'I know about last summer!'

Then a crashing sound, as though something has fallen. As though *someone* has fallen. As though someone has been hit.

She can't help it, she pushes open the door and says, 'Did I leave my …'

Then she says nothing. Theo lies on the floor. A heavy red weal to his cheek.

'He fell off the chair,' Richard says, his tone even, but there are bright spots to his cheeks. His eyes flash in anger and his voice is raised. 'Have you been waiting outside the door?'

'Of course not. I just spotted I was without my bag on the stairs,' Tash says, her stomach in knots.

'Like I said, Theodore and I have got this from here,' Richard says. He strides over to the door, pushes her out and slams the door in her face.

Tash starts to cry, running down the stairs and feeling sick. What had she seen? What did it mean? *I'll speak to Theo. I'll invite him out to the villa with Dom. No Richard. I'll give him somewhere to be himself, away from this pressure.*

As she enters the reception room and looks for Dom, she remembers Theo's mention of Sam.

What has Sam got to do with any of this?

45

Tash

Now

'Can we talk?' she asks, poking her head into Sam's room. He's lying on his bed reading a book. It's like the scene from last night, which doesn't escape her.

'Of course.' He closes his book and crosses to the chairs by the window. The sun is bright, the sea stretching blue and peaceful, like no one's been murdered and the day isn't in freefall. She briefly wonders why he doesn't go out to the shaded balcony.

She settles into the chair opposite him. His expression is determinedly neutral, and she knows she needs to address last night, but she can't, not now. The day is too messy and there are too many things she needs to get straight. All the questions are hurting her brain.

'Can we leave talking about –' She's about to say *us* but realises that's a lot of assumption and a label no one is sure about. She stops and starts again. 'Can we talk about last night *after* all this? Now Kiki's dead I can't think about anything else.'

He nods. 'Of course.' Despite his smile she can tell he's guarded. She knows him so well. She wants to scream the questions – *How do you feel about what happened? Did you mean what you said last night?*

'Let's have a drink. I know I need it. It's after lunch so I'm sure it's allowed.' He spends a minute taking a bottle from the fridge in the room and then uncorks it, pouring the glasses.

The smell of him is faint in here, and she feels a wash of memory of his breath against her neck. She can't look at him as he passes her the glass.

'For starters,' she says, 'what happened with the boys before Christmas?'

'Wait, what?' Sam's mouth falls open and his head rears back. 'What do you mean?'

Tash stares at him. He knows.

Anger flares in her, hot and quick.

'Sam, you knew something, and you didn't tell me?'

'What are you talking about?' he says, but he has the same expression Theo had when he'd asked what she knew at the funeral. She's sick of all this secrecy. There's a woman dead in her home and no one is telling her anything. She's sure it must all be connected. She can feel it.

'Something was happening with the boys before Christmas. Nancy pulled me aside at the Christmas party. She was going to tell me. But she ... ran out of time.'

He flinches. Is it the mention of Nancy?

'Have you asked Dom?'

'Sam! Just tell me!' Her hands clench and her fingernails bite into her palms.

'Tash, I can't. I just ...' He leans forward. 'I would, but I promised.'

'Seriously?' She stares at him. 'I'm his *mother*!'

'God, Tash. You know I'd tell you if I could –'

'Sam!'

'I promised ... I promised Nancy, but more than that, I promised Dom.' He looks distraught, entirely different to the neutral, guarded Sam of minutes ago.

She takes a breath and tries to calm down. 'Sam. There is nothing, *nothing* you cannot tell me about Dom. Nancy was going to tell me, but then she died. It was something bad. I could tell. You *need* to tell me.'

Sam winces again.

Every nerve is on fire, and Tash can't help it, saying, 'Why do you keep flinching when I mention Nancy?'

Sam says nothing. He bites his lip but his eyes crease briefly.

'Were you and Nancy ...' She stares at him. She recognises the streak of pain on his face.

What?

He heads outside. There's a blast of heat in the room as he slides the door open then he stands on the balcony in the sun and faces out to sea.

Tash feels sick. Sam. Her Sam.

No, she thinks. *Not mine.*

Mark had always been prickly about Sam meaning more to her than she claimed. And she would have sworn he never had. But had she taken it for granted he was there when she needed him?

The idea of Sam belonging to someone else feels like a rug has been pulled from under her.

He looks out to sea. She heads out next to him.

For a moment, they look out at the blue – flat and calm. A boat in the distance moves slowly, and a plane crosses the sky, scratching its white trail high overhead.

'Were you ... were you together?' she asks quietly.

He nods. 'I suppose we were. Briefly.' His shoulders sag a little and he glances down, holding the balcony rail and rubbing at a mark that doesn't exist.

'Sam,' she says, placing her hand on his back, forcing herself to be his friend first. 'I'm so sorry. I had no idea. It must have been so hard for you when she died.'

He closes his eyes and swallows. 'It was. For all sorts of reasons.'

She keeps her hand on his back, trying to offer support and ignore the vertigo she feels.

'When did it start? Was it here, last summer? I remember you talking to her when Richard was flirting with Megan.'

He shakes his head, his hands wrapped now round the balcony rail and his knuckles white. 'No. I mean I felt sorry for her. But it wasn't a hardship – she's funny, beautiful, charming. It wasn't exactly difficult. I liked her.'

The words send Tash reeling, but she listens to him. *Now is not the time*, she thinks. *Be a friend.*

'She asked to meet me for a coffee. The boys had started their term at Harvard, and she was worried about Theo.'

Tash makes murmuring noises of encouragement.

'Well, we met again for a drink the next time she was in Boston. We had a couple of drinks. It was the night the snow started.'

Tash thinks back. She'd been in New York, and it had started there too, whitening the park and the dirt on the sidewalks.

'And you and her ...' Tash says.

He nods. 'Yes. It started that night.'

Tash swallows hard. 'I guess you saw her after?'

He stares out again. 'Yes. A few times. Quite a few times.' He looks her. His dark eyes warm and so familiar she wants to cry. 'I didn't tell you because, well, you know. You and Mark were going through so much. There was Emma. And to be honest. I didn't know what to say about it. Plus. It was just about me and her.'

'I understand. You met in Boston?'

He nods and looks down, flushing ever so slightly. 'Sometimes in Boston at the hotel. Sometimes at my flat. Once, when Richard was away, I went to her. She was nervous about Washington hotels – it was difficult to be discreet. But Richard was on the road campaigning, and she was alone.' He takes her hand, very lightly. 'It was the start of something real, Tash. I wouldn't want you think it was just a sordid affair. It was very brief. We can't have met more than ten times, but we liked each other. It felt like it could maybe – well. Who knows? I'm being stupid. I know how ambitious she was. I know she wanted to be in office. I was trying to get her to run for herself – not restrict herself to being the wife of someone successful, but to run on her own. She was so bright.' He closes his mouth, blinks a few times. 'She invited me to the party at Christmas. Initially, I said no, I couldn't watch her play happy families with him. I was getting in too deep. But I went anyway.'

Another plane crosses the sky. Tash wonders how it would feel to simply fly away from all of this.

'It must have been so hard for you. I'm really, really sorry.' She offers it softly.

'It's a relief, to be honest, to tell you. To tell someone, but particularly you.' He looks at her. He's still holding her hand, and she feels colour rise in her cheeks this time. The feel of his stubble on her face last night comes back to her. Had he been thinking of Nancy? Christ. What lie was she living – that all she had to do was whistle? She's been so caught up with herself, living in her own selfish bubble, she'd forgotten other people had feelings, and had feelings about people other than her.

First, Mark arrives with Kiki. A kick to her assumption that she had pushed him away and she didn't want him any more. She'd leaned on Sam, half-thinking he'd be there for her no matter what. Never even guessing that he could be moving forward with someone else – that he could be out of her reach. Had she really ever so determinedly wanted to be on her own?

'I couldn't believe it.' He shakes his head. 'I didn't get the chance to say goodbye. I just didn't know what to do with it all. I contacted Theo – said how sorry I was.'

'That was good of you.'

'Maybe. He didn't want to hear from me, and I haven't seen him since. I've been tied up in knots about the whole thing though. Nothing was right.'

Tash thinks about Theo's face when she'd tried to speak to him at the funeral. 'With Theo?'

'About Nancy's death,' Sam says.

She looks at him sharply. 'What do you mean?'

'I don't know.' He sighs. 'I got the impression that Richard could be ... angry? I know Nancy was very careful what she said to him. Certainly about Theo. I wouldn't say this to anyone else – but you knew her. I just hope that nothing ... happened. I really think it might. He's a powerful man, Tash. I wouldn't want to cross him. He was good at hiding secrets, good at making sure others stayed silent. Nancy told me some of it ...'

Tash thinks of Nancy's face on the stairs before she'd run out in the snow. 'Theo screamed at Richard before he went after Nancy. I didn't see where Richard went. It could have been out the back. The weather was so bad.'

Sam stares ahead, both hands grip the balcony rail now. His eyes fixed and his mouth set. 'Well, I hope to God it was the accident everyone said. With snow that thick, visibility would have been bad. I hope she lost her way and wasn't pushed off course. If he did follow her out – to shut her up after what she saw – well, it's something that's crossed my mind. And now Kiki is dead. And Richard is here. I saw her talking to him last night. I woke and you'd gone, and I was coming inside from here, on the balcony. They were shouting. I'm sure it was him. He was following her down the steps to the beach. I wasn't paying attention – I was wondering where you were. You and me – it was –'

'Mum! Mum, where are you?'

Tash leans over the balcony and sees Dom running down the steps from the patio to the pool.

'Dom! Here! What's wrong?'

He looks up at her, upset and frantic. 'It's Dad! They're arresting Dad!'

46

Tash

Now

'Mark!' Tash shouts, as an officer holds her back. She slips on the tiles in the reception area of the villa, the white painted walls spinning briefly as she flails.

Christos is by the front door, and Mark is in handcuffs.

'Can I speak to my husband?' Tash pleads with Christos.

Jaz and Dom stand back. Jaz is crying and Dom shouts, 'Dad! Dad!'

'Please,' Tash says, 'there must be some mistake.'

'No, I'm sorry. We're taking Mr Cadel in for questioning. He'll be allocated a lawyer if he's unable to afford one.'

'Tash, I'll be OK. Call Smithroe – if he can't come, he'll be able to organise someone.'

Mark has dark rings round his eyes, and Tash can see how hard he's trying to stay in control.

'But why are you charging him?'

Christos nods. 'My superior officer is coming to talk to you. I'm sorry. You can't talk with Mr Cadel directly.'

'But charging him? It makes no sense!'

Mark is led towards the door.

'Dad!' Dom shouts.

'Mark, did they say why? What is it?'

Mark looks at the limit of self-control. His face is set but there's a jump in his cheek, and his blinking is rapid.

'They're saying there are blood stains on one of my T-shirts, found on the beach near Kiki. Blood in the pool house. Tash, I promise, I had nothing to do with it. I have no idea why it's there.'

He's almost at the door.

'Mark, stay calm. I'll speak to the lawyers now. I can come to the station.'

'I'm sorry, Mrs Cadel, but you'll have to remain here.' This is Christos.

'He's my husband!' Tash shouts.

The doors close, and Tash stares in disbelief. Jaz weeps as Dom shouts, 'Dad,' one more time.

The smooth, older officer leans against the kitchen island, the patio behind him, the pool and the blue horizon beyond.

'There are also bruises on the victim. It looks as though there was an altercation. There are traces of blood in their bedroom. I've heard Mr Cadel was irate on the beach, that Senator Fowler and Kiki Sanderson were flirting. A number of people have talked about how Mr Cadel doesn't like to lose. With all the evidence of blood, it looks like an argument that got out of hand. Whatever started there, ended on the beach. We have found enough evidence. It was no accident. Whether it was his intention to kill, we don't know. But the evidence suggests that your ex-husband killed Kiki – Camilla – Sanderson. He has been charged with her murder.'

Hearing her real name – Camilla – lends Kiki a little more gravitas and Tash is cross with herself that such a small thing could make such a difference to her levels of sympathy, which have suddenly elevated.

'There's no way Mark could have done that.'

The officer places the cup of coffee he holds down on the work surface. 'Mrs Cadel, I understand how you feel. But you need to allow us to continue the investigation. We're still considering all the facts. However, the facts point to your husband.'

Tash stares at him. Time presses hard and she can't breathe. It must be Richard. She needs to find answers, now.

47

Jaz

'Becki, wait!' Jaz runs down the steps to the beach.

The section of the cove to the left by the rocks, where Kiki was found floating, is cordoned off, and police are busy.

Becki runs right. There are steps in the cliff, leading up to a ledge. From there, you can access the helipad and the path that weaves up and round back to the villa and the road or leap into the sea in a cannonball if the tide is in.

'Wait!'

Becki makes it halfway up the steps before Jaz gets to her. She manages to get all the way to the ledge, before Jaz can speak again, her breath tight in her chest, the heat making her limbs heavy and the blood pound in her head.

As Becki stops, she stumbles, Jaz blinks sweat from her eyes, a moment of horror as she wonders if Becki will tumble off. But no, she rights herself, dropping something as she sits. A flash of white as Jaz blinks away the sun.

'Fuck.' Jaz collapses next to Becki, who sits, legs dangling over the ledge, staring out across the sea. 'Where are you going?'

'Away,' Becki says. 'I can't stay here.'

'You can't leave,' Jaz says. 'The police won't let us.'

'He'll kill me if I stay. You know he will.'

'What? Who?' Jaz is slack-jawed in amazement.

'For fuck's sake, Jaz. How can you be so stupid? Theo of course. Didn't you just hear them? There's been a murder. She was killed. Of course it's Theo. There's no way it's Mark. What if he knows we know? He'll kill us all.'

'What? I'm missing something.' Jaz's head hurts. No sleep, a hangover, a death ... Her brain is fried. 'Why do you think Theo murdered her?'

'Isn't it obvious?'

Jaz shakes her head slowly. 'What? Isn't what obvious?'

'Theo. He's been hovering round her the whole time. You heard what the bartender said last night. Of course it's her.'

'It could be anyone. We were in a bar.' Jaz speaks slowly, not sure if she's trying to reason with Becki or trying to understand.

'It was her. She must have left here and come over. It's only an hour. She could have taken a water taxi. I asked Natasha what time they all went to bed. It was early. She said they all got drunk on the beach in the afternoon. She said they're too old to take their booze any more.'

Jaz thinks hard – does the timing work?

'Kiki could do it. She could have just waited for them all to pass out, then been there and back. You heard Natasha say she was in the kitchen before we got back. Maybe she'd got back ten minutes before us. She could even have hidden on the boat. Theo could have hidden her there – so no sign on the CCTV.'

'But why?'

Becki squeezes her eyes tight. Tears slide from the edges. 'Jaz, I saw them. I've seen them together off campus. I was trying to tell you in the airport. I hadn't wanted it to be true – I was waiting to see if it was really her when we got here.'

'What?'

Becki looks out, wiping her eyes and quickly shakes her head. The tears stop and her chin lifts. 'She knows who he is – everyone knows who he is. The son of Senator Fowler. Of course she wants to get close to him. He didn't come to the room last night. I looked for him, but I couldn't find him anywhere. And I didn't tell you this, but he was gone the night before. We all got back from the hospital, and I woke in the night for water, and he wasn't there. He came to bed an hour later. I was wide awake, but I didn't let on. I pretended to wake, and he said he'd just been to the bathroom. He lied to me. And he smelt of perfume that didn't belong to me. I don't know if they were having an affair, or if there was something else. But it must be him.'

'You think he's capable of murder?'

Becki looks at Jaz, her eyes sharp and clear. 'I would have said never. But someone did it.'

Jaz is winded. All sorts of moments fall into place.

Becki isn't finished. 'I mean, he brought a knife.'

48

Jaz

Harvard

Fall, last year

'Wait, what? Now?' Dom releases his tight hug as Jaz rolls out of the single bed in the dorm room. She jumps to her feet and runs for the door, laughing.

This is the third week she's been hanging out with Dominic Cadel, and she still can't believe it.

Dom groans and pulls the duvet over his head. 'You're really going? But that means I have to go too. Don't you want to come back to bed?'

'Nope. It's alright for you, rich-boy, but I'm on a scholarship here, and I've promised to go to all the classes. Plus, it's rowing practice after, and you know you won't miss that.' Jaz pulls on last night's clothes which lie in a heap on the floor. 'Do you have a spare toothbrush?'

'Oh God, alright then, I'll get up.'

Jaz's blows air out into her cupped palm and sniffs. 'I really need some toothpaste.'

'How did I end up with such a smelly girlfriend,' Dom says. He kisses her then pulls open a drawer with spare toiletries.

'Don't think you're any better,' Jaz says, poking him in the tummy as he hands her an airline bag – one of the ones they hand out in first class. 'I think curry last night and beer haven't done either of us any favours. Why didn't we brush our teeth?'

'Because it was morning when we went to bed, silly,' Dom says, sliding an arm around her waist and trying to haul her back to bed.

Jaz's stomach does a complete flip. How did she end up with Dominic Cadel? Gorgeous, clever, funny, so very rich. She assumed he'd be a dick when she was introduced to him, but he's … lovely. No other word. He'd kissed almost every part of her last night, and her whole body tingles.

'Sure I can't convince you to miss just one, teensy, weensy little lecture?' he says, wrapping his arms around her and pulling her in close. Then he inhales and exhales dramatically, dropping his arms. 'No! Forget it. You said you need to go. I'll come too.' He stretches and yawns, before finding his own clothes on the floor. 'Can we stop for coffee at least?'

'Sure, I'll buy this morning. I think if I eat anything I'll be sick.' Jaz wrinkles up her nose as she thinks of the food she ate last night. It still sloshes around inside her.

'We'll row it off. Don't worry. Theo is after the new cox – Becki – I think she's called. He'll make us row like crazy to impress her. Theo always gets what he wants.'

As Jaz opens the door and holds it for Dom, who runs a 360 looking for phone, wallet and keys, she wonders again about Dom's friendship with Theo Fowler. Theo is much closer to how she imagined: arrogant, aware of his name. He'd been much more relaxed when she'd met him at the start of term – funny and kind. But in the last few weeks, he's been drinking a little more. One of the reasons they'd eaten so late was because Theo had insisted none of the tables were good enough in the first restaurant. They'd had to wait in the second.

'Fall! So pretty.' Outside in the crisp air, Jaz kicks the leaves that pile on the ground, fresh from last night.

'Look, I have to have a late lunch with my parents. You know it's the parents' thing later. Are yours coming?'

'Nah ... I told them not to bother taking the time off. It's such a trek.'

'You wanna come with me? My parents are over from London; they're working out of New York this month.' He offers, but as he talks, she sees him thinking, so she shakes her head to decline.

'Something up?'

'Nah.' He echoes her, and again she sees the crease between his eyebrows lift and fall, thinking something out. 'I suppose ...'

'Go on.' She takes his hand and kicks another pile of red and golden leaves, stacked beneath a tall tree, its arms stretched and bright, dressed in all the colours of autumn. Students pass by wrapped in thick wool scarves of all colours.

'It's nothing. Well, not nothing. My aunt disappeared at the end of the summer. Mum's convinced she's still alive and is still looking for her. With coming here, it feels quite distant, but it's still very new. Mum says she's sure she'll show up soon.'

'Oh, Dom!' Jaz stops and squeezes his hand. 'That's awful!'

'Yes, it's shit. I miss her. I still can't really believe it. Dad agrees with the police that she must have drowned and is trying to get Mum to accept it. But she won't listen to him. She's stopped talking to him really.' He laughs but there's a forced smile on his face. 'It's a good job you don't want to come for lunch. I don't know what they'll be like!'

He tugs at her hand. 'Let's run. We'll be late!'

The water is cold as it splashes up at Jaz. She mistimes her oar and it whacks her on the chin as Becki, the new cox, calls out another command.

'OK?' Theo asks.

Jaz nods. Her hands are cold, even with the gloves. The air hasn't warmed at all even with the sun out. A cold spell is kicking in.

She wants to get this right. She holds the oar again, watching Becki and waiting for her to lead them.

Becki grins at her – bright blue eyes under blond hair. Jaz would guess Swedish if she hadn't chatted to her already and heard the Canadian accent.

Drying off, after the boats are stored, the two girls watch Theo as he starts showing off.

'He likes you,' Jaz says.

'If he works for it, I might think about it. I'm no push over.' Becki rolls her eyes as Theo executes a perfect backflip into the Charles River from the bank. 'But I need to be sure. I'm the jealous type.' She winks at Jaz.

'That's for your benefit,' Jaz says. 'The way to a girl's heart is through a backflip. I bet he's read that somewhere.'

He climbs out to a group of cheers.

'His dad is Senator Fowler, isn't he? My mom said he was going to be here. She read an interview with him. Not sure she's that impressed with US senators right now.' Becki watches Theo who climbs even further up the bank to go again.

'He's here today with his wife, weirdly. I suppose it's the parents' lunch thing. More for the parents likely to donate. I saw them earlier, after class. They arrived in a fancy car but stopped on campus to say hi to Dom. I think the families are friends.

Both Theo's parents were there – they seem very friendly – at least to Dom.'

'It's another life,' Becki says, then she looks at Jaz. 'My dad's a history teacher and my mom's a dentist. Like, good jobs, but all this is something else. Imagine being part of that – having money whenever you want it. Whatever you want, all the time.'

'Totally mad.' Jaz nods. 'I'm from a farm in the Midwest.'

'Want to get drinks later? I guess your parents aren't coming either so we could hang out. I could do with a beer.'

'Is Dom turning up?' Becki asks, pouring another glass of cheap white wine and curling her legs in their baggy ripped jeans beneath her. She pulls off a sweatshirt and wears a crop top beneath. A flash of her toned stomach is visible in the low lighting – there are candles on the wooden tables, and the floor is a bit sticky. It's an older bar. Cheaper than the ones near campus.

'My God, aren't you cold?' Jaz shivers, sipping her beer and glancing at her phone. 'No, he's not.' She's disappointed, but he mentioned being tired after the lunch. She guesses it's not just their late night – he said his parents weren't getting on any better today, and he didn't sound in the best mood.

'Cold? I told you I'm from Canada, right? This isn't cold.' Becki sits up straight and stretches out her arms over her head. 'OK, one more, then we'll head home.'

The door opens, bringing in a rush of autumn night air.

Jaz glances up and sees it's Theo, buried under a hat and a scarf. He doesn't see her. He looks left and right quickly, but misses them, secluded on the corner table.

She's about to raise her hand, but no, he's not here for them. She sees him head over to a woman sitting at the bar. Her hair, dyed a pale pink, is tied up in a messy bun, and she looks a few years older than them. Maybe a postgrad. She's about to point him out to Becki, who has her back to the bar, but for some reason she doesn't. The whole thing seems a bit off.

She half watches him as Becki chats about snow drifts and minus 11 degrees.

He doesn't greet the woman like she's a friend. A nod rather than a hug. He sits on the stool, and the woman pushes a drink towards him. It's a short one. He knocks it back and orders another.

Becki asks her about Christmas, and Jaz says, 'I'll head home; my sister –' and as Jaz mentions stockings, carols and scrabble, she watches the woman slide a package over to Theo, as easily as passing him a drink.

He takes it with a glance round the room. Then he stands and puts a couple of notes on the bar under his glass. He hands the woman an envelope.

Drugs? Possibly. But Jaz doesn't think so, and she doesn't know why. The package had been so small.

She'll ask Dom. He must know. They're dorm mates.

Theo heads out without looking round, and when Becki goes to the bathroom, Jaz watches the woman scroll on her phone, wait five minutes, then down the rest of her drink and leave.

49

Jaz

Spring, earlier that year

Harvard

Jaz doesn't see the woman from bar again until about six months later, around Easter. She's only just starting to peel down the winter layers. She's walking to Dom's new dorm room – he'd moved after Christmas and isn't sharing with Theo any more. Jaz likes not seeing as much of him.

He'd been out for lunch with his dad, and she bumps into Mark leaving. Mark has been taking him out to lunch a lot recently. Since his parents split, they both seem very keen to make sure Dom is fine. Dom pretends he's fine, then rants when they're gone.

No one is saying what they really think.

But this lunch must be over because there's no sign of Dom with his father – he must be up in his room. He doesn't share with anyone now.

'Jaz!' Mark stops and smiles. 'Dom said you were coming. Sorry to miss you. I'm just leaving. How's term been?' He shifts out of the way as a bike passes them, and a group of students walk by, chattering loudly.

'Good,' she nods, feeling awkward. She's only met his parents a couple of times and the desire to impress is strong.

'Excuse me, do you know Theo Fowler?' A woman stops her. She faintly recognises her but can't place her. She has blond hair, tied up in a ponytail, and it seems wrong somehow.

'I'm not sure where he is,' Jaz says, looking at the woman with interest. She seems out of place, but she has no idea why.

She doesn't look like a student, but Jaz can't put a finger on why. Maybe it's the lack of rucksack. But it's not just that; she's a few years older. She's pale, and despite the cold, she wears low cut jeans and a T-shirt. Jaz shivers in her thick hoodie.

'You're a friend of Theo's?' Mark asks, friendly. He shifts again as a few more students pass, and it takes him a step closer to her.

The woman nods. 'I've been looking for him. He's changed dorm rooms, and someone said they knew his old dorm mate had moved to this building. They pointed me this way.'

'Yes,' Jaz says, 'But not Theo. I don't know where he lives now.' She does know, but the memory of the woman in the bar comes back to her. The sliding of a package. Her hair had been pink, but it's blonde now. It's the same woman.

She doesn't want to say anything else. This whole thing feels off.

Mark glances at his watch. 'Great to see you, Jaz, but I better get going.'

The woman, very pretty, now wears a smile on her face which wasn't there a second ago. She doesn't look at Jaz but at Mark now. 'Hey, you're Mark Cadel.'

He nods. 'Last time I checked.'

The woman takes a step closer to Mark and touches his arm. 'So good to meet you. Are you going in this direction? I'll walk with you. Still on the hunt for Theo, just need to get a form from him. I'm Camilla, Kiki to my friends,' she says. 'I've been counselling here. Not Theo – I'm just chasing some paperwork for the office. But I'm not a student. Bit older than that.' She flashes another smile at Mark – full beam.

'I'd love to pick your brains,' she's saying now. 'My role here is finished, and I know you've got a head for business.'

'I'd be delighted,' he says.

Kiki touches his arm again, and Mark actually blushes.

'Lovely to see you, Jaz,' Mark says again, and he walks away, quickly deep in conversation, swallowed by the campus in spring, and Jaz watches them, uneasy, unable to put her finger on why.

50

Jaz

Now

Jaz closes the door to Becki's room. The atmosphere in the villa is fraught. The police dot around the grounds, still clustered on the beach.

The sun is hot. It's past lunch, but there's been no gathering round the table with Maria bringing out food. It's not like there's nothing to eat – huge plates of Greek delights had been delivered earlier. Olives, tzatziki, moussaka – the kitchen island is laid out like a banquet. But there are just nibbles gone round the edges.

Who can eat today?

Dom won't talk to her. He's been locked in a room with his mum and is going to follow his dad to the station at some point soon.

She hasn't seen Theo all morning.

When Mark had led Kiki out on his arrival, she'd felt sick. She'd recognised her immediately. Dom had gasped next to her.

Her age must have shocked him. But for Jaz, the shock was something else.

Dom had told her a few months later his dad had a new girlfriend. She hadn't for a second thought they might be one and the same.

And then there was Sam.

She'd met Sam that same day. He'd walked out with mojitos when they'd arrived at the villa.

And much like Kiki, she recognised Sam too.

What the fuck? she'd thought, taking a drink, making sure she held her smile in place.

What the absolute fuck was going on, and what was she walking into?

The previous year spools out before her. Not just Kiki, but Sam. She trusts neither of them. Becki is worried that Theo might be behind Kiki's death. Jaz is quietly worried that Sam knows an awful lot more than he's letting on.

51

Jaz

Nancy's funeral

January, earlier that year

Jaz fastens the last button on her jacket just before climbing out of the car. The cameras had flashed at their tinted windows as they'd passed the gates of the church, but the drive up through the graveyard has been subdued.

The January sun is pale, hanging solemnly over the old church on the hill; the grass is frosty, whitening the landscape, muting any attempt at colour. Bursts of breath rise like smoke from the groups who cluster in long dark coats outside the church doors.

They are only one of the many sleek dark cars pulling up. Dom has barely said a word. He stares out of the window, lost in thought.

'You ready?' she asks gently. She touches her hair, making sure it's neat and smooth, and applies a coat of lip gloss as he nods.

'Yeah.' He pauses. 'Except I'm not.' He rubs at his face.

'You must have been close to her.' She knows they're family friends, but she's been surprised by how upset Dom has been about Nancy's death.

'No, not really,' he replies, and he gives the smallest shake of his head, as though preparing himself. 'Look, Mum and Dad are over there. Come on.'

Mark kisses Jaz on the cheek and hugs Dom.

'Sweetheart,' Natasha says, and wraps her arms around him, and they stand like that for a moment.

'Was the journey OK?' Mark asks.

'Yes, thanks,' Jaz says, trying to work out what to do with her hands. They seem to hang like weights at the end of her arms. She tries a hand on the hip but then drops it. Instead, she slides the handbag she'd borrowed from Becki off her shoulder and holds it like a clutch, instantly feeling calmer. She hadn't known Nancy. She'd met her once or twice. But Dom had begged her to come. *Please, it will be like a road trip. Dad's booked us a car from campus. They've arranged a hotel for the night.*

So here she is, feeling like a very small fish out of a puddle of water, surrounded by faces she recognises from the news.

'Jaz, how lovely to see you again.' Natasha squeezes Jaz's arm and her smile is warm.

'Mark, Natasha,' says a tall man in a suit who Jaz recognises but can't quite place. He greets them and leads them to say hello to someone, and then she and Dom are standing together on their own. She takes his hand.

'If you'd all like to come inside, the cars are arriving soon.' A priest in full robes stands on the stone steps that lead up to the tall wooden doors, and the crowd shuffles forward.

'Sit with us,' Natasha says, falling in step. 'We'll just have to say hello to a few people on the way in, but find a pew, and then we'll find you.'

'Do your parents know many people in the government?' Jaz whispers, and she sees Mark shaking hands with a prominent figure.

'They're donors. They gave a fair bit during the campaign before Christmas. They get invited to things. It's Dad's political leaning rather than Mum's, but he maintains it's good for business.'

Jaz walks a little closer to Dom. She can't imagine the sums of money involved or all of the networking that happens even, apparently, at a funeral.

They sit, and Dom bows his head in prayer as Jaz places the bag on the bench next to her. She's never seen him pray. Other than carols at Christmas, she's never seen him in a church.

'Good choice of hymns,' she says, as he lifts his head and looks around. She recognises 'Abide with Me'. They used to sing that at her school when she was small.

He looks at the order of service. Nancy's face stares out at them, smiling. Jaz shivers.

'Sorry, here now,' Natasha whispers, sliding in next to Dom, followed by Mark.

The organ music had been quiet, but now it changes in tone, and the congregation collectively stand, falling silent. Jaz almost daren't turn to look.

Walking down the aisle, Senator Richard Fowler and Theo lead the way, each shoulder bearing the weight of the front corners of the coffin. The dark wood gleams, and the brass fittings catch the light of the candles.

Theo looks like a ghost. His skin is waxy pale, and his eyes stare forward, almost unseeing. She doesn't like him much, but Jaz feels a kick of sympathy in her stomach.

Dom is rigid next to her. The only time Theo's face changes is as he approaches their aisle. His eyes find Dom's, and the look on his face is so hauntingly full of what – regret? despair? – Jaz takes Dom's hand and finds his fingers, but they're locked still and straight. He's as brittle as she's ever seen him.

Once the coffin passes, he trembles, and beads of sweat sit on his brow.

'What is it?' she whispers. If she didn't know better, she'd think he was afraid.

The reception is back at the huge house, gleaming white even in the thin light.

'We haven't been here since the Christmas party. Is it in bad taste to hold the wake here?' Natasha looks out of the window as the four of them sit in the back of the car, heading up the long driveway.

Mark shrugs, glancing at his wife who doesn't look back.

'Is that the pond? It's huge,' Jaz says.

On the left of the car, they pass the pond, which is surrounded by overhanging trees and a small rowing boat tied up neatly near a wooden walkway. Up a bank and some steps, there are two tennis courts. Then the lawn runs up to the sweeping driveway.

Dom turns his head away from the window.

'It *is* a bit full on, seeing the site of her death immediately after the funeral. I don't know how he's stayed here,' Mark says.

'I think Richard will be fine, as he always is. It's Theo I worry about,' Natasha says. She closes her lips, tight and firm.

'A bit harsh! He's just buried his wife.' Mark speaks softly.

'You've always liked him. Me, not so much. I feel sorry for him, but she was in a state the last time I saw her. I wish to God I'd made her stop and sit down and she hadn't got in that car. I could have stopped all this. I had no idea …' Her fingers press the bridge of her nose, and she doesn't finish.

The driver is taking it very slow, behind another car, and he slows further as they approach the house.

'If she drove down the driveway, how did she end up in the pond? Was it a car accident?' Jaz doesn't know the details, and the media has given nothing away. Simply that due to the now famous snowstorm before Christmas, Nancy Fowler, wife of Senator Fowler and mother to Theodore, was killed the night before Christmas Eve.

'They don't know. Looks like she lost control of the car and lost her way trying to get back to the house. There was so much snow, she probably didn't see the pond. Thank God they found Theo when they did.' Natasha shakes her head. 'Luckily the security detail were there. The house was well protected that night, which makes it seem even more strange that she died. I still can't believe we were in there, drinking champagne and partying while she was out in the cold and ice.' Natasha brushes her hand across her face and closes her eyes briefly.

Mark reaches for her, but she shrugs him off. 'I told you we should follow her.'

Mark flinches. 'It wasn't up to us. The weather was terrible, and we had no idea what was going to happen. It was down to you, really, that they found her and Theo. You made them go and look when she didn't come back. If you hadn't, it might have ended badly for Theo. Try to hold on to that.' He speaks gently, and it has the well-worn pattern of a conversation that has settled into the groves of the oft spoken and unlikely to change.

But Jaz notices that Natasha barely looks his way.

'Thank you for coming.' Richard's handshake is firm as he greets them at the entrance to the house.

Jaz follows Natasha and Mark, and Richard Fowler speaks as sincerely to her as he did to them, although she doubts he remembers ever meeting her. But she supposes that with Dom following her, she is clearly identified with the family.

She catches sight of herself in the entrance hall mirror, more groomed than she's ever been. For a split second she doesn't recognise herself. Getting into Harvard on the scholarship had felt unreal but like it had been the pinnacle. Then she'd arrived and felt less than everyone else. Now she's Dominic Cadel's girlfriend, and she rides in sleek private cars. The President is in the adjacent room. The speed of it all makes her dizzy, and she reaches for the banister of the huge, curved staircase that sweeps up from the centre of the reception hall.

'OK?' Dom asks.

She realises it's almost the first time he's spoken to her since they arrived at the church. Maybe that's what's unsettling her so much. Without him, she doesn't belong here.

Her best friend from home had been sceptical about the relationship. *Is it him or his money? I mean, he's good looking I suppose, and the English accent is cute. But without the millions, would you like him so much?*

It had made Jaz angry. It had been Christmas Eve, and she'd been at home with family and friends, drinking eggnog and eating the cookies she and her sister had decorated that afternoon.

Of course! I'm still me! she'd said in reply. But every now and again doubt creeps in. There is so much glamour associated with Dom's family. Most of the time, it's just them, but in certain moments, the light shines on them like the sun has singled them out. The cars are plentiful. Even a private jet ride to Washington for a carol concert a few weeks before Christmas. If she's honest with herself, part of her is unwilling to let all of it go. It's shown her a crack into a world that is compelling, even spellbinding. She wonders how far she'd go to cling on to all this.

All these people here, how far would they go to retain it all?

There's a dangerous edge to a life of ease and luxury.

Getting it is everything. Keeping it could take everything.

She drifts into the main reception room and is handed a glass of champagne. Turning once to collect the glass, she loses Dom. Mark beckons him to follow, but when Jaz tries to move forward, someone tall and important steps in front of her.

Moving back, she finds herself by the wall with no one to speak to. She feels as though all eyes are on her, questioning her right to be here. Nancy wouldn't have been able to pick her out of a line-up. All these faces from important conferences and news reports look through her.

She ducks out of the door she came in and then slides out of a side door. The cold air is refreshing – her cheeks had been hot inside.

The smell of nicotine and maybe something else drifts along the white wall of the house, and she turns the corner towards the back lawns. A frost and low mist lie down the gentle slope. She shivers. A few snowflakes land on her black jacket.

Another few steps forward and she sees the source of the smoke – Theo is smoking next to a man she doesn't recognise. The man swipes at the rollie, but Theo pulls it away. His voice drifts forward with the smoke:

'Get off. You can't make me.'

'Theo, mate. Look.' The man runs his hands through his dark, strawberry-blond hair, and he has an English accent like Dom's. 'You can talk to me. I know it's hard, but you're in trouble, and I'm here. I don't know how much your dad ...'

'You know nothing about my father!'

'Shhh.' The man looks over his shoulder and Jaz flattens herself against the wall, pulling well out of view. There are huge pot plants positioned all the way round the perimeter of the house. She can't be seen.

'Fuck off. Trying me to make me quiet. Who the fuck do you think you are, telling me what to do?'

'Theo, I was there for you. Remember that. When your mum called me, I was there. I'm here now. She'd want me to help. She asked me to help.'

'What did she really ask of you – for you to take her away from all of this? You know nothing. She wanted you for a bit. To take away the sting of my dad shoving his dick into anything he can after a few drinks. She would never have picked you. She wanted to be in the White House. Not this one, the big one. It was all she ever wanted. It was why she put up with him unbuttoning his flies and panting like a dog whenever anyone close to twenty was willing.' Theo hawks and spits. 'He's a cunt.'

The man says nothing. Jaz wonders how right Theo is. Was Nancy really having an affair with this man? Did she know about her husband?

'I read some of his messages – did you know that? I looked into all the messages my dad would send that he thought no one would ever see. I made it my business – after Greece, I'd had enough. Did she tell you what he liked? He liked it any which way.' Theo spins the words like they taste bitter, then takes a drag on the thin rizla paper, limp and fat between his fingers. 'Like I said. A cunt.'

'Look, Theo, she trusted me in the clean-up. You can trust me now.'

What clean-up? Jaz thinks.

'I'm not going to talk to *you*. Whatever stiletto she drove in your heart by dying so quickly –' Theo stalls, and his voice catches for a second. 'If it hurts, then double that, and you're still nowhere near what it's like to lose her. You know nothing. You're no one. You should put some distance between her and you anyway. She was an accomplice to murder. You didn't know that, did you? Because of him. All the shit stuff she did – because of him. Now fuck the fuck off. You weren't there when she died. I was. It was her and me. So just fuck off and let me get stoned in peace.'

52

Jaz

Now

Jaz hasn't thought about it for such a long time. It had made no sense, any of it. Theo had been stoned; he'd just been talking rubbish.

But now someone else is dead. Sam had been having an affair with Richard's wife, and Sam looks like he would pretty much do anything for Natasha. Kiki has clearly been getting to Natasha. Surely that hasn't led to anything else, and Sam has taken it upon himself to be guardian and protector? No. That can't be it. Can it?

Jaz feels sick and her head spins. She can't talk to Dom about this. She can't talk to Becki. Should she tell the police?

Jaz had heard Sam talking to Mark earlier, saying they'd be questioned again as neither of them had an alibi for the time of death. Both had been alone in their rooms.

She's sure she can't tell Dom, because Dom sings his praises. It would break his heart.

But Jaz is sick of sitting around feeling like the small-time farm girl trying to play nice.

Jaz knocks on Sam's door, softly. Nothing.

Does she just go in?

'Jaz, you OK?' Sam says from behind her, and she jumps.

'I wanted to talk to you about Dom,' she says. 'I'm worried about him, and I don't want to bother Mark or Natasha.'

He nods, as though this is the least surprising thing in the world, and gestures to his room. 'Sure.' He smiles.

His room is perfectly made up. Nothing out of place. She sits out on the balcony, under the bamboo shade, and tucks her legs beneath her as Sam pours out water.

'I know Dom's had a lot on his plate,' Sam says, making this easy for her.

She wants to ask him about the funeral, but it feels too much too soon. Everyone else seems to trust him, but she barely knows him.

She watches him sit back easily, ready to listen. He's kind of good looking for someone in their forties. Relaxed – not like the Senator who always looks good – screen ready; always slightly hairsprayed and maybe even fake tan.

'Is there something in particular that's worrying you?' he asks.

She goes in with half the story. 'Dom is worried about Theo. We all came back last night because he didn't want to have to look after him. Theo disappeared at the beach party. And he bought a knife when we got here. He said it was to go fishing with. When Dom found out he said he'd speak to him, but it's been tense between them. Becki and Dom took it and chucked it away, and now we don't know where it is.'

Sam looks at her and blinks a few times. 'That's a lot of information. Theo bought a knife?'

'To fish. I don't know. I didn't really get it. He didn't tell us – Becki found it in his bag and told us.'

'What, Becki took it and gave it to Dom?'

Jaz nods. 'They took it without telling Theo. I don't know where it is. Dom said they'd got rid of it. I talked to Theo to keep him distracted while they were busy.'

'And Dom definitely doesn't still have it?' Sam is standing now. His brow knits.

'I don't know! I think it went in the trash. It might have been taken with the garbage.'

She looks at Sam. Could he have seen them take the knife and followed them, to steal it? It all seems so implausible out here on the balcony, but Kiki is dead, and Theo mentioned murder and Sam in the same breath.

Jaz takes a punt and improvises, pushing for a reaction from Sam. 'I think it seemed to get worse when Kiki and Mark arrived, but I don't know why that would be.'

She watches him. There's the briefest of flickers on his face.

'Look, we need to find that knife. Let's go and speak to Dom.'

Jaz rises. There's some sound from a group of officers walking quickly up to the villa from the beach. They have dogs with them. They strain at their leash and bark, sniffing. The noise of the baying fills the air.

53

Nancy

December last year

Harvard

'Sam,' she whispers into the phone. She can't call Richard, not until she's worked out what's going on. Richard will have the power to make this go away, but she needs to protect Theo first. From Richard too.

She needs some help. She won't tell him what happened. She's going to have to trust him – because of Dom's involvement, she thinks she can.

'Hey, I was going to call, how –'
'Listen, I'm in trouble.'
'Tell me.'
'I went to the boys' room. Something's ... happened.'

His car pulls up to the edge of the park. Theo and the girl wait with her. The young man is in the car.

'What can I do?' Sam climbs out and takes in the three of them. The blood.

'Can you take Theo home? To your apartment? He needs a shower. And to get rid of his clothes.'

She silently pleads with him. He looks from Theo back to her. 'Nancy, what's going on?'

A shake of her head. 'I don't know, not yet. But it's Dom and Theo. They're in trouble.'

'We should call the police.'

Nancy thanks God there's snow falling as thick and fast as it is. CCTV won't get anything here. Two young people catching a lift home. The blood is hidden by the deep mid-winter. The girl obscured from Sam's view.

'I need to take someone to the hospital – they're in the car. I'll talk to the doctors. But I don't want Theo and Dom involved. Neither would Tash. This would ruin them, Sam. They're young. They've got their lives ahead of them. Can you take Theo, get him showered and changed? I'll take the girl with me. She might have information for the hospital.'

The girl stands mute and shivering. She is holding her coat – not wearing it. Nancy could swear her skin has turned blue.

Sam looks long and hard at Nancy. 'Will you tell Richard about this?'

She nods. 'I will. But not yet. It's a fraternity pledge gone wrong. Too much animal blood. You know the kind of thing I'm talking about. It starts innocently but then something goes wrong. I don't want the boys to take the hit on this.'

'OK. I'll do it for Dom. Where is he?'

'Back at the rooms. Cleaning.' She nods to the blood, visible in the white light, the snow catching the yellow of the streetlamps and brightening it. They stand just outside of the halo.

'Fuck. Is he OK?'

She nods. 'I'll go back and get him once I've dropped these two. I'll bring him to you. They can stay with you for a couple of days and give me chance to get the rooms sorted. I'll stay there.' She doesn't say she's already taken the knife she found beneath the body of the boy. It's in her bag. It will disappear in a trash can miles from here.

'What the fuck, Nancy? What's gone on?'

The cold eats into her, hungry and relentless. She has no time for it. Not yet.

'I wish I knew.'

'You said you were taking him to the hospital?' The girl stares at her.

'How old are you?' Nancy tries to calm her tone. She realises too late she's almost barking. She must change tack.

With Sam gone, she needs to find out where the girl lives.

'Twenty-six. What's it to you?'

'I have money.'

The windscreen is white now. Nancy flicks on the wipers. She's wary of a stray police car arriving before she's had a chance to sort this. Her senses are on red alert.

The girl says nothing.

'Look, I'll take him to the hospital. What's his name?'

'Ryan. Is he really alive. I touched him. He feels cold.'

'Yes, he's alive, but in this cold, he'll be in trouble if I don't move quickly. I'll take him now. I'll drop you home first. I can give you some money, to help with whatever you need.'

The girl sniffs. 'How much?'

Good, thinks Nancy. *Good*.

'Half a million. I'll give it to you. If you tell anyone about tonight, then I'll say you stole it. I've got some for him too.'

'You bitch!' The girl screams at her, face creased in rage. 'You fucking bitch! None of this is my fault. You don't even know what they did! You try to buy me off?'

Nancy lets her finish, wipes spit off her cheek. The nails of the girl dig into her wrist.

'I could cut you,' the girl says, her voice as sharp as the blade with which she threatens.

'You could, but you won't. Half a million. Yes? Tell me where to take you. Then we never hear from you again.'

It's such a risk, Nancy thinks. Carrot and stick. Offer her money, threaten for silence. She needs to tighten the whip. Lash it harder.

Leaning forward, she puts her hand on the girl's cheek. 'If you stir up trouble, I won't be able to stop what happens next. I know people, and you have no idea who the fuck you're dealing with. You understand me?'

Wide-eyed now, the girl pulls her hand away from Nancy's arm.

Nancy can see somewhere in there that she understands the situation. She maybe even already knows that Ryan is dead. The money is working here, but this girl hasn't even realised how far down the line she's already gone.

'Where are you taking him?'

'To the hospital.'

'You promise?' The girl looks to the body, and the concern for him is all over her face.

'Yes. If we get on with it, it's better for him. He needs help quick.'

In the end, Nancy drops her at the end of a street. She watches the girl walk away with half a million in notes. If they ever traced her various withdrawals, they'd know something was wrong.

But Richard won't know. She keeps some cash safe always. She didn't come from nothing. She'd brought almost the whole of it in cash anyway – she wondered if money was part of Theo's problem, and she hadn't wanted Richard to notice. She'd taken out the notes before she'd left for Boston.

She'd made her sign the document. She isn't the first woman she's made sign it. She'd cleaned up after Richard at the end of the summer – after Greece. She'd had an NDA drawn up then too.

The girl turns back and looks at her one last time. Finally wearing the coat – it covered up the worst of blood. Nancy had made the girl wipe her face, tie her hair back. She'd given her a scarf.

She keeps thinking *girl*, but with a clean face, and the expensive scarf, she looks like she might really be twenty-six. A woman really. The twenty-six years make her seem dangerous. What hold does she have over Theo?

What the hell was she doing there, in those rooms?

Turning, her stomach tight, she looks at the young man in the back seat.

What was *he* doing there?

Him first. Then she'll collect Dom.

Dom goes to Sam, then she goes back to the rooms. As clean as she can get them. Maybe she'll hire in professional cleaners tomorrow. Say a party had made a mess. Students are reliable in their mess-making.

She's going to be sick. What she's about to do will make her sick.

54

Nancy

December

Washington. Nine months ago

A week before Christmas

Nancy settles into the seat and smiles as Sam sits next to her. She's been looking forward to this for weeks. She can't touch him, not in public. But she'd told Richard that Natasha was going to the theatre with Sam and had invited them along. She knew he'd say no – he's never liked the theatre.

If there are any photos of her here with him, then it's all above board. She'll just say Tash wasn't in the photo or had left early.

He won't care. It will seem like something he got to skip.

But as the dark settles and the stage lights up, she presses her knee against Sam's and her whole body lights up. She hasn't felt like this in years. Maybe longer. There are moments like this, when she's not even touching him, that the intimacy is something that pierces her – stays with her. She knows she'll remember this moment tomorrow, a week from now. No matter what else happens tonight.

She, however, has got some explaining to do. It's the first time she's seen him since the night he took the boys in for her. He'd known about the blood, and the fraternity pledge explanation had held for a while, as it had with her. But he deserves a full explanation. And so does she – only she can't seem to get anything else out of Theo.

These last few weeks have eaten into her like nothing else has. She feels the skin of the boy in the dark. She sees his eyes, opened, staring. She thinks of his mother, somewhere out there, wondering where he is. There's been no news from Harvard about a missing student. If there was ever any truth to the fraternity pledge story, the boy clearly wasn't a Harvard student.

As for Sam, he'd only seen the young woman briefly. He hadn't seen the body in the car – she'd stuck to her story: she had taken him to the hospital. As long as everyone believes that no one died, then they can all live with it.

She's just not sure *she* can live with what she's done, but she's managing to get through the days and blink away the images that creep up on her in the dark. They'll go away at some point. They must do.

She's stuck to the story with everyone. Almost convinced herself.

'Wow, incredible!' Sam says, as they move slowly out of the exit.

'Dinner?' she says.

He nods.

She knows he's waiting to ask her.

The car is round the back. They head up the street and turn into the smaller street, leading to where she's parked.

A hand slams out in front of her.

They are both caught off guard; she flinches, and Sam bats at the hand – a kind of punch, maybe a slap.

'Ow!' A cry. It's a woman.

They both take a step back.

Pink hair, in three long thick plaits, wound up on top of her head. She turns, stares at them.

'You hit me,' she says.

'I'm sorry, I thought you were about to mug us.' Sam is hesitant. 'You threw your hand in my friend's face.'

'Your friend?' Sarcasm drips, oily and full of disdain. 'You should choose your friends more carefully. I had a very good friend once, but I haven't seen him around recently.'

Nancy looks from the woman to Sam and back. She forces herself to stay calm. 'Oh, hi. I haven't seen you for a few weeks. How are you?'

The pink-haired girl laughs. 'That's how we're playing it?' She takes a step forward. Her nose almost touching Nancy's. 'If he's not back soon, I'll come for you. I mean it. I need to know he's OK. You said he was going to be OK.'

Nancy nods slowly, wondering what to say next. 'Maybe he just didn't want to share the money he took.'

'Bitch!' The woman screams at her again, but there's a sound further up the alley and the girl spins, nervous.

'I can't help you,' Nancy says. She can't be drawn into some kind of blackmail drama. Maybe the girl doesn't understand how an NDA works. She speaks calmly, as though she's discussing a domestic cleaner's agreement, 'Remember you signed a contract.'

'I know where you live,' the girl says, looking back over her shoulder. There's a group heading towards them. 'I'll find you.'

Then, as Nancy stumbles a little, the woman is gone.

'What was that about?' Sam asks, taking her arm.

She leans on him. 'Not everyone is a fan of Richard's,' she says, hoping Sam buys this. Did he recognise her from the night?

'Well, they should talk to Richard, instead of you,' he says.

Back at the hotel, after room service and wine, Nancy wraps her arms around Sam in the chair by window. She loves this, watching the city from so high up no one can look back at them. Seeing the snow fall. Feeling as though they're the only people in the world, high above it all.

'I can't tell you how pleased I was when you said it was just animal blood,' Sam says. He pulls the blanket round them both.

'It was some stupid university club pledge that went wrong. It went everywhere. They were terrified. I don't think the boys have ever been faced with anything like it. I'm so grateful you were there.'

He lifts his wine glass, taking a sip. 'They were both very shaken up.'

'I've told Theo he's not allowed to take part in any more of those ridiculous rituals. Why do these big universities make them do such stupid things?'

'There's one in England with a pig.' Sam screws his face up. 'Half the politicians in the UK have exposed themselves to a dead hog. I think they even ... actually, we don't need to go over the details.'

'They do stupid stuff here – all secrecy and fraternity. Boys' clubs. But if any word of that kind of thing got out, it would badly affect Richard. I've told the boys not to say anything.'

'Well, I obviously won't. You wouldn't believe the things I was thinking when I first saw them.'

Nancy kisses him, settling in the chair. She'd brought up the subject wondering if she'd find herself telling Sam more, but no.

She'd stuck to the original story. She tops up both of their wine glasses. They'd eaten then gone to bed. She is hoping there's a repeat performance before sleep.

'Well, I told Richard I was seeing you and Tash tonight. He's seeing someone else, I know it. He was only too pleased to let me go.'

At the mention of Tash, there's a twitch to Sam's mouth.

'Have you told Tash about us?' she asks.

He shakes his head. 'I've told no one.'

Nancy looks out at the city; the snow is fast and thick now. It's just days until the Christmas holidays start. 'And Tash. Has there ever been anything between you?'

'Tash? No!' Sam's face is one of shock, then he laughs. 'God, no. She's a very good friend. I'd never do that to Mark.'

'And if there were no Mark?' Nancy is curious, and a touch of green enters her blood for a moment. 'Do you wish there was no Mark?'

Sam takes her hand. 'Look, I won't lie to you and say it's never crossed my mind. But Tash is out of reach. I'm happy she's my friend. Also, Nancy Fowler, I wasn't expecting this. I mean, you're gorgeous. You're intelligent. You're sophisticated. In the summer, when we got talking, I loved the time we spent together.'

She touches his cheek, follows the line of his jaw with her finger.

'I think I might love you,' he says, quietly, holding her gaze.

'Oh, Sam,' she says, her throat full. She kisses him quickly.

Later, when it's dark, she plays his words over in her head. She trusts him. She whispers that she loves him. He pulls her tighter.

They feel like nothing, the words. They feel empty. She wants to give him something more. She can't tell him about Theo and the blood. But she can be honest with him about other things.

'Can I tell you about Megan?' she whispers.

Sam had been half asleep, his breathing soft in her ear, and she hears a quick intake of breath.

'Megan?'

'In the summer. When you said Richard was flirting with Megan.' She wriggles round, faces him. She lies with her body directly opposite his. She thinks of the intimacy in the theatre. The knee press that filled her up entirely.

'They slept together.'

'What?' Sam sits up. 'They did what?'

Half regretting what she'd shared, Nancy pulls herself up too. Lies back against the headboard of the hotel bed. The room is half lit from streetlights which leak in through the crack in the curtains.

'They slept together in Greece. And again, a few times, when we were back home. He told her we were splitting up. I don't think she meant to hurt me. It's what he says to women.'

'And you knew?' Sam looks at her, a little like he's just met her.

She nods. 'I was upset. I'm always upset. But it's different now – with us. I can't stop him. So, I cleaned up after him. Often, he pays them off. But that wouldn't work with Megan. I asked her to sign an NDA.' Listening to herself aloud, Nancy stumbles over what she says. But she wants to be clean – she wants to be real.

'Was Megan upset? Was she OK?'

'I think so. Richard helped out at her work. She didn't need money. But she deserved something.'

He reaches out and touches her cheek. 'It must hurt.'

She nods, just once. Tight-lipped. This is not a sympathy bid. She will not cry.

'I wanted to tell you. I mean, I can't ask you not to tell anyone, but I hope you won't. But you're so close to the family. I can't ask her to sign it and then lie to you. Not if this is going to count. Not if I'm going to be honest with you. And I want to, Sam. I really want to.'

He is quiet for a moment, and she needs to let him speak. Finally, after Nancy feels the stretch of a thousand years, he says, 'Did he hurt her?'

She shakes her head. 'Not physically. He slept with her. I imagine he told her he loved her. I think he will have given her gifts. And then without telling her, he will have moved on. She will have found out in a way which will have brought her pain. When Richard loves you, it's like the sun is working hard on sending you all its warmth and light. When he pulls it all away, you're in the dark.'

Sam kisses her, just once, on the lips.

'I don't know what to do with that,' he says, his nose touching hers. 'Do I tell Tash? Do I speak to Megan?'

'Do what you must. I won't lie to you.'

He is quiet, in the dark.

56

Tash

Now

'Theo!' Tash jogs along the beach. The sun is relentless – the view stunning. The sea flat and calm. She pulls her cap down as it shifts as she slows. 'There you are.'

They'd told her not to come to the station yet. Megan said there was no point. They had to wait for the lawyer to arrive from Athens, and she wouldn't be allowed to speak to Mark anyway.

If Tash is going to help Mark, she must first work out what's been going on. She still hasn't been able to speak to Richard. He's been locked in with the police for ages. Partly, she thinks, to impress his importance upon them, and to make sure this investigation stays quiet for as long as possible. She needs to speak to him.

Theo sits at the far end of the beach, watching the investigation, perched on a rock. His hands are covered with sand, and there's a pile at his feet. Tash assumes he's been sitting here for some time.

'They've found something,' he says, not looking at her. Instead, he gestures to the police.

'What do you mean?'

'They had dogs down here earlier, and they were showing them something. Whatever they're looking at, they've been a lot more active in the last hour.'

Tash sits on the sand next to him, looking down the beach. *Lulu* is also a hive of activity.

They took Stani to the station hours ago for a statement. Megan called from there to arrange Mark's lawyer, but she hasn't come back yet either.

'I wonder what they've found? I don't believe one of us could have killed Kiki. I'm sure there was some kind of accident. They haven't said why they think it could be suspicious.' Even as she says this, she realises that she's thinking if anyone could have killed Kiki, then her money's on Richard. But she can't say that to Theo.

'They won't. Not until they think they can use it. Dad made me take law, remember?'

'How are you?' Tash drags her eyes from the police and looks at him. So like Richard, but so unlike him. There are marks of Nancy all over his face. The softness of his mouth. The tilt of his nose.

'I'm sorry I haven't seen you since the funeral.'

'I was a dick at the funeral. I'm sorry about that. I know you were trying to do the right thing.'

'Well, I was trying to look out for you,' she says, gently.

The water laps a few feet away from them. Fish, bright colours, visible even from here. The horizon is flat and the huge tourist jets mark their path across the sea to more islands, looking for volcanoes, windmills, black beaches, red beaches, sunsets and ouzo. All summer long, Tash watches them.

'You asked me about Sam at the funeral, about why he was there.'

She nods, surprised he's mentioned Sam.

Theo dusts the sand from his shorts and looks out to sea. 'He was there because he was screwing my mom. I knew about Dad – I felt sorry for Mom. Dad is … he is relentless. But with Mom, I think it was real. Half of me was pleased. I mean, at least she had someone. But it also made me kind of hate her. She didn't leave Dad. She stayed, she gave the speeches, she threw the parties. Part of me thinks she was just as full of shit as he was. Sam was at the party that night. That's why he came to the funeral.'

He turns, stares at the sea. 'That night, when I got in the car with her, I saw him. Out on the road. Before we drove away, she got out of the car to speak to him. Apart from me, he was the last person to speak to her alive. Ask him. Ask him why he was there.'

Tash stares at him, not able to process what he says.

But Theo isn't done. 'And ask him what he knows about Emma and my mom. Ask him that.'

'But –' She starts with a question, but the dogs are barking now. A cacophony of hounds.

A glint in the sun. Something in an officer's hand.

She rises, slowly.

A figure from the steps, running, red hair flying behind her.

'Natasha!' Jaz screams, jumping down the beach. 'Come!'

The hive of activity has intensified. Phones are out. A drone appears overhead.

Tash looks from them to Jaz, running ever closer towards her.

Tash knows. The look on Jaz's face.

'They've arrested Dom!'

57

Tash

'But I don't understand? How can he have had *anything* to do with it?' Tash is frantic.

The salt-and-peppered detective, with all the authority, nods in the face of her rage. 'I understand your anxiety. But we have found the murder weapon, and it has your son's fingerprints all over it. Plus, there is more.'

'But you've got it wrong!' Tash's throat is raw.

'Ms Cadel. I need to go. But I'll be back with more information at some point.'

Megan pulls on her arm as the detective disappears.

'Tash, get it together. Now is not the time for emotions. Listen, the lawyer is still in with Mark. Another one has been called for Dom, but until then we can use him. The firm in Athens is excellent, one of the best.' Megan takes Tash's hand. 'They don't want to pull any punches. I've spoken to Inspector Carrass – he's the older one leading the investigation who you were just speaking with – he said he's happy to tell us what they've got. You ready?'

Tash nods. Despite it all, Megan's poised: hair swept up, a matching shorts and top set, straight from some designer store they'd looked at in Athens last year. She looks up to the job. When did she get the chance to pull herself together? Tash feels like she's melting.

'They can't have anything. Fingerprints is nothing ... so maybe he touched something but –'

'They've got into Kiki's phone.' Megan's face is unreadable.

Tash's stomach turns to ice.

'There are messages on there. To Dom. He knew her, Tash. And more than that, he's threatened her.'

Dom faces the wall in the cell.

Entering quietly, Tash sits on the end of his bed.

He doesn't turn his head and look at her. He stares fixedly at the wall, his shoulders hunched and his legs up on the bed, his knees high – he hooks his arms around them.

'Sweetheart, it's time to tell me.'

He starts to cry.

'I didn't know how to stop it all, Mum. Once it started, I just didn't know –'

She leans forward and wraps her arms around him. His tears land on her neck, making the back of her T-shirt damp, his six-foot frame curled into her, like he would do when he was small.

'I'm so sorry, Mum ...'

58

Jaz

Now

On the ocean

'You sure we're allowed?' Jaz says, staring at the boat, unsure who to trust.

When Dom had been arrested, she'd screamed at the police. But he'd shaken his head – locked eyes with her. *I'll be OK*, he'd said.

They stand on the beach, *Lulu* at the end of the jetty. Stani is on board. She can see him moving around.

Becki nods. 'With Mark and Dom at the station, both arrested, the rest of us are free to go. Theo's gone back with his dad to the hotel room he booked. Most of his luggage is there. They're booked on a flight later today.'

'You're OK with that? You've barely spoken to him.' Jaz looks at Becki; she can't tell anything from her tone.

The sun reflects off her blond friend's sunglasses, huge and round. Her hair is braided down her back, and she wears a pink bikini with a pale pink throw. She isn't wearing the necklace

Theo gave her for Christmas. Jaz can't remember the last time Becki took it off.

'I don't want to see him again. I don't trust him. I can't see how Dom did this.'

'Of course he didn't!' Jaz says, then forces herself to listen.

Becki carries on, 'I know, but the police won't listen to me. I've got no evidence. I told them we moved the knife that Theo bought. That's surely why Dom's fingerprints are on there.' She looks confused. 'But we chucked it. I threw it away, with the necklace.' Her hand goes to her throat. 'I don't know how it ended up under the jetty. Maybe Theo saw us and took it – or whoever killed Kiki saw us. It could still be Theo … But not Dom. Why would he? They'll have to let him out. We can't leave Dom and fly back – we need to support him. Let's stay for a few more days.'

Jaz nods. She has no intention of flying home just yet. She'd be at the station now if she could. She'll stay here until they let Dom go.

There's a gentle breeze, and Sam jumps from the boat to the jetty and waves at them.

Becki steps forward. 'The police want to go over the house again. It's an hour or so until sunset. Stani will take us out on the boat. Sam suggested it. We can have a break. You'll want to go to the station to see Dom later, I'm guessing. But Natasha asked for family only right now. I don't know about you, but I can't face going to the village. An hour on the water will be much nicer than sitting on the beach, near where she died.' Becki glances left, where tape marks out the spot.

'Sure,' Jaz says, tired and hungry – she hadn't realised she was hungry, but she can see Sam lift a picnic basket up from the jetty, and it makes her stomach rumble. He must have sorted food earlier. She'd told him Dom had moved the knife. He'd spoken to the police, tried to explain but the police don't want any of the rest of them in the station at the moment. They'll try again tomorrow.

'I don't trust him,' she says.

'Who, Stani?' Becki swings a bag over her shoulder. 'Why not?'

'No, Sam. I don't trust him at all.' Jaz climbs up on to the walkway of the jetty. Her rubber flip flops make a padding sound on the wood. The sea, the sky, the other islands dotted in the distance. Everything looks so perfect. She feels sick.

'Really?' Becki looks confused, but Sam walks towards them and Jaz can't say anything else.

'Ready?' he says. He looks tired but he offers them half a smile. 'I told Tash I'd look after you both. Come and let's get out of the way of the police.'

Jaz looks over her shoulder, at where the police are combing the beach. They'd found the knife under the jetty, stuck into the wooden boards from underneath. They're going over every inch of the beach and house again.

With Becki and Stani on board, she should be safe from Sam. She hopes he doesn't know half of what she knows. She'll tell the police later.

'OK,' she says, pulling her attention back to *Lulu*. 'Let's go.'

Stani helps Sam set up the food at the front of the boat. He heads up to the wheel and gives a call to Sam to let him know they're ready.

The sound of running feet, landing heavily on the jetty slats, comes from behind them.

'Wait!'

Jaz turns to see Theo arrive just as Stani is about to steer out.

He grabs the rail of *Lulu*, and Stani shouts down to Sam to open the rail again.

'No one falls in this time!' Stani calls.

'I thought you'd booked to go home,' Sam says, surprised and not looking very pleased.

'I talked Dad into staying a little longer,' Theo calls. 'OK to come aboard?'

Sam looks back at the girls. Jaz feels Becki tense beside her, but she nods.

Theo climbs aboard, looking up to the prow of *Lulu* where Becki and Jaz sit, food spread out on a picnic blanket. The galley kitchen is in the centre of the boat, where the steps lead down to the two bedrooms and the bathroom. Up front gets the evening sun.

Becki kneels up and looks wary.

'I'll only come if it's OK with you,' Theo says, speaking directly to Becki.

Jaz feels Becki take her hand. Her head rears back a little, as though she's flinching.

'You don't have to say yes,' Jaz whispers, seeing Becki's reluctance.

'It's fine. What's one hour on the boat.' Her tone is resigned, and she looks no one in the eye.

Theo smiles. That big smile, the blue eyes, the blond hair. Tall. Of course he gets away with so much. Who doesn't believe the handsome rich hero. It's what they've all been brought up to believe.

'Ready now?' Stani calls.

The sound of heavy footsteps again, running.

Richard Fowler.

Jaz sees Sam stiffen now. She's not sure she trusts Richard Fowler any more than she does Sam. Do they cancel each other out?

'Theodore, if you're going, then I'll come to. I want to keep you close by.'

Theo doesn't even look back at his dad. Instead, he leaps up the steps to the prow and takes position on the picnic blanket with Jaz and Becki, dropping to a seated, cross-legged pose, and he pulls out a box and offers it to Becki. 'Earrings, from the market near Dad's hotel. They're handmade.'

He's almost shy, Jaz thinks, not able to reconcile this man with the drunk one from the beach, chasing a blonde woman away from the club.

'Shall I pour us a glass of wine?' Richard is saying to Sam.

Does he know about the affair? Jaz wonders. This whole charade of politeness, of manners. When they're all capable of lying to each other. It's all just surface crap. No one says how they really feel.

With Dom held at the station, there is nothing to keep her here. She might be better off booking herself into a hotel when they get back to villa. She'd feel a lot safer.

59

Tash

The police station

'What threats? Why would you threaten Kiki?' Tash stares at Dom. None of it makes any sense.

He looks away from her, biting his nails as he speaks.

'It was once we were here. I couldn't believe she'd come.'

There's a knocking on the door. 'Mr Cadel, we'll need you in a few minutes for blood tests.'

Tash takes Dom's hand. 'Tell me.'

'I recognised her, Mum. When Dad brought her out. Theo and she had some beef. She's some kind of hacker, and she got some stuff on his dad. Theo paid her for the information, but I think she must have copied it – kept it in case it was useful. Her boyfriend said they should get more money. He came with her. He was pushing for a huge pay out. They came to our room, at college. It was the first I'd heard about any of it.'

'What happened?'

'It went wrong. Nancy came, and she sorted it. We got in a fight with him. Nancy took the boyfriend to hospital and took Kiki away.' He covers his face with his hands. 'For a moment we thought he was dead in our dorm – we thought we'd killed him. It was awful – it was the worst. But Nancy came. Thank God he was alive. I don't think I could bear it if I'd killed someone. Even in self-defence. It was all too much. I changed dorms. At Nancy's funeral, when I saw the coffin, all I could think was when I'd seen her there – all the blood – and it could have been that man I fought with in a coffin. I could have killed him.'

Tash stares at him. How could Nancy not have told her straight away?

Dom continues. 'I think Nancy must have paid Kiki off. But then she appeared here. I couldn't talk to her, not here. Theo tried. But he kept getting pissed. It might have been her at Mykonos – I have no idea.'

Tash is hushed and quick. 'So, what, you told her to leave?'

He nods, looking down. 'I told her to leave and stay away from you. You've had enough to deal with, Mum. I don't know why she came. She must have found Dad and made a play for him.'

Tash thinks back to Kiki in the kitchen. She'd said she got together with Mark first for a specific reason, but then she'd ended up liking him. Mark is easy to like. Maybe it had started one way and ended the other. Tash is convinced Kiki hadn't been faking her affection for him. She really did have feelings for Mark. Her jealousy of Tash and Mark was real.

Also, she's fairly sure Mark was making use of Kiki. Yes, he fancied her. That was clear to see and unpleasant to watch. Kiki was punishment for her. If she was going to reject Mark, then she would have to watch him with someone young and beautiful.

Mark has always had a touch of the cliché.

If anything, Kiki was the one being paraded rather than the one taking advantage. Dom wouldn't understand this. He would see his dad for what he was – naïve and gullible. But he wouldn't see the wound Mark was carrying, the kick Tash had given him by rejecting him. Dom wouldn't understand that Mark was big enough to take care of himself. He might be generous with his cash, but he was also clever. He was no victim.

And, by the sounds of it, neither was Kiki. If she had being trying to blackmail Richard or his family, then she was dancing with the devil. Richard was nobody's fool. He had a streak in him that Tash would never cross.

'Mr Cadel, are you ready? I'm coming in.'

'I couldn't speak to her. Theo promised he'd fix it, but I texted her to tell her to leave. Her number was on Dad's phone. I don't think she knew it was me. I tried to sound threatening; I just wanted her gone. Before she upset everything. I don't know where her boyfriend is – she must have split up with him. I said she wouldn't like what would happen if she stayed. But I didn't *mean it*. I just tried to frighten her away.'

The door starts to open.

'I didn't kill her, Mum. But the message I sent her – they might think I was implying I would.'

60

Tash

Megan's face is the colour of ash as she brings Tash weak machine coffee in a thin plastic cup. It's been an hour since she saw Dom. They've given her a small room to wait in. The chair is hard. There's no window. The air con is almost antiseptic.

'I've spoken to the lawyer. He said Dom is happy to share everything with us – all the evidence they laid out for him. He's talked me through it.' She touches Tash's hand. 'It's not good.'

Tash drinks the coffee, and it's so hot it scalds the top of her mouth. She winces. 'Go on.'

'The police have accessed her phone. Fuck, Tash, it's mad. That poor girl.'

Megan stops for a moment, takes a breath. 'She was working as a hacker in Boston. A lot of it was for people thinking their partners were having an affair. A good chunk of it was students at university trying to impact their grades. That must have been how Theo got her details. They've sent a car for him. They want to talk to him about it. But it seems when he asked her to hack into his dad's phone to see what he was up to, well, it seems to have been the catalyst for all this.'

Tash stares at Megan, who will not look her in the eye.

'Why did he want to hack into his dad's phone?'

'It was after last summer.' Megan looks at the floor. 'They found a file on Kiki's phone, with Theo's original request. He said he thought his dad was having an affair, and could she find any evidence. It seems, from the information he gave her, that when they were here, and Richard was drunk, flirting ... well, it was the first time Theo's ever really seen his dad like that, and he was worried about Nancy.'

Tash looks at Megan. She still won't look her in eye. 'Who did he think his dad was having an affair with?'

'Fuck, Tash, you know the answer to that. Me, of course!' Megan's hands are tight in fists. 'I'm not very proud of it.' Her voice is small.

'Was there evidence? Did Kiki find anything.'

Megan gives the smallest of nods. 'Richard took photos. He kept photos. He must have taken photos when I didn't know. It's like his phone has been positioned on the side – it's clicked at intervals.'

Tash feels so many different things. She doesn't know where to start. 'You slept with him?'

Megan nods again. 'Yes. The day Emma went missing. We had sex on the beach. Then again, back in the US. I'd been in New York for about a year. He would come to my apartment. It went on for a few months. Then he went quiet.' She looks at the wall. 'I knew; you know when you know – I knew I was dropped. It was all lies. He was still with Nancy. But I'd bought into it all. I thought I loved him. Then one day, Nancy arrives with an NDA.'

Tash is so tired she just stares at Megan and shakes her head.

Megan will still not look at Tash.

'But why did you sign it?' Tash can't get her head round any of it.

'Nancy said that she was sorry. Imagine how I felt – I'd slept with her husband – she said she was sorry to ask, but she'd found out about it, and she was worried about the press. How it would look. She said that Richard knew the head partner of my firm. They would be able to put in a good word. I got the impression Richard was used to paying people off. Maybe even threatening them. I didn't need their money. I suppose Nancy thought a different tack might work with me.'

Tash stares at her sister in disbelief. 'She said that? And you went along with it?'

'What was I supposed to do, Tash? I'm on my own. My heart was broken. I felt like shit and the wife of the man I slept with was in my apartment. She said either I signed it, and they helped out, or I refused, and Richard might have a different kind of word with my boss. She said Richard was capable of being cruel, and she didn't want me to get caught in the crossfire.'

The hum of the air con is the only thing Tash can hear for a moment. They both sit in silence, letting the words rest, sink in.

'You signed?'

'Yes, and within six months I was made partner. I suppose it's all true: the rich get richer; it's who you know, not what you know. All that bullshit is true.'

Richard's words on the beach come back to Tash. 'He told me Emma had got the wrong end of the stick. What does that mean?'

Megan takes hold of Tash's hand, squeezes it gently. There are tears at the corners of her eyes. 'There were photos of Emma, too. The man she told us about – it seems it was him. Richard had been with both of us. I swear, I had no idea.'

'Oh my God.' Tash feels sick. She shakes her head. 'Richard was with Emma last summer too? But she must have seen the flirting. Was Richard the man she was seeing – she wouldn't say who it was. Oh God. Then she watched it all crumble before her eyes – here, at the island.'

Megan wipes tears away roughly. 'I know! I know!'

'So, what happened that day? Why did she go missing?' Tash has a flash of fear. Had Emma been depressed? Was Megan right – that the bracelet she left wasn't a token to keep safe until her return, but a message of goodbye?

The world shifts a little. Spins.

Megan gives the smallest shake of her head. 'The worst-case scenario? Somehow, she found out about us. And we broke her heart.'

Tash closes her eyes. The day has replayed itself so many times.

61

Emma

Last summer

She can't describe how it feels. The ache is like a hole inside.

She'd met him first at Tash's apartment in New York, at a dinner party. Richard had arrived with flowers and charm. He'd listened carefully to her plans to become a journalist and said he'd be happy to show her round the White House if she wanted.

She wanted.

She'd rocked up in her smartest outfit and gone round open-mouthed at the history in front of her. Then he'd taken her to lunch in some fancy Washington restaurant, and the VP had come over to say hello.

Emma was used to fancy places. Since Tash and Mark had been catapulted into wealth and success, things had been different. But this was something else.

Richard had offered to do an interview with her, so she could place it somewhere. They'd met a few times.

How had it started? Slowly, she supposes. She wasn't attracted to him to begin with. He was so much older than her, and she'd met Nancy.

Then very slowly, she'd been flattered, he'd sent gifts. They'd had dinner one night at a hotel, and somehow, she'd ended up in his room. She can't really remember what he'd said but she remembers that whatever it had been had worked. He hadn't forced her. The suite was huge. The bathroom bigger than her apartment. He'd bought her diamonds. He'd also known what he was doing, and after some terrible fumblings at university, she found herself lost in pleasure, in an ocean of space and silk.

Coming here, to Greece, had been hard.

It was so new, and he told her Nancy was only staying with him until the latest campaign was over. Then he would leave her.

They'd managed a few stolen moments. Behind the rocks on the beach on the first night, when everyone else had gone to bed. Even one afternoon in the water, they'd swum out, and they'd been so far from the beach no one had seen. There had been a kind of thrill being naked in the water outside. Having him breathe her name.

But it was also shit. Chatting to Nancy made her feel hollow. Lying to Tash – it was taking advantage of her hospitality. She knew what Tash would say.

Also, Theo had a crush on her. It was so blindingly obvious – what would he think when his parents split up next year and she got together with his father?

The worst moment was when Megan began flirting with him.

At first Emma had barely noticed. It was hot and they'd all been chatting.

Then the laughter grew a little louder. Nancy looked over at Megan and Richard once or twice – the expression on her face sent ripples of shock through Emma. If Nancy minded, what was *she* supposed to think?

Still, what could she say? She had no claim to him.

Then this afternoon at the Acropolis she couldn't bear it. Megan had sat next to Richard at lunch. Sam had kept Nancy entertained, and Emma had hit her limit.

'I'm tired,' she told Tash. 'I'll head back early.'

'I'll come in a bit,' Megan said. 'I've seen the Acropolis a few times. Meet you back at the villa?'

Richard said nothing, but when Emma had gone to the bathroom, he'd found her. 'It's nothing,' he whispered. He'd put his arm around her waist and pressed her close to the wall.

She turned her face away from him. 'Look, I don't want –'

'I bought this for you.' He stepped back and held out a box. 'I know I've seemed distracted, but I'm just being polite. You know we can't sit next to each other all the time. It would be too obvious. I can't keep my hands off you.' His voice had been low and intense. 'All I've been thinking about is you. Those moments in the sea the other day were the best I've ever had.'

In the velvet box was a slim rose gold ring, with a black diamond glistening atop.

'It's a placeholder. For next year.'

Emma's voice had caught in her throat. She'd started to go off him – a brief ick every now and again. The odd moment last night, on the beach, when he'd been laughing with Megan, she'd seen the wrinkles at the corners of his eyes and felt his age. Even Mark was younger. What was she doing? She was worth more than this. And watching Nancy's face when Megan was laughing at Richard's joke. Well. Emma could feel her own self-respect withering a little. She'd always believed that falling in love with the right person would make her like herself more. Help her become her best self. That wasn't always true with Richard. He roused a shame in her that was new.

But here – in her hand. She slid it on. The echoes of her shoes tapping the corridors of the White House sounded in her ears. She was twenty-four. The love came flooding back. Who gets this chance? He'd picked her – out of everyone. It was both flattering and overwhelming.

'I've spoken to someone about an internship,' he said.

She was divided. But she was also in love. Or maybe infatuation – she couldn't decide, but the pull he had was magnetic, and she could do nothing about it.

The night before, he'd come to her room. Afterwards, she'd worried if Tash had heard. Megan had been joking round the pool about being able to hear Tash and Mark at night. They each had a room either side of Tash and Mark's. Did that mean Tash might have been able to hear her? She wasn't good at being quiet. When Richard wanted, he could make her scream.

Being wanted was addictive.

The helicopter had brought them back. The first ride was just her and Richard. Megan had gone to a bar with the boys for a drink first.

The whole place to themselves.

'No staff. Tash said they were finishing after breakfast.' He kisses her. His breath is rich in red wine and garlic.

'Just us?' She hates herself for hearing a catch of neediness in her voice. This is her first love affair. She's not good at the rules.

He kisses her neck, her bare shoulder. 'I'll go and change. Meet you at the beach? No one else will be back for a couple of hours.'

'First, I've something to show you.' The gift he'd given her earlier had given her confidence. She takes his hand and leads him to her room. She slides open the bedside drawer and shows him what is inside.

His face is impassive, and she feels a flash of fear.

'OK? Is it OK?'

They both stare down at the pregnancy test and its two bright lines.

He takes a step back. 'If I said no, would you deal with it?'

There's a look in his eyes she hasn't seen before. A touch of steel to his tone.

'I'd think about it,' she says. 'How about I get ready and meet you on the beach?'

He leaves without a word.

She showers, music from her room distant beneath the showerhead; the faint buzz of a passing helicopter muffled by shampoo in her ears.

Dressing slowly, rubbing in cream, her hand lingers across her belly. Flat like a pancake. She had been topping everyone's drinks up all week so no one would notice her not topping up her own. She'd been sick a couple of months ago – food poisoning. The doctor had said that must have been the reason for the pill she took each day to stop working. Did she want to look into other arrangements?

No.

If Richard asked her to get rid of it, would she?

No.

She wants this baby. She craves it.

Richard loves her. She can talk him into it. She can prove to him they can make it work.

Tash had given birth to Dom at the age of twenty-one. She is twenty-four. Tash is generous. She might be at the start of her career, but she can do both. Richard will come around but she can't tell him her decision. Not yet. Not until he's left Nancy. She doesn't want to complicate anything.

Another pang for Theo. She knows he's fond of her. But then, who doesn't want a sibling?

The sun burns as she takes the steps slowly. Butterflies rise up and catch in her throat. The whole beach to themselves.

She loves him. She wouldn't have chosen to. But nevertheless, they are where they are. She dreams of him, thinks of him.

He had pressed hard – she'd pushed back to begin with. He isn't her type. But he'd flattered, convinced, spent hours on the phone, listening to her stories about her day, her sisters, her dreams ...

It's love.

'Richard?' she calls, but there's no sign of him.

She kicks the sand as she wanders up towards the top end of the beach where they'd all been diving from the ledge the other day. There's a cave hollowed out in the rocks. They'd gone there the other night, after everyone else had gone to bed. With no one out on the beach so late, it had been sexy as fuck.

'Richard?'

Did he call? She can hear a noise.

'Richard?'

A laugh. It's a woman. Oh no, did they come back early? Was the helicopter she'd heard in the shower someone landing here?

The sun is hot on her shoulders now. She's only in a bikini. She hadn't wanted to smell of sun cream, so she was going to put it on afterwards.

'Richard!' Someone calls his name and more laughter.

The butterflies in Emma's throat are gone. Bile kills them. She walks right up to the entrance to the cave. The hollowed-out mound is safe from the sun.

She knew he was drunk. He's worse when he's drunk. She doesn't always like him so much.

Naked, he's on all fours, hovering, kissing the thigh, the arm, whispering... *Megan.*

It's Megan who lies on the sand of the cave. Where Emma had lain only a few nights ago.

Megan who laughs and calls his name.

Not just a distraction then.

His flirting had been real. He'd lied.

She's told no one. She'd only told Megan that there had been someone.

She takes a step back. And she can't stop it. The bile in her throat rises, catches in her mouth, and she half chokes, half cries. They mustn't hear her. She just needs to leave.

He looks up, catches her eye. Carries on. Thrusts. Lets out a groan.

She's gone before Megan sees her.

She runs the length of the beach.

Going to be sick, she wades into the sea. Vomits. Needs the cool. Needs to think.

She strikes out further. Who is this man she gave her heart to? What is he capable of?

A figure on the beach – it's Stani, heading to *Lulu*. Of course, they're all using the helicopter today. Stani is always kind.

She strikes out, the strength in her arms fading. The world a little dimmer. Her limbs so heavy.

She can make it. She's sure she can.

62

Jaz

Lulu

Now

The sun is low now. Theo has tried to talk to Becki, and she isn't giving him anything. They've eaten food, drunk beer. It's been awkward to say the least. Jaz has focused on the watercolour sky and thought of Dom.

She's sure Sam is behind some of this. She's watched Sam and Richard carefully. They haven't said much to each other. Richard took a call. Sam stared out to sea.

A boat drifts into view. A single person craft.

Theo catches sight of it. He stiffens, and the first person he looks to is his father.

Jaz looks from one to the other, then back out to the boat.

It's coming this way.

63

Tash

The car drops Tash and Megan back at the villa late. The police have finished for the day. The search is done. The evidence is gathered.

Sam had sent a message to say they were out on *Lulu* and would be back soon. Mark and Dom were still being held at the station. It looked as though the police believed Dom had tried to kill Kiki, and either Mark had helped, or he'd helped to cover it up.

Tash is more tired than she has ever been. Her limbs pull and her eyelids close. But she can't rest yet. Nothing is finished.

'I'm going to sort this,' Megan says as the police car pulls away behind them and Tash fumbles with the key in the lock.

Tash has lost count of the times she's heard her sister say that this afternoon – it's relentless. Megan keeps pushing forward, trying to fix it. There's been no time to really go over what happened. The revelations that had been so … crippling.

'Stop.' She lets the door slam behind her and strides into the kitchen. She takes wine from the fridge and sits at the kitchen island. She pours the wine into two glasses and pushes one towards Megan who trails in and takes a seat opposite Tash. For the first time since she arrived, Megan is coming undone. Her hair spills at the edges from the knot on the top of her head. Tendrils curl, and her eyes are bloodshot. The expensive shorts and top – matching pieces of linen – are crumpled.

'I *can*, I can sort it.'

'I want to talk. About Emma,' Tash says. She swallows a gulp and closes her eyes for a second. She waits for the cold in her throat and the warmth in her belly. 'What do you think happened? If Emma was seeing Richard, and then you slept with him ...'

Megan stares at her, wipes her face with her hand, rubbing again at her eyes. 'Yes. I know. You think I don't know? I must have hurt her. I must have crushed her.'

She drinks the wine; she holds Tash's gaze. 'I've been so jealous of you for so long. The son, the husband, the business. I've been so jealous of you, I wanted to tear you down. I hated you at times. I'm sorry. I'm sorry because when you told me to stay away from Richard, it spurred me on. I mean, *who is she to tell me how to live my life*? Well, Emma watching me with Richard must have been a thousand times worse. Because she loved him. She told me she loved the new man. And she had to watch me take him away.'

Tash whispers the next bit. 'You think she's really dead?'

'You mean did I push her to end her own life?' Megan closes her eyes. 'One of the reasons I can't think about it, every time you ask me, is that it will tear me apart. Now isn't the time anyway. What we need to do is to think about Kiki because there's no way it could be Mark or Dom. It must be Richard.

I spoke to the police about it, and there's no evidence against him. But, given what we know about the hacking and that boy, she might have tried to blackmail him. With Dom's fingerprints on the knife, and Mark's T-shirt at the scene with her blood on it, the DNA evidence is too powerful to ignore. But you told me she cut her foot here.'

Tash takes a swallow of wine and gestures to where Kiki had sat. 'Yes, just there. She smashed her glass. She could easily have gone back to the pool house and tried to clean up. It's not impossible she didn't wake Mark. He could sleep through an earthquake after all the wine. Maybe she went out to meet Richard on the beach? Richard has no alibi. I think he slept in the beach house. I've told the police all of this. But they say there's no evidence. Even Sam thinks he might have seen them together – I didn't really think of it properly. I was distracted when he said ... it must be him.'

'Yes. It has to have been him. Thank God he's at the hotel now. But we can't let the police allow him to fly home. We need time to find some way to prove it.'

Tash refills the wine glasses. After no food and shit coffee, she's starting to feel human again, but she will pay for this tomorrow.

Tomorrow makes her flinch. If her family are still behind bars ... 'You know I don't think there was a meeting planned. She was in her PJs. She came up to the main house to get water – she didn't need to do that. I wonder if she was coming over here just to see if the kids were back. Could it have been Theo she was looking for?'

Megan rubs her eyes. 'I don't know. One of them. But you're right. She's unlikely to go down to the beach in her PJs for an arranged meeting. Richard might have gone looking for her. Theo might have been caught up in all of this, but I don't think he's a murderer.'

Tash remembers what Dom had said about Ryan – Kiki's boyfriend – almost dying in their dorm. Situations can get out of hand quickly.

64

Jaz

Lulu

The small boat is so close Jaz can almost see who is on board. It's strange, that it's coming in so close to them. They're on their way back to the villa now, and other than their beach, there's not much that comes this way.

Jaz looks up at Stani to see if he's noticed.

Yes, he definitely has. In fact – she looks around – it seems as though *Lulu* has stopped. She places a hand beside where she sits. No vibrations. It's a very quiet engine, but even so – silence. Nothing.

Darkness is falling.

Sam and Richard have noticed the boat too. Sam leans out over the side. His head tilts a bit, like he's squinting to get a better view.

Richard follows suit. He stares – rears his head back a little, then he looks up at Stani. 'Take us back to the beach now, would you.'

Richard and Sam lean out over the rail at the starboard end of the *Lulu*. Stani sits up near the wheel and says quite calmly, 'I'm just sorting a problem out here.'

The smaller boat now is very close. Jaz watches as it passes them, heading towards the beach. There's a blonde woman on board. Theo sits still like stone then looks back to his father.

Richard watches the boat. 'Take us back, now.' His tone brusque.

Sam looks at the smaller boat, then at Stani and to Richard. 'Don't speak to him like that. He's the captain.'

'Don't tell me what to do, Sam.' Richard's voice is like steel now.

Becki sits upright and stiffens. Jaz feels cold. Theo is watching the smaller boat, which now sails between them and the beach. The woman looks directly at them, locking eyes with Theo. Is it the woman from the beach in Mykonos?

The boat is on its way to the shore. It looks small enough to sail straight onto the sand – the centreboard on small boats lifts easily.

'I won't let you speak to Stani like that,' Sam replies.

Richard takes a bottle of beer and drinks it down in one. Jaz can see where Theo learned it from.

'Stani,' Richard stares at Sam as he speaks, 'take us back now.'

'No,' Stani says. 'Not yet. I need five minutes.'

'I am ordering you to take us back.'

Jaz looks out at the smaller boat. It's heading to land. To the villa.

'Not yet.'

Richard chucks the bottle down, and there's the sound of breaking glass.

'Sit down,' Sam says. 'You're drunk. You're being a menace here.'

'You can't make me,' Richard says.

'I will if I have to.'

Becki looks at Jaz and whispers, 'What's going on? I don't understand?'

Sam takes a step forward and it's difficult for Jaz to see. She rises on her knees.

'OK, Sam, you want to do this? You sleep with my wife and think you get the upper hand here?'

'Don't make out like you care,' Sam says. His tone is hard. 'You destroy women.'

'I,' Richard says, 'can destroy you.'

There's a scuffle, a thwack. The men shout. Jaz jumps up to see what happened. Following the commotion, there's a loud splash.

'Man overboard! Throw out the float!' Stani shouts.

It's Sam, out in the water.

'Why did you do that?' Theo runs down the side of *Lulu*, towards his father. 'Is there nothing you aren't capable of?'

'Don't speak to me like that, Theodore.'

'I will speak to you however I like! This is all your fault! All of it! If only you hadn't –'

The second sound of a thwack. This time Jaz sees Theo fly back and hit the deck. Richard Fowler stands over him.

'Everything I've done has been for you!' he bellows.

'That's such a crock of shit!' Theo screams. 'You break everything! You broke Mom, even before she died!'

'How dare you!' Richard screams now.

Becki grabs Jaz's arm. They look at each other – what do they do?

'Did you kill her?' Theo scrabbles back, pushing himself on his heels, and sitting upright. There's blood on his face. 'Did you kill Mom?'

Jaz feels the bite of adrenalin. She leaps down the steps on the starboard side of *Lulu*. Theo and his father are on the port side, and she ducks round and into the small, luxury galley kitchen. She grabs a flare from the emergency box and, heading out to the rails on the beach side of the boat, lets it rip up and high, into the sky.

65

Nancy

Winter, nine months ago

The Christmas party

Theo climbs into the passenger seat. His blond hair is dark and heavy with snow from the time it took to walk from the house to the car. She feels drips down her own neck.

He closes the door as he sits, his voice soft and tired. 'Mom, don't go without me.'

'Oh, sweetheart.' She leans over and kisses him on the cheek, pulling him to her. Her throat is tight. 'Let's get out of here. Let's go to a hotel. Leave all this behind.'

'I hate him, Mom.'

She holds his hand. 'Me too.'

'That night –' He stops.

All there is to do is wait. She sees the front door open a crack. They don't need anyone else right now. She needs to get them away.

'Tell me while I drive.'

A figure runs at the car.

'Wait a moment.' She opens the door, and the snow lands on her eyelashes, on her tongue as she calls out, 'Sam!'

'Nancy, don't. We'll go together.' He looks back at the house then back to her. 'Please. I love you. You don't need to put up with any of this. It's all just meaningless shit. Come with me.'

'Sam.' The snow makes his hair darker. 'Call me later. I need to be with Theo now. But please, call me. Come and find me. I'll be waiting.'

'We can make this work, Nancy.'

His eyes carry the flakes, and he touches her cheek. She takes a step back, blinking as the snow covers her footsteps quickly, the bite of cold dimmed a little by the look on Sam's face.

She powers the car up as Theo looks at her. 'Him?'

She nods. 'But you are the most important. Remember that. You first. Let's go and find a hotel. Hot chocolate and a new start.'

The car turns slowly in the deepening drifts of the sweeping drive. It's fresh fall, and the car is a good one, so they move forward fairly easily, but very slowly. Carefully. The snow tyres are already on, and they purr steadily down the drive. The sound of the party behind them. All those people. There's a hotel just down the road. It won't take long.

All she wants is Theo.

It's over with Richard. She can't unsee what she saw tonight. And she can't get her head around any of it. She's been able to ignore his indiscretions when they've been out of sight. It's not like he's been sleeping with someone else and coming home to sleep with her. She couldn't have borne that. The thought turns her stomach – she won't even sip from someone else's glass.

Plus, they've been business partners more than anything for some time now. All those dreams she had of love have kind of slipped away – or been erased. She'd almost not noticed. The love had been eclipsed by the glow of being a parent, the bright lights of the oval office.

She's made excuses for him in her head. Tried not to mind. Even cleaned up after him – the NDA she had Megan sign. The bribes.

But seeing him tonight ...

The expression on his face. Ugly in desire; twisted in need. That girl could have been his daughter. And his trousers down around his ankles, his naked ass raised for the whack ... The sound of the beating. The look on the girl's face was pure loathing. She had despised him.

Nancy has been raised one way. Family pride was everything. To be kneeling and despised, in his own house, begging – she's not sure she can look Richard in the face again.

Whatever the girl's motivation for it, none of it had been pleasure. By coming to their home that night, she'd wrecked it all. She'd put the nail in the coffin of a relationship that had already been skin and bone.

Along with it, so much else had died. Things hanging by a thread she hadn't even realised.

She's done. Maybe she'll do as Sam suggested – maybe she'll run on her own. If Richard has a fall from grace, then she can stand for office on her own terms. America loves a strong figure, a survivor.

Right now, she needs to be here for her son.

'Tell me,' she says. The look on his face when she'd entered the dorm room comes back to her. He'd been lost. It had been a scene from a horror show.

'After the summer, after Greece, I found the woman who came here tonight. The one who was in the dorm room that night. I paid her to find out what Dad was up to. She's not so much a private investigator, as someone who can track tech. She gets into his phone with my help, into the video doorbell, can look at his emails. I knew last summer he was seeing someone else. I saw him with Dom's aunt.'

'Megan?'

'No – not at first. The other one. I didn't know what to say. I couldn't tell you – I'm so sorry, Mom. I should have just told you straight away. She was pregnant. I guessed. She didn't drink – threw up a few times. I didn't know until later it was Dad's. It was bad enough when I knew he'd been cheating on you, but when I realised it was her, and I saw the photos Kiki found, I lost it. I just couldn't stop drinking, Mom. I properly lost it. I've been so angry.'

Emma as well as Megan? A baby?

She grasps his hand tightly. Tears stream down both their faces, and she slows the car. Lights from the beneath the snow edge the driveway. Only a very dim glow – the white of the air is light, but the flakes catch the glare of the headlights and fly at the windscreen in such thick succession it's impossible to see much of the road ahead. The expensive engine turns beneath them, and it skids only a little as it slows.

'I knew – or rather I guessed. Your dad and I haven't been like a normal couple for a while. It's not something I ever hoped you'd find out about. He promised he was going to be better. I didn't want to leave him and ruin his chances at office. And I wanted to keep us together – a family – for you. I love you. You've always been the most important thing ... always.'

It's true. Everything she's done had been to protect Theo – from the shame. From the family name being dragged in the mud. They'd be a laughing stock. It was all for Theo, wasn't it?

She grips his hand, the other steady on the wheel.

She hears herself as she tells him that he's what she was thinking of. But if she's honest with herself, she knows she's let him down. She's put the campaign and ambition above Theo. If she really wanted him to be OK, she wouldn't have lied to him when she found that dead boy in his dorm – Ryan, his name is Ryan. She needs to face it. She didn't kill him, but possibly she did worse. The least she can do is call him by his name.

Her first thoughts were blank – a whitewash of panic. But once she'd been able to make plans, to formulate something like a course of action, it had been about hiding the truth from Theo. It had been about hiding the body.

All of it was about hiding from view – because the perfect view had always been the most important thing. How they appeared to everyone. To the public. A whitewash of truth, a cover of their flaws: Richard's straying, her loneliness – Theo's desperation to do something.

The young aren't good at ignoring the truth in favour of a lie. They want to act and to make right the wrongs. She should have remembered this. She should have thought about this as she tipped the boy over the bridge and watched his body plunge down to the icy water and bile had made her gag and she'd tried to remember who she used to be.

'What happened?' She stops the car.

Theo's voice is small 'I paid her. I paid her for the information that showed Dad was cheating. I don't want to upset you – it's why I didn't tell you. He was paying the women too. He paid them for their silence. And threatened them too. Kiki found sums mentioned on a different phone he had. She printed out some of the things he'd say to them. I found his phone – once I knew it existed, I looked for it. Reading it made it so real. He slept with women, then when he was bored, he paid them off. He hit them – a few. To show he meant his threats. And I think he was paying someone else to do the heavier lifting – to keep them quiet.'

'Oh, darling.' Nancy looks at his profile, hair slicked and damp, cheeks wet with tears.

'I paid Kiki the money she'd named as her price for the job she did. But I think she realised there was more. She asked for hush money. She said she'd made a copy of the information she'd found, and she'd expose him.'

Nancy feels sick. 'What did you do?'

'I told Dad. I had no choice. I couldn't pay her. I told him, and he went mad. But he gave me money to pay her. He said he'd give it to me in cash so it couldn't be traced to him. So I took it and banked it until I had enough to pay her off. She wanted one lump sum. I told her to meet me that night. I was going to do it outside, somewhere else. But she wanted to come to Harvard. She wanted to come to the dorm room. She insisted and I didn't know how to say no.'

Nancy imagines him trapped – caught by trying to unearth secrets that became his prison. Richard has so much to answer for.

'What happened?' she whispers. Her heart is in her throat.

'Mom, it was awful.' He lifts his palms over his eyes and cries; his shoulders shake. 'Dom wasn't going to be there. He was supposed to be out with Jaz. But he came back. He said Jaz was feeling sick. I tried to make him leave – I pushed him out the door. I told him I was cheating on Becki, and a girl was coming round. He told me to get my shit together and started trying to have some kind of heart to heart – then she came. Kiki and her boyfriend. She said she'd brought him for protection. He had a knife.'

'Fuck,' Nancy whispers. She never swears, and she's never sworn in Theo's presence. She imagines his panic. 'What did Dom say?'

'He didn't know what was happening. He assumed at first she was the girl I was meeting behind Becki's back, but when Ryan came in and flicked open the knife, he didn't know what to do. He started shouting.'

Nancy shakes her head. She shivers. The heating in the car is turned right up but the wind is blowing now, and snow has banked quickly on the windscreen, obscuring the outside world. It's just her and Theo.

'What happened next?'

'I tried to do it all quickly and just make it all go away. I gave her the money, but she insisted on counting it. And Dom kept asking what was happening. He pulled out his phone at some point.' Theo turns to look at Nancy. 'Honestly, Mom, I tried to stop it all. He held the knife out at Dom – the point was almost touching his chest, telling him to be quiet, and Dom freaked out. Kiki was counting out notes, and Dom threw himself on Ryan. The knife fell to the floor. Kiki screamed and started punching Dom on the back. They were wrestling on the floor.'

Nancy doesn't breathe.

'In the end, I lost it. I grabbed Kiki and pulled her away. The knife was about a foot from Ryan, and he was reaching for it. So I picked it up.'

Silence sits with them for a moment, and Nancy wishes she could press pause. She doesn't want to hear the rest.

'I went to cut him, just to warn him. But he rolled free. He grabbed it.' Theo cries harder. 'He lifted it up, and crouched, pointing at me. Then he launched. I thought that was it.'

Nancy feels sick.

'Dom saved me. He threw himself at him again, only this time the knife didn't fall to the floor. It hit Ryan – it must have gone backwards with Dom's weight. There was blood everywhere

– even in the moment I was thinking it must have been an artery. What should we do … So much blood. Kiki was screaming and started wailing. Dom was covered in blood. He fell to the floor – pushing himself back against the wall, sliding on his ass, and all I could see was tracks of blood. It all happened so *fast*. The dude was pulling at the knife – just pulling and pulling. It came out and … Then he kind of lay down, and he didn't get up.'

Theo's voice is high now, as though he's ten years younger. 'Kiki started screaming. Dom was just still then. I don't think he moved. It was dark.'

Nancy stares at the dark – the fringes of the world peep from over the edges of the snow lying thick on the windscreen. Cold sits in her stomach like ice.

Theo speaks so softly she can barely hear him. 'He just lay there. He didn't move. I just watched. I didn't know if he was passed out or what.' His eyes are bright with tears, and he looks at her. 'Then you came. You said he wasn't dead, and you took Kiki away. I haven't seen her since that night. I thought she'd come to kill me tonight. I thought it was all over.'

Nancy looks at her son and wishes she could rewind the clock back to last summer. She wishes – instead of ignoring Richard's flirting and finding some solace in the attentions of Sam, instead of wondering how it would be to be in the arms of a man as simple and honest as Sam seemed to be, – instead, she wishes she had gone to find Theo and dealt a round of cards and made hot chocolate. She wishes she had taken him home to the US and just hung out by the pool and put a movie on when it got dark. What was it about competitive sex? When she'd seen Richard flirting with Megan, she'd made a plan to sleep with Sam. She'd promised it to herself like you tell yourself you deserve a massage or the expensive dress. She'd needed to even the stakes in her failing marriage. She planned on feeling Sam inside her and knowing that when that happened, she'd feel as though Richard would be forgotten, would be unimportant.

She'd never really needed the touch of another man to make her better. She'd just needed to walk away.

What she should have done was to hold on to her son.

'Theo,' she whispers, the cold outside nothing compared to the heat of her heart. She burns to make this right. She will do. She will make all of this go away. She'll be there for him always. She'll never let him down again. She'd made Megan sign an NDA, and she'd paid Kiki off. Enough. She is done now. She will not be part of Richard's world any more. She will be with Sam. She'll hold her son tight.

Tonight is the start of tomorrow.

She starts the engine. Powering forwards, the snow is thick and it's hard to see. From seemingly nowhere, a figure appears on the road. Nancy swerves the car, and it spins, flying out of control and catching some ice.

They spin up and over, landing in a drift. Before she knows what's happened, she's wet and lying in the snow. 'Theo?' she screams. She can't see him. His door is open and the white whips in. He must be out there somewhere.

The figure appears again. She can't make out who it is. 'Help me!' she shouts. 'My son!'

66

Nancy

Last Christmas

The snowstorm

'Richard!' Nancy staggers back against the car. Theo is somewhere, thrown on the snow-covered lawn. She'd swerved to avoid a figure – is Richard here too?

'What are you doing here?' she screams.

He whacks her hard across her cheek, and the pain explodes down the left side of her face.

'You think you can leave me? And take my son?' The snow has drenched him. He wears a security detail black coat. He grabs her arm and pulls her towards the house. 'You're coming back with me now!'

'No!' She pulls back. She must get to Theo. He will be cold. He needs checking. 'Theo's out there!'

Richard's eyes are tiny, like beads. How could she ever have thought him attractive? He's vile. Inside and out. Nothing is worth this. No house. No power.

'We're leaving. We're not coming back,' she screams. The snow is cold, but the fire in her throat lets fly the words. They do not freeze in her mouth. She will speak now; she will not be silenced by him. She will not silence any other women. She is done with him.

A figure in the road emerges, dressed in another security detail coat.

'Help!' she calls.

Richard takes a step back and shakes his head.

'I'm going back to the house.'

The other man approaches. 'Sir?' he says.

Richard nods to Nancy. 'You know what to do. No one sees. Call me when it's done.'

Nancy screams.

The pit in her belly widens, and fear, like a snake, wrestles and writhes.

She knew he had some people in his employ. She knew he'd done some awful things to smooth his way.

But not her. Surely not to her.

The man lunges, and she feels his hand close around her throat. She gags, struggles against his fingers. Tries for air.

'It will be quick,' he says, pulling her forwards, his other hand grabbing her by the waist. He pulls her across the lawn, to the pond.

Richard is nowhere to be seen. He will be seen by everyone in the house.

Theo must be out there, lying in the snow.

She kicks and scuffs the snow on the lawn; the cold eats through her skin, fast to her bones. The water makes her gasp, fills her mouth, her nose.

Theo.

As she closes her eyes, she thinks of him. Of all the life she won't get to see. The most precious thing she has ever done. The most precious thing she has.

Theo.

67

Tash

Now

Greece

'There's trouble on the water,' Megan says, standing quickly. 'Look!'

Out through the patio doors, which look down on the pool and out to sea, Tash sees the fading flash in the sky. It's quite close to shore.

'It's them,' Tash says. 'They must be in trouble. Call it in. I'll get the dinghy. Meet me on the beach.'

Tash pulls the knot free and climbs into the small wooden dinghy that seats three at most.

'Come on!' she screams at Megan, who runs across the sand. 'The police?'

'On their way.'

They push away from the jetty, and Tash steers the dinghy out, towards the flare.

Night has come in apace.

The sea is calm, and it won't take long to reach them.

As they get closer, she wonders if she's going mad, or if there are two boats out on the water?

68

Jaz

Lulu

'Stop! You'll hurt him!' Becki screams as Richard and Theo wrestle on the deck of *Lulu*. Traces of blood smear out and spread. Sam is still in the water, and Jaz hopes someone saw the flare. They need help.

'Stand back,' Stani says, gently pulling Becki out of the way. 'This never fails.' He turns a deck hose on the two figures, and a stream of fierce water shoots out, drenching them.

'What the fuck?' Richard rolls off Theo, and turns to face Stani, his hand up in front of his face. 'Turn it off!'

Becki runs to Theo and helps him up. The water is now on Richard, but the spray is everywhere.

Jaz is soaked and leans out over the rail. Sam is in the water and hanging on to the float, but he's not swimming back to them. Instead, he seems to be treading water. Is he hurt?

'Sam, are you OK?' she shouts.

A whack to her shoulder, and she's knocked down to the wet deck. Her hand is sharp and sore, and when she looks, blood leaks out quickly, spreading out into the pools of water from the hose. Richard's smashed beer bottle, it must be.

'What's happening?' she says; her shoulder aches. But no one hears. She crawls away, cutting herself again. She turns to see where the blow came from. Richard has thrown himself at Stani, and they'd fallen into her. They fight up against the rail. Stani is pushed backwards and falls on Jaz again – another whack.

'Put it down!' This is Becki.

Jaz spins. Richard has picked up the bulk of the broken bottle and holds it up to Stani's face.

'Stop what the fuck you are doing.'

Stani goes very still.

Jaz hears her breath come in pants. Her shoulder is aching, and her hand is still bleeding. It's the water that's making it seem like so much blood, she thinks, it must be. She hangs on to it – she feels weak and dizzy.

Richard waves the bottle closer to Stani. It's up against his cheek, his eye.

'Stop!' Becki screams.

Jaz daren't move. She doesn't want to jump-scare Richard. He's drunk and angry.

Stani doesn't flinch, doesn't speak.

'Dad!' Theo shouts.

A flash – blinding and so close – sparks up just overhead.

Jaz blinks – she can't see. She's lightheaded.

A man's scream. Thuds.

Then there's the sound of a boat banging into theirs, a clatter on the rails.

'What's happened?' Becki screams. 'It's so bright.'

'I think it's another flare,' Jaz says, but again, she's not sure anyone can hear her. Her voice is weak now. The flash is dazzling. Dots appear behind her lids. She blinks.

A shout.

A thump.

A splash.

The light goes out, and they're left in the dark again. Blacker this time. The flare has momentarily blinded them all.

Someone must have turned off the main lights on *Lulu* – only the pale deck floor lights illuminate now.

What's going on?

'Help!'

It's a man's voice, but it's fading.

The sounds are distant, muted. Jaz blinks once, twice. Tries to focus.

But is taken in by the darkness again.

69

Tash

The ocean

'They're fighting! Oh my God!' Tash screams as their dinghy approaches *Lulu*. All they can see are figures wrestling in the moonlight.

She can see the sharp cut of glass that Richard is holding, the recognition on Stani's face that Richard wouldn't hesitate to use it.

The glass flashes, catching the moon.

'Megan, what do we do?' Tash is almost crying. The dinghy isn't going to get there fast enough.

But Megan is quick. Always calm in a crisis, she ducks under the seat of the dinghy and pulls out the wooden safety box, lifting the lid.

Megan pulls a flare, trying to fire it above the heads of Richard and Stani.

The flash is bright, and it burns Tash's eyes. She turns and cries out.

There's a scream from the boat. Like an animal, wounded.

A bang. Tash feels a weight land close to her, and the dinghy lifts like paper on a breeze, high and briefly flying in the night air. Her stomach rises and falls. Then salt water, sharp and cold, flies up her nose, soaks her clothes, pulls her down briefly, before turning her and pushing her gently back up towards the surface.

They've both been thrown into the water, and Megan had been so close to the boat, she's been thrown against the side of *Lulu* as their dinghy upended.

Tash flaps her arm forward, but she can't lift it any more. Her shoulder is like lead – heavy and immovable. Her arm burns.

The moon lights up the sky. Rays of pale gold and silver spin outwards, and the heavens are alive. Please let the gods be on her side.

'Meg,' she whispers.

Her sister's hair, always so perfectly dried, so smooth, floats up in strands and touches the surface of the water. She is face down.

'Meg.' She tries to shout, but nothing will come. There's simply not enough air.

She's already lost one sister. How can she lose two?

A mouthful of water.

A kick at the back of her throat.

She coughs and flaps one arm in the salt water. She's closer. She reaches Megan's foot. Kicks again and manages to grab her waist, pulling and half spinning her.

Megan gags.

The shimmer of silver in the sky blurs. Salt stings Tash's eyes and her head aches.

Someone had fallen from *Lulu* and landed on their dinghy, capsizing them, and Tash wipes at her eyes – blood, not just water. She must have banged her head as they'd fallen in.

'Meg!'

Could Tash have done more? For both of them?

In looking for Emma, she had overlooked Megan. She never gets it right. She's got everything wrong, for so long. Mark, Dom, Sam.

There's a light now – softer than the sunset. Brighter than a flame. It burns in her brain. Her limbs are heavy, and the pull of the water is too much.

70

Jaz

The ocean

There's a scream. Jaz can only hear from what feels like underwater as she lies, dizzy, on the deck, bleeding. *Lulu* rocks heavily but doesn't overturn.

'Megan!'

It sounds like Natasha, in the water.

Sam had been in the water. Is he still there – can he save her?

Jaz blinks and tries to push herself up. She sees Theo, climb to the edge of *Lulu* and dive in towards what looks like Megan. She's face down, not moving.

People could die – Jaz must do something. She bites on her lip as standing makes her want to scream, but she forces herself, holding the side of the boat. The ocean spins around her; she's so dizzy. Leaning over the side, she tries to climb up the rails to see what is happening. A small dinghy is overturned – it must have been what the sisters were in.

Richard has fallen. Did he land in the middle of the dinghy and bounce into the ocean? Is that what flipped the boat? All she can see of him is his back, floating up in the water.

Megan and Natasha must have been coming to rescue them. But now both of them are in the water.

One of them must have shot the flare.

'Tash!' Sam shouts.

He swims to the dinghy and pulls it upright. Jaz watches, blinking, and climbs higher, trying to see where Natasha is.

Blinking once more, she swoons, so light-headed. Then she's falling, sinking, salt water stinging her eyes.

Someone grabs her arm. She kicks to the surface, the pain in her leg sharp, but the cold clarifies the world for her. She manages to hold the side of the dinghy.

'I'm OK!' she says, as she's sees it's Theo who grabbed her, and he also holds Megan, his other arm looped beneath her shoulders.

'Where is she?' Sam scans the water, right and left. 'Tash!' He flashes a torch from the dinghy, swimming out and scouring the water.

Theo, through some superhuman means, pushes Megan up and onto the dinghy.

'Come on,' he says to Jaz. 'Climb up; use me.'

Jaz will never know how she managed to haul herself up, but Theo pushes hard as she's almost there, and then she falls to the bottom of the boat.

Theo is quick behind her, knocking himself hard on the floor of the boat as he lands.

'Natasha,' Jaz tries to call, but it comes out as no more than a whisper.

She sees the flash of Sam, the torch blinking over the dark sea.

Jaz shivers on the dinghy. She finds some towels at the front and first wraps Megan, who is being sick, but is breathing and her eyes are half open.

Then she drapes another over Theo, who lies on the dinghy floor. His eyes open and close. A single tear slides on his cheek.

'Tash! *Tash!*'

Jaz looks out at the water – black-blue and still. She can't get warm. Her teeth clatter and snap.

Becki has stayed on *Lulu* with Stani. The flare had shot into them. Stani must have been caught by fragments. Becki has wet a towel for him to hold against his head and helps him sit up. The emergency lights are soft enough to make it out.

Richard is still face down.

It's so dark. Theo is bleeding. His dad had hit him hard. Whatever energy he had left, seems to have disappeared. In saving Jaz, he's exhausted himself.

The dinghy spins as they look for Natasha, out in the water, in the dark.

Something up ahead.

'What's that?' She lifts a finger, as even she struggles to hear what she's saying. Her words disappear, dissolving against the weight of the night air.

The blood from Theo's head leaks a little more into the striped towel. Red, white and blue. She squeezes her eyes shut tight.

'There.'

Theo follows her finger but can't lift himself to see.

With nothing left for her to do, she wraps a towel tightly round her shoulders, and she kneels, the boat rocking, down on the wooden floor. She lies down next to Theo.

She lays him out – splayed in the recovery position next to Megan. His body warm, even as it breaks. His breath steady, though shallow.

'We'll save you,' she whispers.

71

Tash

The ocean

'Tash, Tash.'

The sound, like a wave, washes over her.

A crack of light, as her eyelids – heavy and salt-stung – open. 'Tash, can you hear me?'

Eyes brown. Milk chocolate pools. His hair darker than usual, wet, and hanging over her face. Drops fall as his head moves, scanning her. 'Can you hear me?'

'Sam.' Her throat hurts when she speaks. A creak rather than a word.

'Oh, Tash. I thought you'd gone.' He wipes at his face, clearing his eyes. Not just sea water, she realises.

'Tash. I can't lose you. Not you as well.'

Sam. Always there. His hands warm on her cold cheek. He lifts her head and rests it on a towel, rolling her to her side. Her eyes close again.

She's not here for him.

'Megan?' she asks. She'd been going after Megan.

'She's safe,' he says. 'You might be sick again; focus on breathing. We'll be back to shore soon.'

The light of a boat drifts closer. Not the dinghy. The other boat. The one she'd seen earlier. It had been heading for shore, but it must have turned round.

'Tash!' a voice calls.

Tash can hear that she's crying. 'Tash, please let her be OK!'

It's a voice she recognises.

Sam says, 'Help me get her on board.' Then he says, 'Oh my God!' as they reach the edge of the boat and he sees who's sailing.

Nothing makes sense. Tash spits out water as Sam helps her up into this third boat. To the voice she recognises. The voice she's dreamed about.

The engine purrs beneath them. The vibrations rumble through Tash's bones.

It can't be?

'Emma?'

72

Tash

The ambulance waits up by the villa as the paramedics check them on the beach. Tash is exhausted, but the joy. Oh, the joy. She trembles and will not let go of Emma's hand.

'But where have you been?'

'We,' Emma says, her blue eyes wet with tears. 'We've stayed with Stani. He found me in the sea that day last year. I told him what I was going to do and begged him. I needed to get away. He took me to his home. I wouldn't let him call anyone. I wanted to disappear. I begged. He didn't want to keep me a secret. He said it would break you.'

Tash shakes her head. 'Who is we? You mean you and Stani?'

Emma squeezes her hand. 'Me and the baby.'

'Really?' Tash's voice is soft and Emma nods.

'I was pregnant. It was Richard's ....' She drops her head and takes a breath.

Richard. Tash doesn't know what to think. Of course Richard is behind this. He's behind everything.

Emma speaks quietly. 'He broke my heart. But he also threatened Stani last year. Stani had seen him with me, and then with Megan. I suppose Richard's not the kind of man to notice staff. Stani pulled him aside and said he should sort himself out. Richard hit him. He said he had broken bigger men than Stani – he said he had so much power Stani should watch out. That no one gets to speak to him like that.' She shakes her head quickly. 'Tash, I was so frightened. I told him about the baby, and he told me to get rid of it. I just couldn't. I thought he'd make me get rid of it – properly make me. It would screw over all his political wet dreams. How could I be so stupid?' She shakes her head. 'You have to forgive me.' She grabs Tash's hand. 'I know what I will have put you through! I followed you on the internet where I could. I got Maria to sneak my bracelet into your room. I thought if anyone would know, you would know.'

Tash squeezes her hand back and holds her heart in her mouth – too full to speak.

'I didn't care about Megan. I mean, I thought I hated her. Not now. I know who he is now. She didn't know about me.'

Both of her sisters, going through so much.

'I thought if Richard was done with me and had moved on, all I could do was hide to protect the baby. I can only imagine the pressure he'd put on me – to get an abortion. Maybe even something worse.' She shudders. 'I thought I'd wait, until the baby was born. Until I felt stronger.'

'Really?' Tash looks down the beach where Stani sits while two paramedics check him over. Megan is next to him. 'Stani looked after you?'

'And Maria. Both of them. I went to a local hospital. Not the private one in Athens. Stani told them I was working for him. He paid for the healthcare. The baby is Greek. She can have a British passport too.'

The paramedic nods at Tash. 'OK, you're ready for the ambulance. Your head is cut but no signs of concussion. We'd just like to get you checked over properly. There's an air ambulance on its way back.'

The paramedic moves away.

'On its way back?' Tash repeats, confused. 'Who has it taken already?' She can see Theo and Jaz being looked over; Megan sits with Stani. Becki and Sam are talking to the police, giving statements.

'Richard,' Emma says. She looks up towards the dot in the sky that gets bigger as it approaches them. 'They took Richard first. The police insisted.'

'The police?'

'He's dead, Tash. He was dead in the water. Megan shot the flare, and it scorched his face. He fell in the water. It all happened quickly. He was face down by the time we got to him. We pulled you and Megan out first. He'd been face down for about ten minutes. There wasn't any hope.'

Tash looks back up at the light in the sky, the blades louder now. She thinks of Richard and his casual use of both her sisters, how he'd hit Theo at Nancy's funeral. His lazy, thoughtless treatment of them all, like they were all just there for his amusement. Like he was some kind of old-fashioned god, playing with the mortals on earth.

Maybe it was for the best.

'Do you know about the murder here?'

Emma nods. 'Stani told me. He messaged to say Richard was on the boat tonight. That's why I came. I was worried. If it was him – and I assume it is, then I didn't want to leave you alone. Not with Dom and Mark being held in custody.'

'We think it *must* have been him. Maybe they'll let Dom and Mark out now. He threatened Stani on the boat, knocked Sam overboard and hit Theo. They must know what kind of man he is.'

Tash touches Emma's face. 'What's her name?'

Emma smiles. 'Lulu. For mum. Might be time to change the name of the boat.'

73

Jaz

Becki sits with Jaz in the helicopter. The noise is loud, and Jaz looks out of the window and down over the sea. It looks black from up here. Just the odd flashing light from the islands as they pass overhead. Athens on the horizon. There are hospitals closer; they are heading to the one the family use – the same one Theo was taken to on the first night.

Jaz's wrist is bandaged up. Her head aches. The flash from the flare is still bright in her eyes. And the sound of the cry, bestial, the sight of Richard Fowler, floating face down.

Becki's face, pinched and white.

Jaz wonders.

'You'll be good as new in a few days.' The doctor is English. She sounds a lot like Natasha. She looks much brighter than she should this late in the day. Jaz feels like she's been awake for a century.

It's technically Monday now; it's 2 a.m. – officially Dom's birthday.

'Can I go back in the morning?' She'd like to see him. She hates thinking of him in a cell.

The doctor smiles. 'I'd suggest twenty-four hours here at least. You've had a nasty bang to the head, and we'd like to change the dressing on your wrist – the stitches are good, but the wound is still angry. But it's up to you.'

As the doctor walks away, Jaz leans her head back on the pillow. A private room and a plate of toast and jam. After the craziness of the weekend, the peace and safety here are a relief.

But it's not over. She can't stop thinking about what Becki said.

When Jaz goes over what she actually saw that night – instead of what she'd been told – it doesn't stack up.

She'd checked on Becki in her room after they'd got back from Mykonos, but she hadn't actually seen her. She'd seen the bed, which looked as though someone was inside – a rumpled duvet and a raised shape, as though someone was underneath. That could have been anything.

Jaz had seen Theo argue with his father. Richard had stormed off away from the house, towards the beach. Theo had been standing by the house. Becki had supported this – mentioning she'd seen it too. But if Becki had been asleep in her bed, how had she seen Richard heading to the beach with Kiki?

Becki hadn't been wearing her necklace since the Mykonos night. But then she said yesterday she'd thrown it away with the knife. The knife was thrown away the night before the Mykonos beach party. Unless Becki had got the knife out again. Why would she throw it away twice?

And the day before, she said Dom had been the one to get rid of it.

Becki had been so sure that Theo had killed Kiki.
She had tried to leave when the police had arrived.
None of it adds up.
All tiny details that, when mixed together, leave an unpleasant taste in Jaz's mouth.
Dom can't be in jail on his birthday. None of this is fair.
Jaz presses the button by her bed and asks for a number when the nurse arrives. It's a long time since she had any idea where her mobile is, but there's a phone by her bed. The nurse advises her that the call will be charged to the account.
Jaz is pretty sure Natasha won't mind.

74

Tash

The villa is far quieter than it should be on Dom's birthday. Emma has gone back to look after Lulu and will bring her over this evening. Maria has been babysitting, and Tash can't wait to hold her. A whole year of missing Emma. Months of Lulu being in the world without her knowing. So much to catch up on.

But before that, there is her own child to think of.

She looks out of the huge kitchen windows. The doors are closed to keep the cold in, but in a moment, she'll open them and hopefully all this will be over.

Jaz, Theo, Becki and Sam sit with coffee on the patio, and the shades are raised over the pergola. No one wants to be in the sun today. Everyone needs rest and gentle light.

'OK?' Megan asks quietly. Her hair is tied up in a ponytail and she wears denim shorts and a white T-shirt. Her face is clear of make-up, and dark circles ring her eyes. She'd been in hospital last night then had provided statements about the firing of the flare. She's lost her polished sheen over the last few days. Tash hopes not all the fight has left her. She relies on Megan to have an edge. Not everyone should be sugar and spice. That's not what girls should be made of.

The salt-and-peppered detective – who by now Tash has learnt is called Giannis – had talked with Tash last night, Christos next to him, by Tash's bed in the hospital. They'd flown there to speak to her. With someone of Richard's status, they needed to get the details of his death wrapped up quickly. There were press statements to be made, the President to inform.

Giannis had been relaxed – she can't imagine him doing stress. Christos sat up ramrod straight.

'We've had someone look at the body in the last hour. We need to do a full post-mortem but I thought you'd want to know that the doctor's provisional report states the alcohol levels in Richard Fowler's blood were very high. And there was salt water in his lungs. There are marks where the flare appears to have glanced against his head, but it's not a mortal wound. It was death by accidental drowning. That's what we're looking at. Maybe the autopsy will throw something else out, but the doctor isn't expecting it. The death will have been quick – and inevitable, given the circumstances.'

'A quick death is more than he deserved,' Tash had said, unable to stop herself. 'You must know by now he's the one who must have killed Kiki.'

'Actually,' Christos had looked at Giannis, who had nodded, 'we had an interesting chat with Jasmine when we arrived. We have a few things to check, but we might need to come to the villa in the morning, if everyone is back by then.'

'Ready?' Megan asks, lifting a coffee up and nodding to the patio.

Tash nods. 'I'll call them. They're waiting nearby.'

Sam taps on his phone as Tash and Megan take a seat at the table.

'There are flights with spaces this afternoon. I suppose it just depends how quickly you want to leave.' He finishes speaking to the group; they've been discussing the return home.

He looks at Tash as she settles. His brown eyes are neutral – he had held her so tightly on the boat until the rescue services had arrived. They've never actually talked about Saturday night. It seems years ago. She looks at him, trying to smile. But she's spent – she's running on empty.

'I'm in no rush,' Theo says. 'I'd like to spend a bit more time here. I'll need to do some paperwork I guess ...' He trails off. Glances down.

Tash reaches out and takes his hand. 'He was your father, Theo. It's OK to grieve.'

'Even though he could be a piece of shit?' But Theo's words lack the bite to make them land.

'He was your father. He had his good points. I mean, most of America loved him. It's OK if you did too.'

Theo is quiet for a moment, then he looks at Tash, his face brighter. 'And I've got a baby sister to get to know.'

'I can't believe you knew all along.' Tash still can't get her head round the story.

Theo nods. 'It was Kiki who told me. She didn't even realise. There were photos on Dad's phone of Emma. When Kiki gave me the information she'd taken, back last Fall, I saw Stani in the background of one of the shots of my dad and Emma. I guessed he must have been the only other person to know. I flew out here, after Mum died. I felt like I needed to know it all. I liked Emma.' He looks down at his plate.

Tash remembers the glow on his face when he'd talked to her sister last year. 'And Stani just told you, just like that?'

Theo shakes his head. 'I didn't tell them I was coming. I knocked on Stani's door and Emma answered. Lulu was in her arms. I mean – it was crazy.'

'It was. But thank God,' Megan says, quiet but happy. 'We've got Emma back.'

Theo says, 'I sent her some money. What Dad should have provided – for his daughter. She will need more. My sister shouldn't be denied anything.' He looks at Becki. 'It was Emma on the beach in Mykonos. Stani had told her about my behaviour. She couldn't come to the villa, not until she was ready. She wanted to speak to me. Stani told her where I was. She met me on the beach. She told me to get it together.'

Becki stares at him, her blue eyes wide. The glass she holds slides the few millimetres to the table. It clatters but doesn't break. Orange juice spills on the table. 'That wasn't Kiki?'

Sam coughs, as there's a sound behind them – footsteps on the paving stones. The sun is bright and Tash squints to look.

Giannis and Christos. Both are dressed smartly and look well rested, and not at all as though they'd been up most of the night. Each beard is neat; their clothes are smart and pressed. They smell of olive groves.

'Morning,' she says, rising. 'Any news?'

'Just a few things.' Giannis nods to the group. 'If you don't mind, we won't take up much of your time.'

Tash can't help it. She glances at Becki.

'We found this,' Christos says. He holds up a necklace.

Tash hears a gasp.

'We were wondering who it belonged to.' Christos sounds professional. Not accusatory, but direct. He looks round at the group.

Becki says nothing, and it takes Jaz to say, 'Isn't that the necklace Theo gave you?'

Theo looks at it, leaning in. 'It is. Did you lose it?'

Still, Becki says nothing. She doesn't move, frozen to the chair. *She looks terrified*, Tash thinks.

'It's yours?' Giannis asks. Then he pulls up a chair and sits down.

'Coffee?' Tash pours him a cup, and he nods, thanking her.

'You see we found fibres on this necklace, which was down on the beach, near the steps. And some fibres on the knife that was stuck underneath the jetty. The same knife that delivered the killing blow to Camilla Sanderson. One stab. Then she drowned and bled out – both killed her.'

Becki pushes her chair back from the table. She stands and looks wildly round the group. Her fingers fly to her mouth, as though to push a cry back in. When she speaks, the words are part strangled. 'I didn't kill her!'

Giannis takes a sip of his coffee. 'I'd be interested to know what *did* happen.'

'Becki?' Theo looks confused. 'What's going on? I thought Dad killed Kiki? Sam saw him following her to the beach? You said it too?'

'We think he did follow her there. Kiki, as you know her, had been blackmailing your father since Christmas. There were details on her phone. Notes, and photos. It seems she went to your Christmas party, the same one where your mother died, and she took photos of your father in compromising positions. She has been receiving money for these last nine months.'

'Fuck!' Theo sits back down and stares at Giannis. 'Well, it must have been him then?'

'In his statement, after her death, he said he admitted he did confront her. She agreed to stop the demands. He had threatened to tell Mark Cadel what she was doing. It seems she was in love with Mr Cadel. More than that, she had blamed Senator Fowler for the disappearance of her friend, Ryan Gibbons. There was a newspaper article she read here, from an American paper, that came with someone on the plane, that said a body was pulled out of the Charles River only last week. She believed it would be identified as Ryan. She confronted Senator Fowler about this. But he knew nothing about it.'

'What the fuck?' It's Sam's turn this time.

Theo is fixed. He stares at Giannis. 'I read that article on the plane. Have they identified the body?'

Giannis shakes his head. 'No, I called the Boston police. But based on Kiki Sanderson's diary notes on the phone, I've suggested they check it against Ryan Gibbons. The notes say that Nancy Fowler had found him, trying to blackmail Mr Fowler, and that Nancy Fowler had taken him to hospital and paid Kiki Sanderson a lump sum to stay quiet. That was when she decided to go their home. She began blackmailing Senator Fowler with these new photos. If Ryan Gibbons has ended up in the river, then we'll never know to what extent either Mr or Mrs Fowler were involved.'

Theo remains absolutely still. *He is grey*, Tash thinks. Dom had told her about the dorm room. Dom was sure Ryan was alive, and Nancy had taken him to hospital. He must have been dead. Between them, Dom and Theo must have killed him – self-defence, but still. He must have found out on the plane if that's when he read the article. Is that why he'd started drinking so heavily again?

Tash offers a silent prayer up to Nancy. She had saved them. The truth doesn't matter when it comes to your own kids. Richard was the dangerous one. Everything around him spoiled – he leaked evil. *No matter what the boys had done*. She closes her eyes. She will *never* let Dom ruin his life over this.

She can say that Nancy had finished him off. Nancy killed him to save the boys.

The pang for Kiki and her friend Ryan, who had tried to blackmail someone who went on to crush them. Why had Richard left Theo to deal with this? Why couldn't he have faced his own music?

Theo says now, 'And Kiki hasn't put anything else in her diary, about what happened to Ryan?'

Giannis cocks his head a little, appraising Theo. 'No. Is there anything else you want to add?'

Theo says nothing. The briefest of head shakes.

75

Jaz

Looking at Theo, Jaz wonders about the plane ride. He had read the paper on the plane, the same as the rest of them. Dom had said that was when his behaviour changed so much. Did he suspect the identity of the body in the river?

Giannis turns to Becki, and Jaz sees her friend take a step back.

A white scarf, stained a pinky brown, dangles from Christos's gloved hand. He must have discreetly pulled it from a bag. He wasn't holding it before.

Jaz stares at it, then stares at Becki. Her eyes fasten on to it, wide. Her hand shakes.

When she'd chased Becki up to the ledge the other morning, Becki had let something drop. She'd told the police last night. Whatever it had been, they'd found it. Jaz doesn't want to betray Becki, but she can't leave Dom in jail, suffering.

'Dom gave us a statement saying that he'd left the knife in the trash. We traced it to the shop – it was a fishing knife.'

Theo looks at them. 'My knife? Yes, I bought it so we could go fishing. We went at Easter when I came to find Emma, and I broke Stani's. I bought another one so I could replace it. I wondered where it had gone.'

Jaz looks from Becki to Theo.

Becki is open mouthed. 'But you pulled it away when I looked at the bag?'

'Well, I didn't want you to cut yourself on it. I was pissed, I think. I didn't think anything about it. It was nothing, Becki.'

Giannis looks back to Becki. She takes another step back, and she reties her hair, up in a high bun. It piles on her head, and the sun catches the threads of gold which spill out of the band.

'The necklace was found near the beach steps. Why did you get the knife, Becki?'

She is crying now. Her hands cover her face. 'I just wanted to talk to her. I couldn't talk to Theo – he was so different. I felt like I was losing him. He just wasn't himself. I thought maybe Kiki was the problem. I was sure it was her on the beach. I'd had a lot to drink. Theo was missing. I saw Richard follow her to the beach house, and I went and got the knife then, because I didn't know what was going to happen. Theo and his dad had just had a row; Richard and Kiki were shouting. I was frightened. I thought if I just had it, by my side, I'd feel stronger. You don't know that it was me who used it!' She takes another step back.

Jaz pushes her chair back, but Christos leans out and places his empty hand on hers, gesturing for her to stay where she is.

Giannis's voice is soft. 'We can move to that. You went to the beach?'

Becki nods. 'She was crying. I think Richard had been hard on her. I followed her down to the beach, and she saw me and laughed. She said something about me being a child, about not knowing anything at all. I asked her if she'd been at Mykonos and she called me stupid.' Becki covers her face with her hands.

Giannis sound kind. 'We have the scarf, Becki. There's a blood match. It's OK. We know. There's no reason for you not to tell us. You'll feel better. It's easier all round.'

'I didn't mean it! I was so angry! She said she could ruin Theo if she wanted. She could break him, and then what would I be left with? She said I was as bad as the rest of them – take, take, take. She has no idea about my life. She knew nothing!'

Jaz feels sick.

'She saw the knife in my hands. I didn't do anything with it. I was holding it wrapped in my scarf. Then she got *really* angry. She said the last time she'd seen a knife her friend had gone missing, and why was it always this family, and she went to grab it. I pulled it away.' Becki gestures as though remembering the fight. She looks confused. 'I don't really know what happened. We were in the sea, and I fell. Then she was face down. I ran back onto the sand. I still had hold of the knife. But there was blood on it. I ran and stuck it under the jetty. I dropped the scarf. My necklaces got tangled up, it flew off. I grabbed it, then when I looked around, she was quiet. Just lying there. Floating. I felt sick …' She gags now.

Jaz can barely breathe.

'I ran back up the beach. I threw the necklace somewhere. Then I ran to the room. I just stayed there. I didn't know I'd killed her. I wrapped the scarf round my waist until I could get rid of it. I didn't realise. I just wanted to make her feel ... I wanted her to feel like I did. Powerless. Out of my depth.' She looks at Theo. 'I loved you, and I thought you were leaving me. You were everything I'd ever dreamt of. All this. What would I do, if I lost you?'

76

Tash

A week later

In the end, there had been no birthday party. Dom and Mark had been released from jail. Becki had been charged.

Sam had flown back to the states to deal with some work issues. Mark had gone to London for the same reason.

Jaz had gone home. Back to the farm. Tash thinks they'll see her again. Dom has moped a bit without her.

Emma had moved in with Lulu. Theo had stayed to be with his sister. Dom with his cousin. They were all knit now. One family. There was so much time to make up for. So much to say.

She will be more careful about who she invites into her home in the future. Even if they come bearing gifts. Richard had arrived with champagne and had destroyed them all – for a while. She likes to think they are stronger now. They are where they should be.

*

'I've quit the firm,' Megan says, as she and Tash climb out of the sea after a morning swim.

'You haven't!'

Megan nods. 'The firm in Athens, who were so good with Mark and Dom. They had an opening in their commercial department. It's less money, but I like it here.'

Tash laughs. 'You mean you like who lives here.'

Megan blushes. 'His eyes really are like tiny pieces of the ocean. It's only been a week, but I can see it being much longer. And even if it's not, I'm sick of New York. My fucking firm. I'll always wonder if I only got the partnership because Richard told them to give it to me. It's all bullshit.'

Tash bats her arm. 'Nah, you might have got it sooner, but you'd have got it.' Looking at Megan, she thinks it suits her, this more relaxed look. Stani suits her.

'The flare gun,' she says, 'when you shot it. Did you aim it, or just shoot?'

'Richard was going to hurt Stani,' Megan says, shrugging. 'I mean, it's not like I'm a crack shot or anything.' She pauses, then says quietly. 'I do think about what I did. But I don't regret it. I'll carry it. I'll have to bear its weight.'

Tash touches her arm, just once.

'What about Mark?' Megan asks.

Tash flops on the sand, stretching out and closing her eyes, letting the sun dry off the salt water. 'Oh, I don't know. Of course I still love him. But I think we're beyond repair. You know when he took my name, so that Dom could keep his, and we'd all be the same, a family, I thought, if he would do that, then I'd stay with him for life. But when we thought Emma was dead, I pushed him away, and he just went. If the roles had been reversed, I think I would have hung around. At a distance. I don't want to compete any more – always having to prove myself. I just want to be.' Mark had spoken to her quietly, sincerely, before he'd got on the plane. *I only half said what I wanted to say on the beach. I wanted to say that you asked me to go, but if you asked me to come back, then I'm yours. I'm yours, Tash. I think I'll always be yours.*

But she's not sure she wants someone who will go when she asks and then, to rub salt in any wound she'd opened up, bring someone new and parade her in order to win a race that no one had started.

'And Sam?'

Tash stands up, brushing the sand off her. She doesn't want to talk about Sam. Not yet. Not until she's ready to talk to him.

'Come on. Maria said she'd come and make us breakfast. I can't keep her away now Lulu has moved in. She should be awake soon, and I need more cuddles. I'm still in deficit.'

They approach the villa, white and clean in the morning light.

'What about Dom? You and him had a heart-to-heart last night?'

Tash sighs. 'He's been meaning to tell me for weeks now. He failed all his exams at the end of the year. He's had a rough time.' She doesn't tell Megan that the guilt of what had happened to Ryan Gibbons has been weighing him down. That he was struggling to focus on work. 'I've suggested he take a year off. He can work with Mark – learn some of the basics of the company. Harvard have said he can resit the year. He's got time to work it out.'

She also doesn't tell Megan that Dom had said he needs to go to the police. He's planning to fly back to Boston soon and tell them what happened. He wants to tell the story, to clear his conscience. She's both proud of him and terrified of what could happen. But it was all an accident, and Kiki's notes hadn't mentioned anything about him. Who knows what will happen – but Dom will be able to at least look himself in the mirror without hating what he sees.

Tash pushes open the huge glass doors to the kitchen. 'What can I help with?'

Maria is surrounded by plates of fruit, fresh bread, honey, yoghurt and meats. Theo is making coffee and Dom makes pancakes.

Tash feels something inside of her slide over and relax. The last year has been too much. For them all. It's time to press pause.

Her phone buzzes. She looks down. A message from Sam. She'll look at it later.

Right now, this is where she wants to be.

Emma comes in, carrying Lulu. 'I barely slept!'

'Well give her to me and go back to bed.' Tash takes Lulu gently in her arms, kissing her head, breathing in the baby smell.

'*Kalimera*, little one.'

Acknowledgements

Thanks are due to my incredible agent, Eve White, and Ludo Cinelli, Steven Evans and Emmanuel Boakye.

Thanks also to the incredible team at Bloomsbury Publishing, Head of Zeus, including my editor Bethan Jones, Peyton Stableford, Lydia Gittins, Jo Liddiard, Nikky Ward, Lydia Forbes, Jessie Price, Simon Michele, Jenni Edgecombe, Rachel Rees, Emily Champion, Simon Michele and Tania Doney.

Sophie Ransom PR is brilliant and much appreciated.

For the feedback, thanks to Kate Simants. Supportive author friends provide a lifeline: Jo, Heather, Dominic, Clare, Niki, Fliss, Lou, Harriet, Rob, Liz, Susie, Barry, Howard, Angela, Erin, Anna and Kate.

And thanks to Rob.

About the Author

RACHEL WOLF grew up in the North of England and studied at Durham University. Before turning to writing, she worked for a holiday company and travelled widely. Her thrillers take inspiration from some of those travels.

Did you love *HER PERFECT ESCAPE*?
Then don't miss Rachel Wolf's other glamorous, twisty thrillers.

A POWERFUL FAMILY.
A LUXURY CRUISE.
A KILLER ON BOARD.

'Totally gripping... *Succession* on the high seas.' **HARRIET TYCE**

'Addictive, claustrophobic.' **ERIN KELLY**

BE CAREFUL WHAT YOU WISH FOR...

'The perfect escapist read.' **CLARE LESLIE HALL**

'Chilling and taut.' *SUN*

Available to enjoy now in paperback, eBook and audio.